Angelfi... ...s, Book 4:
Only the Lonely

by Karen Wiesner

Writers Exchange E-Publishing
http://www.writers-exchange.com/

Angelfire Series, Book 4: Only the Lonely
Copyright 2023 Karen Wiesner
Writers Exchange E-Publishing
PO Box 372
ATHERTON QLD 4883

Published by Writers Exchange E-Publishing
http://www.writers-exchange.com

Cover Artist: Odile Stamanne

    The unauthorized reproduction or distribution of this copyrighted work is illegal. Criminal copyright infringement, including infringement without monetary gain, is investigated by the FBI and is punishable by up to 5 (five) years in federal prison and a fine of $250,000.

    Names, characters and incidents depicted in this book are products of the author's imagination and are used fictitiously. Any resemblance to actual events, locales, organizations, or persons, living or dead, is entirely coincidental and beyond the intent of the author.

    No part of this book may be reproduced or transmitted in any form or any means, electronic or mechanical, including photocopying, recording, or by any information storage and retrieval system, without permission from the publisher.

Chapter 1

Too tired? When is my boyfriend ever too tired to see me? We've been apart for longer than four months. An endless amount of time with hardly any phone calls! And now Robert is finally here and suddenly he's too tired to be with me? Unacceptable!

Diane Hoffman started after her boss of ten plus years and her boyfriend almost as long as that. They both worked for Global Pharmaceuticals. Robert Drake was a "pharma sales rep"—a pharmaceutical sales representative who sold company products all around the region he was responsible for. His job involved a tremendous amount of travel. In an average year, he returned to the home office in New York City maybe three or four times. He traveled so much, he didn't have a true home. He lived in various hotels. His job involved giving elaborate presentations that sold their products. He checked in by phone and email more frequently, of course, but even that couldn't be personal enough for Diane.

Right out of college, she'd joined the company as the administrative assistant for District 2 sales reps. It was exactly the position she'd imagined for herself in college, and she loved her job. But even she had to admit that, since becoming involved with Robert, she'd been thinking about a lot of things she'd promised herself she wouldn't even consider until she was thirty years old—long enough to enjoy her career satisfactorily. Thirty was the age she'd deemed crucial to start having a family before it was too late. Unfortunately, being in love made her want to be married and raising lots of babies. She'd turned thirty-one recently, and her dreams seemed to have come and gone in the ten years she'd been working for and loving her boss.

Wanting more from the relationship certainly qualified as the hardest part about being in love so deeply. Robert traveled so much, his argument against getting married had unfortunately made perfect sense to her this past decade. Having her happily-ever-after put on hold if they were married and he couldn't be around much to be a husband to her and a father to their children would be infinitely harder than what they had been doing together. *But I've been waiting in anguish to be with the love of my life. Hasn't he missed me as much? Or is he being playful? He wants me to follow him to our usual hotel in town so he can surprise me?*

After very little consideration, Diane decided that had to be why he'd returned after four endless months and immediately left her again. Usually, they enjoyed at least a day and night together before he had another presentation scheduled and had to fly or drive out again.

Grabbing her purse, figuring she was leaving only a few

minutes early, she rushed out of the building in time to see Robert getting into his red Lincoln Town Car with the custom license plate that said Drake 8. Surprisingly, a cab pulled up almost as soon as she made it to the sidewalk. She hopped in. "Follow that red Town Car please," she said, feeling slightly giddy. In seconds, she was questioning her decision, but ultimately she always came back to the same conclusion: Even if Robert was as exhausted as he'd claimed, he'd be thrilled to see her once she arrived in their hotel room.

The bottomless gap of time since they'd last seen each other had been so hard on her. She'd fallen into her usual funk whenever her sweetheart had to leave town again. This time, he'd been gone longer, checked in less frequently even at the company, and she always gained weight when she was depressed.

She looked down at her ultra-feminine, pale pink business suit. No denying it felt much tighter than usual. Would Robert notice how many pounds she'd packed on? *Why do my mom and sister always have to send me so much fudge? I can't resist it. I gravitate to the freezer constantly, sometimes without even thinking. Because it's pre-cut into such small squares, I always eat more than I should. And I've gone through a truckload in Robert's extended absence.*

Diane sighed, feeling ten times larger than she had a moment ago. She reached into her purse to get out her compact mirror. As she checked her hair and makeup, she wondered if her face looked fatter than usual. She made her hand into a shelf and put it under her chin. *This is bad. What have I done to myself? Enough binge-eating! But maybe if Robert's here, I'll be able to control myself...at least until he has to leave again. Ugh!*

Permanently dissatisfied with what she was seeing in the

small mirror, she touched up her lip gloss and combed back her long, wavy mahogany hair, anticipating her arrival at their hotel in a few minutes. But when she looked up, she saw the cab was heading away from Manhattan. Up ahead was the bright red Town Car. *Robert said he was so tired. What's he doing? If he's as exhausted as he claimed, wouldn't he be going to the hotel to get some sleep?*

Long minutes passed and she saw the Town Car signaling toward the off-ramp—toward New Rochelle! Diane frowned, totally confused. Were they following the wrong car? No, that was Robert's license plate. Did he have a meeting? He hadn't mentioned it and, as his assistant, she usually scheduled any appointment he needed, including those for dentist and doctor.

More time passed, and they were definitely heading out of the city. Diane wrestled with whether or not to continue with this spontaneous little surprise. She'd rushed out spur-of-the-moment, planning to follow him to their hotel. Robert clearly wasn't going anywhere of the sort. So shouldn't she call this off?

Though her heart fought her head, she couldn't deny the vague sense of disquiet in her chest. She couldn't define what she was feeling. Nevertheless, dread filled her until she couldn't have spoken to say "Turn around" to the cab driver even though she desperately wanted to.

More than a half hour passed, and they were nearing New Rochelle. The cab driver periodically asked if he should continue following. She only nodded, experiencing a burning sensation in her heart. The Town Car entered a city Diane couldn't remember ever being in before. She knew a lot of New Yorker's moved here because it was an ideal place to raise a family.

What was Robert doing here though? Did he have family in

New Rochelle? He almost never spoke of relatives. She'd gotten a strong impression the few times they spoke of family that something had happened—some kind of horrific rift—that brought him pain. And so he, and she, avoided the subject altogether. *Or is that what I wanted to believe because the alternative was that he was hedging?*

What am I thinking? This is Robert. My love. He's a good man. I know him...

Her thoughts shut off as they entered a residential area with elegant, stately older homes. The landscaping was almost too perfect. Diane's throat closed as an alarm wailed in her head. The Town Car drove into the attached two-car garage that opened just as he pulled up to the old-fashioned house. *He has a garage-door opener for this home. Why? Why is he here? Who lives here?* The red car parked inside the far right slot and, a moment later, the garage door started to come down.

The cab slowed, then stopped, and Diane felt the driver looking at her expectantly in the rearview mirror. Her gaze barely strayed from the house out the passenger window. The mailbox they were parked almost right next to said "Drake" with the address. That address burned into her brain even as she thought there could be only two explanations for why Robert's name was on the mailbox: 1) He had family, a sibling or parents, that lived here and he was visiting them...and they allowed him to use their garage while he was here—though they were presumably estranged. *Right. That sounds about as logical as a convertible on a rainy day.* 2) He had family that lived here. *His* family. A *wife...*

Diane found herself rolling down the window of the cab, and immediately she heard the squeal of young children nearby. A young boy and girl appeared around the side of the house the cab was closest to, but then a female voice called for them to return to the backyard. A baseball-size lump filled her throat. *Robert's children. Robert's wife...*

"Lady, what do you wanna do?" the cab driver demanded impatiently, making her realize he must have spoken this same sentence more than once in an attempt to get her attention.

"Go back," she whispered painfully. "Back to New York City." Her lips wooden, she gave her address in the city.

The driver muttered dismissively, "It's your dime, lady," and made a fluid U-turn.

Ten years. Ten years and nothing but lies. All of it lies. Robert Drake, the love of my life, the man of my dreams, is married with kids. He used me. I'm a...God please no!...a mistress.

Her mind was scrambling and she knew if she didn't talk to someone right this minute, she'd burst into tears or unending screams. What would the car driver think of his passenger wailing all the way back to the city?

It's my dime.

Diane got out her cell phone and called her best friend and roommate, Roxanne Hart. At the moment, she didn't care what the driver heard over the rap music playing on the radio. She knew Rox was supposed to be packing for her trip to the Christian Dior Haute Couture show in Paris, where she would be modeling, but her friend sounded half-awake when she picked up. Diane and Roxanne had met at Columbia University in New York, as roommates then, too, and they'd been fast friends ever since. With her long white-blond hair, golden skin and killer body, Rox had been discovered as a model before she'd gotten a Bachelor of Arts degree majoring in music. After securing her degree, she took up modeling full-time and her career took off.

"Roxanne...it's over," Diane said quietly, not looking at the cabbie.

Strangely, that was all she needed to say. "With Robert? Mr. No-Show?" her friend guessed immediately. "Where are you?"

"In a cab. Coming back to the city."

"Hmm. How long until you're home?"

"Forty-five minutes or so."

"Okay. I'll call Darlene and Cherish. We'll be here when you get home."

Darlene Radcliffe was Diane's other best friend. Cherish had become part of their circle in the last couple years, though Diane didn't know her that well. She owned the flower shop Darlene worked. "Why?" Diane asked nervously.

"Look, you know I'm leaving for the Paris show soon. You're gonna need someone who knows what's going on so you're not alone through this."

Diane couldn't argue. She'd never felt more alone in her life and she wanted to be surrounded with the people who cared about her now.

The rest of the cab ride was surreal and she barely had enough ready cash to pay the fare, making the cab driver even more impatient and rude with her considering how low his tip was. She stumbled inside the security building and into the elevator.

Oh, Robert. Not my Robert. He's the perfect man. I fell in love with him within days of coming to work for him and the other District 2 sales reps at Global. He was so charming and mature. I'd never met a man like him, especially not in the small farm town I grew up in rural Wisconsin or in college where all the guys I dated were so childish and stupid. Robert always knew exactly what to say and do to make me agree to anything he suggested. He said he never intended to fall in love with me either, but we spent so much time together outside work that first year. The company frowns on inter-office romances. But his attraction to me was too strong to deny. Still, he said we had to be careful not to let anyone at work know about our personal relationship. He's been unyieldingly stringent about that, even when several of our co-workers openly paired off.

Both Darlene and Rox came to meet her at the door, Darlene saying that Cherish was sorry not to be present, too, but there'd been an emergency at work. Roxanne's face looked lined on one side, as if she'd been sleeping away the day instead of packing. Even her gorgeous eyes had dark circles under them.

"Where are Jace and the kids?" Diane asked, glancing Darlene's way and feeling guilty for dragging her friend away from her young family over something so embarrassing. *Over what? My life being finished? And now it's to be public humiliation for my decade of blind stupidity.*

Darlene waved her hand. "Jace is watching them."

Her two friends led her to the sofa in the luxurious living room of the high rise apartment Roxanne's salary as a supermodel easily afforded. Rox wouldn't hear of Diane paying more than a third of the rent, since she'd been the one to insist she didn't want to live alone here.

"Tell us everything," Rox demanded without preface as they sat down, bracketing her.

Darlene spilled her guts to her friends, somehow managing to do so without sobbing her heart out. Some part of her felt numb with shock. This couldn't be happening. She must have misunderstood somehow. *I've been eating so much fudge in my misery. Maybe he noticed how fat I've gotten and he didn't want anything to do with me.*

Diane groaned at her own ridiculous thoughts. *That's insane. What an idiot I am. This isn't about me. This is about* ten years *of deception! Ten years of being in the dark. Ten years of being someone's fool.*

Diane didn't know her own mind. She wanted an explanation for what she'd seen, something simple—something she could fix herself, like going on a much-needed diet. *How, without an ounce of discipline? I've never had any. Especially where Robert Drake is concerned.*

"I gave him ten years of my life. He was so good to me. I love him so much. He's so sophisticated and handsome. You should see him in his expensive suits…" She shook her head, her mind scattered and jumbled with too much at once.

"See him? We've never even met him!" Darlene hooted in disbelief, glancing at Rox. "Well, you did that once when you showed up at the restaurant he was trying to hide her in the back corner of." Roxanne had said she'd wanted to see this reputed "prince" for herself.

"I knew something was wrong. All these months. He barely called this time. Checked in at the office with emails instead of calls. We haven't seen each other since March! Or was it late February? And look at me. I'm so fat I barely fit in my clothes anymore!"

She jumped up and rushed to her bedroom to put on her go-to comfortable slobwear: loose terry cloth capris and a much-stained, oversized tank top.

Darlene and Rox followed her into the room. "He doesn't wear a wedding ring," Darlene pointed out, her tone gentle as she finger-combed her short cap of dark hair. "You told us he doesn't wear any jewelry."

Diane shrugged with extra force. "Some guys don't. Some guys don't like wearing jewelry." Robert had always said that. She'd tried buying him a present once—a gold watch. He'd refused to accept it. He'd never accepted any gifts from her, not even on his birthday or at Christmas. He insisted that the price of living in New York City was too high and she needed to save her money, as he was, for the future. *Their* future.

"Oh my gosh..." she murmured, the truth dawning so bright, she felt as if her eyes were being burned right out of their sockets. "He didn't want to leave a paper trail for his wife to find. That's why he never accepted any gifts from me and never gave me so much as flowers. Why we went Dutch on everything. Why he wanted me to categorize his hotel in Manhattan as a work expense—his wife would never see the receipt because it only came through the office. He never came here to the apartment, not even when you were on assignment, Roxanne. He didn't want anyone to see him. Anyone who might know him or know his wife and family. That's why he always reserved tables in the darkest, furthest recesses of any restaurant, even when I visited him for a day or two when he was on a sale pitch. Mostly we ordered take-out."

The expressions on her two friends' face stunned her and she burst out in the midst of her realizations, "You knew! Both of you knew he was married!"

"Oh my good golly!" Darlene croaked, shaking her head as if she couldn't believe this conversation—and how dense Diane had been. "Are you serious? You never had the *slightest* clue? Come on, Diane. I never met the guy and it couldn't have been more *screaming* obvious."

Diane looked at her oldest friends, blown away that neither of them had ever said anything to her like this before. "Did you know, Rox?"

Rox snorted, un-model-like. "Of course. Meeting him that one time solidified my guess."

"But we'd only been dating a few weeks at that point. What could possibly have led you to that conclusion?"

With more tact than she usually had, Rox muttered, "It was pretty obvious even then."

"Did *everyone* know?" By everyone, she meant their close circle of friends: Jamie Dubois or "Doobs" as everyone called him, Darlene's husband Jace and her brother Brett Foxx, Brett's relatively new wife Savvy, and Mikey Lund who worked at the mechanic shop Brett owned.

Neither Rox nor Darlene spoke, saying "yes" loudly with their expressions.

When Diane moaned in distress, Rox put her arms around her shoulders from the back. "Babe, would us telling you what was *so* obvious have changed anything for you? I mean, seriously? You never would've believed it. You were too stupid in love."

Diane cried out, half spluttering, "Yes, something would have changed! I never had the slightest clue. It never occurred to me. I wouldn't have imagined he was married for a split second. I didn't see any of these obvious things. Not then. Not until now. They weren't tell-tale to me. We never see each other. A couple times a year, if even. His absence is legitimate. I know—I'm his assistant. If he went home to his family between presentations...well, he didn't log those vacations in with the company. He didn't take them as work expenses." *Our entire relationship could be considered one long phone call—because that's mostly where our love affair has taken place. But in the last four months, even that's been few and far between.*

Diane wasn't sure which was worse: That she'd been in the horrifying position of "the other woman" or what her dearest friends must have thought of her. She wasn't lying. The realizations she'd had a moment ago had never come before, never been triggered by anything Robert said or did. She'd been almost completely in the dark. Everything that might have led her to wonder if he had a wife and family had been accounted for—explained by one thing or another that was genuine, or at least had seemed utterly authentic.

"Can I ask...?" Darlene started.

"What?" Diane demanded, flouncing away from Roxanne and out to the freezer in the kitchen. She grabbed the Tupperware container she kept her ample supply of fudge in.

Darlene and Rox trailed close behind again. "Well, if you never guessed he might be married," Darlene went on "what excuse did he give you for not marrying you this whole time?"

Rox jumped in, "Because he'd have been a complete moron not to realize you're one of those nice girls who get married and have two point five babies."

Darlene shuddered with a vocal protest at the idea of that "point five". Diane was too busy prying off the lid of the Tupperware and going right for the peanut butter fudge she adored most. "He travels so much," she defended with her mouth full.

"Eleven months of the year, he's somewhere other than here. It's part of his job. He wanted to wait until he could settle down, put down roots with me. I wouldn't have handled his absence as well if he was traveling all the time once we were married and had kids, and he knew it."

"Yeah. He was just thinking of you," Rox said, sounding like she was spitting. "Come on, Di, he's a sales rep. What're the odds of him ever 'settling down'? Besides, the dude's middle-aged, isn't he? Forty or forty-five years old? His job is the best he's gonna get at his age. It's not likely he'd quit and find some desk job."

Diane glanced at Darlene who appeared to be agreeing with Rox without reservation.

Another chunk of fudge filling her mouth, Diane shook her head. "I'm jumping to conclusions. I could be completely wrong about all this. What if he's just visiting someone? A sister or parent?"

"You said his name was on the mailbox."

"Okay, a brother or his parents?"

"Has he ever mentioned a sibling before?"

Diane swallowed a huge amount of the sugary concoction. "No. He never wanted to talk about his family. He implied there were painful situations. That something traumatic happened between him and his family that he wasn't healed from."

"Of course he did."

"Look, it's not that convenient," Diane insisted, almost through her teeth. Rox was determined to cast Robert as an ogre here. "He's never met my parents or sister either."

"Did you ask him to?"

Diane shoved another square of fudge in her mouth, irritated.

Of course she'd wanted the love of her life to meet her family. He'd never been able to get away. Even when they'd made plans, he'd canceled at the last minute, always with some job situation being the cause. She had wondered about that, but not too hard.

Her parents knew she and Robert had been dating for ten years and they'd asked almost constantly for the last nine and a half years of that time when they were getting married. Diane had worried that her parents somehow suspected their baby girl whom they'd raised with a solid moral compass was sleeping with a man she wasn't married to. She'd always been afraid of them finding out the truth and dreaded more than once whether they'd know just by looking at her and Robert together that she'd relented in insisting they wait to have sex until they got married.

The fact was, Robert had seduced her completely. She'd known marriage wasn't an option for a long while, but she'd loved him and she'd been committed to him with her whole heart and life. She'd believed he felt the same for her. So what did a piece of paper mean?

She'd given him her virginity barely a year into their relationship. The time before had been torture—as difficult for her as for Robert, who'd been beyond impatient for her to be ready.

Rox stepped closer, pushing the bucket-sized container of fudge aside. "Listen, babe, you didn't wanna know the truth. You like your head firmly buried in the sand. As long as it meant he didn't dump you, you wouldn't have considered anything like this."

"No. You're wrong," Diane insisted. "I have to be wrong. I didn't see what I thought I did."

Her own words echoed back to her in mockery. What Roxanne had just said about how she loved to stick her head in the sand and hide from the truth couldn't have been more accurate. She didn't want to know this reality. Wilting like a flower under a relentless sun, she dropped into a chair. "What do I do?"

"You know, hon," Darlene said with more tenderness than Rox usually displayed. "You know you can't go on with this relationship now that you know the truth for sure...don't you?"

"*Do* I know the truth for sure?"

"We will tomorrow," Rox said, her tone unwilling to accept an argument. "Tomorrow we're going back to that house and we're gonna find out the truth. That's that. If you won't save yourself this time, I'll do it for you."

Diane knew how forceful Roxanne could be. She was a tank when she made up her mind. If Diane didn't accompany her, she'd go alone after needling the address out of her with her clever manipulation.

I have to go along. I know I do. But Rox is right. She's absolutely right about me. I don't want to know the truth. Ever. Firmly buried in the sand is the most comfortable place for my aching head and too-forgiving heart.

When Diane woke late the next morning, she found her eyes were as bloated as her body. Between endless tears and fudge, she was a mess. *That's not even the worst part. I want to talk to Robert so badly. I want to hear him tell me I misunderstood everything. I didn't see anything I thought I did. I want to go through life with rose-*

colored glasses on.

And she fully intended to talk her best friend out of dragging her to New Rochelle. Unfortunately, by the time she emerged from her bedroom, Rox was already dressed, looking beautiful and ferocious instead of tired. She took hold of Diane's shoulders and shoved her toward her own bedroom. "You are not going to see if your cheating boyfriend has a wife and family dressed or looking like that."

"I am what I am. I'm fat and ugly. I can't go anywhere. Why did you and Darlene let me eat all that fudge?"

Rox chortled. "Oh, we let you, did we? I hid it five different times, Lady Jane. You found it every single time." Whenever Roxanne scolded her, she used that nickname.

Diane didn't have the energy to fight her determined friend. When Roxanne got done with her, she was wearing designer jeans that somehow fit her bloated proportions and made her appear slim with a top that Rox had gotten from a big-name designer she was on a first-name basis with, flirty sandals, and wearing makeup so naturally no one could possibly tell how red and blotchy her face was beneath.

"Wait a minute," Diane said in shock as Rox hustled her toward the door. "I can't do this today. I have work."

"I already called you in sick. We're going. You're not getting out of this, so stop trying. It's time to wake up and move forward in your life. You've been in limbo for ten damn years already."

"But I have been moving forward for ten years, waiting to get married and start a family with the man I love" was at the tip of her tongue. Then she realized, if Robert was married and had children with his wife, she'd been at a standstill from the moment her heart

set itself on him.

What a waste. I love him so much though. How can I still love him so much? I want nothing more than for the chance to turn back time, not to follow him at all yesterday. If I'd called that off, tonight I might have been in his arms, hearing him tell me he loves me and someday we'd have the most beautiful house and children...

He already has both. With another woman. Oh, Lord, save the stupid! Me!

The drive to New Rochelle felt contradictorily endless and too short. Diane felt so sick, she was afraid to throw up inside the tight confines of Roxanne's rarely used, custom lavender sports car.

It was nearly noon when they reached the same residential area Diane had seen from the backseat of a cab yesterday. As before, she could hear the squealing laughter of little kids. That sound got louder when Roxanne forced her out of the passenger seat and herded her to the front door of the stately home. Instead of invigorating her appetite and memories of childhood the way it usually would have, the scent of grilling meat made her stomach churn sickly.

Rox kept a firm hold on her arm as she pushed her index finger against the doorbell. Diane wanted to close her eyes at the sound of sandals on the other side of the door. The middle-aged woman who appeared when the stain-glassed paned door opened had a page-boy hairstyle that bounced lightly when she walked. She couldn't have looked more like the girl next door if she tried. *And I'm the bad girl. The other woman. Some married man's mistress! Me!*

"Yes? May I help you?"

She even sounds sweet and intelligent. I'm the dumbest person alive.

"We're looking for a Mrs. Robert Drake," Rox plowed forward, looking pleasant and casual. At the same time Diane wondered what she'd do without her friend, she wished she'd been allowed to stay home and sulk.

Abruptly, the most familiar voice in the world to her called, "The burgers are almost done. Where are those buns, my d…"

Robert appeared through a patio door Diane could see on the opposite side of the house. He held a grill spatula and wore cargo shorts and a polo shirt. In the background, the sound of kids playing enthusiastically carried through the open patio door. *Robert. My Robert, who's never, ever worn anything so casual in all the time we've been together. My Robert, a family man…*

All the strength in her legs gave out, but somehow Roxanne held her up as the woman who'd opened the door turned back from her husband and said, "I'm Mrs. Robert Drake. What's this about?" Though she still smiled, there was something wary in her tone now.

Diane fixated on Robert, who'd halted in the center of the house and gaped at her in obvious shock and terror. The truth was displayed in that expression. There could be no mistaking it. He'd never expected her, his mistress, to show up at his home where his wife and kids lived. Diane had wondered a time or two whether he'd seen her following him in a cab yesterday. It was apparent he hadn't. He never expected to be revealed in this way while relaxing with his beloved family.

As smoothly as a Jehovah's Witness, Roxanne said, "We're in your neighborhood today, sharing the Scriptures, Mrs. Drake. If you wouldn't mind, we'd like to share some good news with you. We have some pamphlets in the car…"

Just like that, the door slammed shut in their faces. Rox hustled her to the car, obviously struggling because Diane didn't feel capable of anything but collapse. Somehow she was in the passenger's seat, all but incapacitated by shock.

Hours later, she felt sick to her stomach after too much fudge, ice cream, a greasy double cheeseburger, cheese curds and wine. She was curled up on the couch, verbally going over every second of the time she and Robert had spent together as a couple. There were so few of them. Most were memories of intimate, heart-stealing conversations. "My happiest moments these ten years have been spent with him, mostly on the phone. He was my whole life. He was my future. Now I have nothing. All the memories are tainted. Whenever I remember us together, I'll see the shadow of his wife, those happy children..."

"His dripping grill spatula and gorilla-hairy legs in those shorts," Roxanne added without the slightest bit of sympathy.

Diane barely heard her, though the picture of Robert's naked—shockingly hairy, white body—filled her mind. "You know..." she mused, "he never answers the calls I make to him from my cell phone. I don't have his home phone number. I never have had it, because he told me he didn't have a house or apartment—just random hotel rooms—and I'm the administrative assistant of the whole sales division now, instead of a single district. How could he have gotten away with not giving a home phone and address to his employer all these years? He'll only answer my calls when I call him from work and not even all the time then. Otherwise my calls go directly to voice mail and he calls me back later. The phone he uses for me must be a secret phone. One he uses only for me and his wife had no idea he even has it. He makes sure my calls never come in while he's with that phone, which means he must hide it, maybe in his glove compartment. It is a work expense, too, now that I recall. That cell phone, I mean. That has to be why I can never get hold of him—not even for work-related things. Do you know how many times I've called his phone and left messages? Countless. He must hate having to wade through all of them when he's finally in a place where he can listen to them without his wife overhearing. But he always does seem to have heard all of them. Funny because some nights when he calls from a hotel room wherever he's staying, I'll hear another phone ring. He always claims it's not for him or the TV. How does a person live a double life like that and not feel like…like they're suffocating or going crazy?"

"Like he's a total creep and can't meet his own eyes in the mirror? I can't imagine," Rox intoned.

"Oh my goodness, how often did we talk about getting married, having children together? Endless phone conversations that made me fall in love with him over and over. He went along with all of it whenever we talked about it. Every single time. Sometimes we'd go through a magazine and pick out furniture for our home once we got married and settled down. He was so serious about it all, so emotional about the prospect. So tender when we finally saw each other…" Diane paused to blow her nose and toss a tissue in the scattered heaps all around the sofa she laid out on like a beached whale.

"I wonder now, has he really been in Newark these past four months, closing a major deal and increasing visibility and sales volume of Global's products with pharmacists, hospital personnel, physicians, patient advocacy groups, and retirement homes…?"

Roxanne rolled her eyes.

"Or was he off on some family vacation all that time?" Diane shook her head. "No, he must have been on the job. The paperwork for closing that one huge deal must be what was in that oversized envelope he left on my desk when he stopped at the office after his flight got in yesterday. Usually he gets home and stops at the office, then we go to our hotel. Instead, this time he rushed to the office, dropped off the paperwork and went straight to see his family from there. Was he hoping I wouldn't be in my office and he could drop the paperwork off without seeing me? If that doesn't prove where his loyalties lie..."

"Diane, please tell me you're not seeing this through the eyes of the jilted mistress."

Diane whipped her head in Rox's direction again. "I don't like that word. Do you know his wife never once set foot into Global Pharmaceuticals? Not once. Did he lie and tell her he doesn't have an office at the company he works? He doesn't have pictures of his wife and kids on his desk. He doesn't have them in his wallet. I've noticed that. I looked in his wallet more than once at the hotel, hoping he had a picture of me inside. I even slipped one inside it once and he claimed he didn't know and that it must have fallen out and a hotel maid threw it away. But why doesn't he have pictures of his wife or kids in his wallet? Does he have a separate wallet for home and one for being with me? He puts mine in his car with his secret cell phone when he's home?"

"He's good. I'll give him that," Rox said. "In ten years, it's obvious he never slipped except yesterday when you followed him. But it's also obvious the clues were all there, sweet pea. How could you not have seen it? Not even considered it once?"

"I told you, I didn't have a clue. Not even a shadow of it. He's so good at keeping his life with me separate from his other life. I believed everything. I'm really dumb, aren't I? How could I not have seen something? But I didn't. I honestly didn't."

"At the very least, you've never seen he wasn't exactly a catch?"

Diane sat up, squishing a pillow tighter to her bloated middle. "Why do keep talking about his looks? He's the most handsome man in the world. He's so sophisticated…"

Roxanne barked. "Come on, have you ever really seen him? I mean, without the rose-colored glasses? He's middle-age, closer to fifty than forty, and you're only thirty-one. He's old, Diane. He's more than half bald on top and hairy as Chewbacca everywhere else, short—hell, he must be two or three inches shorter than you!"

"He's barely an inch less than me," Diane defended heatedly. It was true that since meeting Robert, she'd been wearing flats exclusively. He was so bothered by being shorter than her. He wore slight lifts in his shoes, insisted she wear flats, but when he took his off, she was again slightly taller than him.

"I don't see *anything* that could make you find him attractive. Seriously, it's true that he somehow manages to be in decent shape in clothes, but he's not muscular in any way. What in the world do you see in him? You must be in love."

"Of course I'm in love. But he *is* the most perfect man in the world."

"Oh, Di, he's just not your type. He's not the right guy for you at all. It's glaring."

"He's everything I ever dreamed of."

Rox shook her head, dubbing her hopeless without the words. "It's time for you dream bigger and better, Lady Jane."

"Who else could possibly be more perfect for me than Robert Drake?" Diane threw the pillow at her friend almost as a gauntlet.

Rox caught it easily. "Well, go ahead, Roxanne Hart. You're always saying you're so good at picking good men for all your friends, so you pick one for me. You chose Jace for Darlene years before anything serious happened between them, then predicted Brett and Savvy, and they all actually did pair off. What about me? What man would you pick for me?"

Roxanne chuckled, raising an elegantly arched brow. "That one's a no-brainer, sweet pea. Mikey."

Diane's fudge and alcohol saturated mind whirled at the name. "*Mikey?* Mikey Lund? Our Mikey?" Mikey worked for Brett at Foxx Body Shop. He'd hung around with their crowd as long as Diane could remember. But Mikey...*boyfriend* material? While it was true that he'd forever had a crush on her, he'd had crushes on most of the women he'd come in contact with—probably all his life. Roxanne, Darlene, Savvy for sure. If he'd met Cherish Stephenson, Diane was sure he'd fallen for her, too.

"First of all, Mikey's your friend, Diane. He respects you. Hell, he worships you. Better yet, he cares about you. He loves you. In case you haven't noticed, he's cute as the dickens, too."

Diane's entire face wrinkled. "*Mikey?* Mikey Lund?"

Rox grinned. "You haven't seen him for a while, have you? Even if you haven't, I've always thought he was beyond adorable. If he was in any way my type..." Her eyebrows wiggled suggestively. "Maybe."

Diane shook her head, finding all of this unimaginable. While Mikey was the sweetest, shyest guy on the planet, he wasn't...well, he was hugely obese and he drank like a fish! "He's not your type, Rox, but somehow you think he's mine?"

"Heck of a lot better choice than Robert Drake."

Diane's cell phone rang, and she fell off the couch unceremoniously in her haste to answer it. By the time she heaved herself up and retrieved it, smacking her head in the glass coffee table, Rox was roaring with laughter. Diane ignored her. In her clumsy maneuvers, she'd somehow seen the display with Robert's name. Stumbling more than once, she ran into her bedroom to take the call. By the time she pressed the button and gasped, "Robert!", she was breathing laboriously.

"Diane, please don't hang up. Listen to me…"

A hand snatched her phone away, and Diane twisted to see her best friend hanging up and throwing her phone onto her bed angrily. Aghast, Diane spluttered, "I needed to take that call! How could you?"

"You little idiot. Why? Because of course you plan to take him back. What, after he promises to leave his wife?"

Diane was eying her phone, wondering if she could reach the bed in time to get it before Roxanne tackled her. No, she was in no shape to be cat-quick.

"You're so stupid about this guy, Diane. He'll charm you into believing one of his patented lies, and you know it. You can't give him the chance to hook you in again. Even if he did leave his wife for you, is that what you really want? To break up a family? To be with someone who's committed adultery for ten years? All while his wife is having his children and caring for them with utmost nobility? He's done all this, lived two separate lives, without blinking an eye, so if you're still telling yourself he's a good man, think about that for a second. He'll lie and cheat again once he makes you his wife instead, only this time some other woman will be his poor, unsuspecting mistress. I guarantee he'll have another port in some other city in no time after he's got you chained with a ring on your finger and a baby in your belly—if he doesn't already."

Diane gasped and shuddered at the same time. Sobs burst from her as her mind tried to rebel against every cruel word Roxanne said. *Robert is mine… But he hasn't been, has he? I'm nothing to him. Nothing but the mistress he tries so hard to keep hidden from his family. From his poor, unsuspecting wife. That poor Helen Housewife didn't deserve to be cheated on so barbarously. And she's probably just as oblivious to his affair as I was. He's played her for a fool, just like he has me.*

Roxanne hugged her as she cried T-Rex tears. Her tone was softer when she said, "You have to protect yourself, babe. You can't see or talk to him again. You have to end the whole thing now. Don't let him get his foot back in the door."

"But I work for him," Diane blubbered.

"You work for the same company. You don't work for *him*. Can you transfer to another department?" Rox had barely asked the question before she was shaking her head. "Second thought, it'd be better if you got out of there altogether. You can easily get another job. And I heard from Darlene yesterday that Brett's mentioned hiring someone to organize and handle the office duties at the body shop."

"Receptionist? You want me to downgrade to receptionist? I'm an administrative assistant. I run an entire sales office. I make a…well, pretty good salary." At one time, she'd commanded the salary she'd expected to once she got the perfect job as a college graduate. The company had been down-sizing continuously for the past few years though. She made nothing like she once did starting out.

"Oh, seriously, you're a secretary there just like you'd be at the garage. Basically, you'd be doing the same job. Paperwork and phone calls. And Brett would probably hire you full-time. You haven't done that for a while now, have you?"

"But I love my job. It's everything I went to college for."

"Yes, and you've spent the last couple years terrified they were going to lay you off or fire you outright instead of cutting your hours left and right."

"It's mostly the sales reps they've been firing. They're downsizing pharma sales reps. Mostly." Robert's job was the one she'd feared for the most, even as she'd wondered if it might mean they could get married sooner if he was fired or laid off.

"No, you said you thought your own job would be eliminated soon."

Roxanne was right, but Diane didn't want to see reason.

"You can't see him again. You know that, right? You realize that?" Roxanne asked in a firm but strangely gentle way. "Because if you go back, you'll have to act like nothing happened. You'll have to face him over and over and somehow continue insisting it's over to him. His betrayal will affect every part of your life, sweetie. You know that yourself. You're not gonna be able to work with him without being crushed or catapulted back into the role of mistress."

Diane shuddered, revolted at the word and its ramifications. "I can't be that."

"Of course you can't. You're not that kind of woman. But you love him so much you'll cave if you see him. He's seduced you consummately for ten years. His charm is your downfall."

"My parents would be so ashamed," she murmured. "They're always talking about how New York will corrupt me. I guess I've proven them right."

"It's not your fault. You're too sweet and innocent to have seen what was right before your eyes all this time. But now that you know, you *can't* go back."

Easier said than done. Roxanne held her, and Diane wanted nothing more than to go home to Wisconsin, where her plump mother would wrap her in darkly tanned arms and tell her everything would be all right. Whenever she was home, she felt like the world righted itself.

But they know. Mom, Dad and Penny all know about Robert. They've never met him, but they know we've been together ten years, that he's my boss and he travels a lot. That he's my whole world. What will I tell Mama when she calls next? She always asks about Robert. "When will we meet him? When are you getting married?" A skipping record every time.

At the prospect of admitting her relationship with this man she'd loved to the exclusion of all else—*to the exclusion of my own morality*—was over, Diane felt like she was suffocating. She had no future left without him.

Roxanne pulled back and clasped her face in her hands. "Look, Diane, I'm leaving the States tomorrow and I won't be back for a week or more. You need to have a backup while I'm gone. Someone to call if there's a Robert emergency. Unfortunately, Darlene and Jace are taking the kids to Buffalo to see their parents for the next couple weeks—they're leaving Friday just like I am. Brett and Savvy are heading there with Darlene, too. They won't be staying as long since you know Brett can't take more than a short time being with his and Darlene's parents. So they're all out as your rescue options." Rox sighed. "Cherish has family visiting her at her apartment, and she's already stressed out about it, so she's not really a good choice." A grimace captured Rox's expression. "I can't see you calling *him*…"

Diane cringed at this tender area in her and Roxanne's relationship. They almost never talked about Jamie Dubois because of something that'd happened years ago and yet still felt raw to Diane after all this time. She braced herself whenever Jamie came up in conversation.

Though Rox refused to say his name and Diane always knew she meant Jamie when she said *"him"* in that loathing tone, her friend went on as if she wasn't in the least bit bothered…and Diane always told herself Rox probably wasn't; *she* was. "That leaves Mikey. You know he'll be there for you at a moment's notice. You need this, babe. Promise me you'll talk to Mikey instead of throwing yourself into the lion's den again with Old Faithful."

Taking a deep breath, Diane muttered dully, "You'll talk to him first, won't you?" Roxanne was too stubborn not to get her way about this.

"You know it. But I want you to go along with this. If you can't protect yourself, you have to be willing to let someone else protect you. I can't be here this time. You're weak where this guy is concerned. Let Mikey handle it."

Diane didn't feel right about the prospect, in part because she couldn't remember the last time she'd seen or talked to Mikey Lund. It'd been months. She hadn't thought about him once in all that time either, and now Roxanne wanted her to force him to step into a situation like this? The fact was, she didn't know if she was ready for that any more than she was to let Robert go cold turkey. Still, Rox was right. She couldn't see or talk to him ever again. That was crucial. Diane just couldn't imagine how to shut off her heart and dreams like they were emotionless light switches.

Chapter 2

Mike Lund felt inward pride as he finished up the low-fat chicken salad he'd made for himself at home the night before. In the past, his lunch had consisted of ordering in a whole pizza or some other junk food and eating every bite himself. *Never one to leave behind so much as a crumb.*

Though he had more than a twenty-minute break left, he got up and made his way back to the brand new Camaro he was detailing. On his way, the intercom went off. Tentatively, Mike walked to the wall unit. "Yeah?"

"Get up here, Lund," Brett Foxx ordered.

Mike held himself rigidly, realizing he wasn't likely to get out of this summons in the end. "Gotta get back to work, boss," he said into the intercom...then hustled away.

Since Brett—The Man himself, as Mike referred to him in his

mind and sometimes even verbally—had married a couple years ago and had a kid with his wife Savvy, the two had moved into her fancy-smacy penthouse apartment. Brett's own place upstairs in the garage got transformed into a gym for employees to work out, get away from "the fam", and in general shoot the bull.

Mike had been avoiding that particular area of the body shop for almost three months now. He saw it as the hole where he'd once upon a time stuffed his face with all the crap Brett left lying around. Potato chips, booze, pity. All the seriously bad mojo Mike—for the first time in his thirty years—had been trying to avoid.

Hell and damnation, he was still shocked at how well cleaning out his apartment, avoiding his "friends", his old haunts and habits, had changed his life in a few short months. The extra weight had come off faster than he could have anticipated without beer, carloads of French fries and pizza, and triple cheeseburgers. After the first month of his transformation, he hadn't owned a single scrap of clothing that fit him anymore.

Sighing in relief, Mike went back to the Camaro. Shoot, he'd known his glass bottle existence wouldn't last. One of them would call him on the carpet sooner rather than later. He'd evaded his friends because being around them made him realize just how much he'd never fit in with their elite crowd. Brett and Doobs and Jace were the popular dudes, the ones all the gorgeous ladies drooled over. Mike wasn't that guy. Not at all.

Honestly, he'd thought a lot about how he'd gotten into such a crowd in the first place. The only conclusion was that Brett had hired him at the garage right out of high school. Mike had never wanted to do anything but fix cars, even when he was a kid. Shop had been the only class he'd aced in school. He was good at anything and everything cars. *The only thing I am truly good at.*

Mike had hung around Brett after that without any real permission. Doobs, Brett and Jace allowed his presence, tolerated it, just as their mainstay chicks—Rox, Darlene and Diane—always had. Savvy had been folded in with open arms as soon as she and Brett hooked up permanent-like. *Thirteen years in this group, and I'm still the joker in the background everybody pities.*

Keeping his distance from Brett had been the hardest part of the past three months. The dude was his boss, and he came in, maybe not as much as he had before Savvy and his baby girl Harley became his life, but he was involved in the business regularly. In this time, Mike had become pleasantly aware of how easy it was for him to stay in the background, how to get in and out morning and evening without going through the usual greetings.

Pshaw, not like any of 'em would notice my absence anyway. The past three months prove that. I'm not a vital part of the group. I was just the drunk, tub-a-lard in the background. The loser who put his life on hold 'cause I never really had a life of my own anyway. I spent my time wishin' I was anybody but who I was and always would be. Maybe I was right about that in the first place. After a few months, maybe that part hasn't changed at all.

The intercom intoned loudly again, and Mike glared at it. He hauled himself over to the comm system a second time, punched the button, and barked, "Yo?"

"Get your ass up here, Lund. Now. Who's payin' your bills anyway? 'Sides, since when would you rather work than bullsh*t with us?"

Mike all but groaned out loud. "Us" meant Doobs was here—probably came in the back way. Mike couldn't refuse. His job was the most important part of his life. Sometimes he wondered what would be left of him without it. He didn't have anything else. But he'd been trying to have a life, a healthy life, a *real* one instead of one lived vicariously through those men he wished he could be. His job was still central, regardless of the changes. If Brett fired him, he'd be royally screwed. But he hadn't really done anything to deserve termination. His boss would have a hard time without him in any case. Mike ran circles around the other mechanics in the place. There wasn't a car on the planet he couldn't fix…

Resigning himself to the inevitable confrontation, he adjusted the old coveralls he knew he'd have to replace soon. He all but drowned in the triple XLs now. Swinging up the steep staircase at the back side of the garage that used to have him panting like a half-dead dog, he made his way to Brett's old bachelor pad.

When he entered, Doobs was lying on the bench, pressing a hundred and seventy-five pounds. Brett was spotting. His unfathomable hooded gaze met Mike's scattered one. Without a word, he handed Mike a soda from the fridge behind him. If it'd been after work, it would have been a beer. He wasn't ready to face that situation yet. He'd been drinking a case a night for most of his adult life—only slightly less than that when he was younger. Cutting out booze had been hard. Yet he'd realized without his friends there, he hadn't felt the self-pressure he always had to fit in. When he was half-wasted, he stopped caring whether or not he belonged. Maybe his friends had never truly pressured him on that point. Regardless, he'd come to accept he just didn't fit in and never would, even with *kegs* of beer inside him.

Mike took the non-diet soda but didn't open it. He leaned in the doorway of the huge, open space that used to be Brett's living room slash kitchen but was now empty save for an old sofa, some chairs, and all the exercise equipment.

Without looking at the other men more than a few glances here and there, he waited for whatever would happen. Doobs finished his reps, sat up and grabbed the towel nearby. Wiping sweat from his hands and face, he settled his attention on Mike.

Jamie Dubois had earned the nickname "Dr. Feelgood" from all the women he'd effortlessly made fall in love with him. He, Brett and Jace called him "Doobs" (certainly in part because of all the joints they'd smoked together when they were younger) or "Doctor". Even Mike could admit the guy was blow-the-gaskets good looking. He was tall, trim and muscular, tan as some Greek god, and he'd always had that long, blond hair that made most girls insane. Beyond that, he was charming and fun-loving—always knew what to do and say to work himself into the bed of any chick he desired for five meaningful minutes.

Brett had a dangerous thing going on that made the women crave him. He didn't have to speak a word, and they were all over him. Or had been before his marriage.

Both dudes were beyond cool, while Mike was a perpetual goof. More than once, he'd wondered what made them tolerate him. He wasn't cool. Never had been and sure as shooting never would be.

Doobs stood up with a friendly grin on his face as he approached Mike. "How the hell are you doing, buddy? *Where* the hell have you been?"

Mike couldn't understand why Doobs would ask either question. The way he always did around these two—and drank to drown—he felt like a complete fool as he went along with Doobs' cool handshake. He couldn't get himself to say a word.

Doobs stepped back, frowning slightly now. "Seriously, man, where have you been? I haven't seen you at all for I can't remember how long."

Was this the first he'd noticed? Or had seeing Mike now made him realize it'd been awhile? He clearly hadn't given him the slightest thought prior to this.

I'm not kiddin' myself anymore. These two aren't my friends. Jace never has been either. We're not close. In the past, I called 'em my best friends 'cause they were the only dudes who'd talk to me whether I was wasted or not. I never had a basis for that assessment. I was just pathetic. No, I can't see Brett or Doobs "sharin' feelings" over a helluva lot of beer, though maybe Jace would. They all just felt sorry for me. That's the only reason they let me hang around with 'em. Why they threw me a bone when they talked the women kneelin' at their feet into sleepin' with me. Hell, those girls must've been desperate to please Brett and Doobs if they were willin' to go that far with me.

Humiliated, Mike looked away, forcing himself to shrug with an indifference he wished he could really feel. "I been around. Just like always." *Always where you only see me when you wanna see me.*

Though he was trying not to look at either of the other two men, he felt them staring at him with the concentration of lasers. Had they noticed he'd let the hair dye fade, cut his greasy mop that grew *out* rather than *down* but never looked as cool as these two rock stars? The first time Mike met Diane Hoffman, she'd told him she had a thing for long-haired blond guys. She'd been looking at Doobs that whole time. She'd always had a secret crush on him, like most girls did, though Doobs was only interested in being her friend. Mike had run right out and gotten his hair dyed blond, and he'd tried to grow it out so it'd fall over his shoulders, like Doobs's did when he didn't have it caught back with a leather thong. Instead, Mike had ended up with a blond, white-man's Afro. It'd looked like a bird's nest for far too long. Not that Diane would ever look at him, let alone *like* him that way anyway. Even if not for the crush on Doobs, she'd been blind in love with some phantom dude named Robert that none of them had ever met.

Another thing Mike had changed in the last few months had been to let the hair dye fade back into his natural shade of dull brown and he'd gotten a decent trim. Paired with his shocking weight loss, he supposed he did look different—maybe even radically so. But that implied anyone had noticed what he looked like in the first place.

"There's something different about you, man," Doobs said. "Did you shave off a beard or moustache?"

Mike had played around with various styles—none of which suited him like a clean-shaven face or day-old scrub. He shook his head.

"You got new coveralls?"

He barked a laugh at that one, and Doobs went on, trying to figure out what'd changed about him. Like he couldn't stand another minute of it, Brett growled, "Try he's half the man he's always been."

Doobs looked him over critically and his intelligent eyes lit up in recognition. Another thing that'd always awed and annoyed Mike about his three male friends: All of them were so much smarter than him. Doobs was book smart. He had a Master's degree from some huge college in New York. He read everything he could get his hands on and could speak multiple languages. He was always quoting some author or famous person or another. Brett was street smart. Jace had done everything at least once so his experiences made him wise. Mike couldn't hold his own in anything but fixing cars.

Doobs's expression reeled. "Whoa. Dude, this is *serious*."

Mike flushed again, but he couldn't deny that he'd always resembled a big, fat barrel with short, stubby arms and legs. With the weight loss, he finally looked normal. In fact, he sometimes thought he looked taller than ever before. Maybe that was wishful thinking.

"Yeesh, this isn't a few pounds, man. You're a shadow of yourself." Doobs glanced at Brett. "Half the man you were. But it looks good on you. What happened? Are you sick?"

"No. Nothin' happened," Mike ground out, growing more humiliated by the second.

"Something happened, man. Did you shed all that weight and your friends at the same time?"

Mike hadn't expected that. Never anticipated Doobs sounding so offended and Brett standing there with no expression at all and yet making it obvious he'd noticed Mike's long absence—and was just as insulted by it. *Why can't I master the expressionless face? I've wanted to be able to do that my whole life, but instead my boyish, plain looks give away everything. Not that anybody cares what I feel anyway. No one notices me one way or the other. I fade into the woodwork until I disappear. And that's okay with everybody. Three months ago, it stopped bein' okay with me.*

Swallowing hard and mad as hell that he should have to feel any guilt, Mike averted his gaze again. He couldn't say what'd changed for him months ago. Maybe it was as simple as realizing his life meant so little to anyone in the world, if he died in his apartment, the only way anybody'd notice was when his stench leached out into the hallway.

Doobs made a sound that Mike accredited to guts. He had a lot of guts acting put out now when Mike knew he didn't mean anything to him. Oh, nobody in "the group" had ever been mean to him. They'd never made fun of him or played cruel jokes on him. They just hadn't considered him, beyond feeling sorry for him. In three months, he hadn't had a single visitor come to his apartment. They expected him to come to them—and bring a couple cases with him while he was at it. He'd gotten a few messages from them in his cell phone voicemail, but they never took their time calling back when he didn't respond. He'd seen Rox only because they'd met up by chance at the gym he'd become a member of to avoid this place.

Rox... Maybe she was different. She was nice, even sweet to him. She made him feel like the center of the world although he knew she wasn't interested in him and never would be. She saw him as a friend, no more or less than Darlene and Diane did. But the fact was, his absence had gone virtually unnoticed by her as well.

If he lived or died, what did it matter? So why were these two dudes acting like *he'd* done something wrong? "What's it matter to you?" Mike muttered, unable to hide his annoyance.

"What's that supposed to mean?" Doobs spit.

Surprising him, Brett stepped between the two of them. "Look, dude, you were workin' some stuff out. We left you alone so you could get a handle on it."

"Maybe I was."

"And?" Doobs demanded.

"And what?" Mike could feel his willpower collapsing. He'd never expected this attitude. *I expected 'em to act like they saw me yesterday and nothing's changed. They'll always see me as the pathetic, fat dude without feelings who could drink 'em all under the table. I don't know what this reaction is.* His guilt increased, warring with his anger.

"And…" Brett shrugged, speaking in a surprisingly soft voice, "we're here."

"You're *here*?" Mike asked, no longer sure what was going on. Were they fighting? Or something else?

"Where else would we be?"

Brett moved away again, grabbing a chair and sitting on it backwards. In truth, he looked bored out of his mind with the argument or whatever it was.

Feeling stupid and yet still furious, Mike looked away once more, wondering if he could leave now—preferably without saying anything further. But he knew he couldn't do that, not until he knew what was going on.

"You forgot your friends? Is that it?"

"Could ask you the same thing," Mike said under his breath, not looking at Doobs.

"Are you implying *we* forgot *you*? Because Brett's right. When we called and you never answered, we all kind of assumed you were working your s@#t out. But now you can't be bothered to come out from under the hood of a car when we get together up here. What's up with that?"

Mike swallowed again, his throat feeling raw. "Didn't think you'd notice."

Over-exaggerating—or at least Mike told himself he was—

Doobs sighed. "Why wouldn't we notice?"

"Why *would* you?"

Doobs snorted, lifting his hands like white flags. "Forgive me. I thought we were friends."

The guilt that'd been growing blew up in Mike's face. He'd never felt more like an ass. Okay, so Brett and Doobs *had* noticed his absence. The only reason they'd kept their distance was because they'd thought something was wrong that he needed to work through on his own.

Had they really both been here for him, waiting until he was ready? If that was true… *Do they actually consider themselves my friends? Do they even notice I'm alive?*

His face burned like acid cutting through steel. He couldn't look at either of them. He'd never wanted to run for the hills and never look back as much as he wanted to now.

"What's going on with you, Mikey?" Doobs asked, sounding not quite as unapproachable suddenly. "You look like a completely different person. If your name wasn't sewed on those coveralls, I might not have recognized you. I've never seen you without a beer gut. Seriously, have you been sick?"

"Do I look sick?" Because he needed to do something, Mike opened the can of soda and drank, cringing slightly at the sugary bite he'd gotten used to living without.

"No. I don't know. You look good, all things considered. But if you're not sick, what's going on?"

Mike wished for a laser to incinerate him on the spot. He had to answer. He just didn't know *what* to answer. Maybe he'd been all wrong. About everything. They didn't talk about their feelings with each other. Mike had never had another person to talk to about his feelings. Sometimes the girls encouraged him to, but he'd always assumed they forgot everything he said the second they left him. What did they care?

He shrugged. "I've always been..." He shrugged carelessly. "The joke of the group. I knew that. Didn't think anybody'd notice when the laughs stopped for me." Because he had to, he sneaked a peek at Doobs and Brett and saw they both seemed shocked—behind Brett's mask lacking expression, that was.

Doobs shook his head. "I don't even know what you're talking about, dude. Since when are you a joke to us? Since when did we ever laugh at you?"

Kill me now. Please, God. "Pitying," he managed.

"Okay, I have no idea what's going on here. Maybe you're not the Mikey Lund we all know and love anymore. You sure don't look anything like him."

Know and love? Since when? But Mike had to admit none of them had ever laughed at him or treated him like a lapdog trying pathetically to get their attention—to his face anyway. He'd presumed they did that when he wasn't around. As much as was possible for dudes, they'd been affectionate with him. The girls certainly had. For the years he'd known all of them, he'd convinced himself they really liked him, cared about him just as much as they'd pitied his bad luck with woman and general pathetic nature.

Maybe I transferred my feelings about myself onto them. Maybe I'm being unfair to them. I've never exactly encouraged them to open up to me so we could get to know each other beyond the surface stuff either. Dudes don't do that. But, if I don't know these two, how is it I know, though Brett's face is blank, he's accepting me with that gaze—warmly?

"You're all right, aren't ya, Mikey? You just learned a few new things about yourself. That's all. And maybe a couple new things about us."

Countless times in the years they'd worked together, Brett had made it clear he didn't believe in change. People couldn't change. In his mind, that was impossible. He believed human beings merely learned things that shaped their perceptions and the directions they moved in. *Street smarts.* With his words, he seemed to understand what Mike had been through, alone, and he was okay with it all.

Maybe the dude wants me to know he'll accept me no matter what. Fat joker or...something different.

Mike kept his gaze averted as he said under his breath, "Sorry."

Brett shrugged. "We all go through our own s*#t."

The forgiving way they'd always been with each other, Doobs nodded, looking as chagrinned as Mike felt, "Yeah. Understandable. And the weight loss looks good on you. It really does. It's natural?"

"I'm not sick. Okay?"

"Good. So...are we cool?"

"Yeah. We're cool."

Doobs got up with the same easy grin he'd had at the beginning. They shook hands again, and Mike couldn't keep himself from grinning, too. Doobs held on longer than usual to say, "Don't forget your friends again, dude. Maybe we can help."

His face burning once more at what a colossal fool he'd been, he nodded. *If I got it all wrong, I'm glad. Even when I assumed no one really liked me or wanted me there, I liked being part of this cool, likeable group.*

"In the words of Erich Segal, 'A true friend is someone who thinks you are a good egg even though he knows that you're slightly cracked'."

Mike couldn't help laughing out loud, feeling all the tension that'd made him feel rigid as a post leave him. Brett and Doobs were also laughing companionably, and Mike realized this felt familiar. *We are friends. I'm not a fifth wheel. I belong.*

A part of him still didn't quite believe it, but, before he could let himself consider anything different, his cell phone rang. The device had been all but silent for three months. He couldn't imagine anyone except maybe Jace calling him. Doobs and Brett were with him and there was no one else left who might. He sure didn't expect to see Roxanne's number in the window.

The same giddy rush he always got when Roxanne Hart, Supermodel, called him flooded and then paralyzed him. He managed to say to his friends "Rox" with his head in a whirl. He turned away from them and headed down the steps. He noticed only subconsciously Doobs's inevitable reaction to the sound of his former girlfriend's name.

The ladies in the group only called Mike to say things like "We're getting together for a party at so-and-so's house. Be there at seven"—nothing personal. Or they called him when something broke down and needing fixing. He told himself Rox was calling for that reason, not because they'd seen each other fairly recently and her words "I've missed you" actually had any meaning beyond something to say in parting.

"You got Mike," he said when he answered but instantly after the words were out, his tongue got tied in a Chinese crown knot. His mind went blank, the way it always did whenever a female talked to him, looked at him, *anything'd* him. Since he'd moved away from all things past, he'd ignored the calls from his male friends. He didn't even consider doing that now. If any of the girls had called him, he would have answered. No question about that.

"Mikey," Rox said, her voice naturally hoarse and seductive.

Mike ducked into the office on the same floor as the apartment, grateful he'd left so he could be alone. *Alone with Rox. Her voice anyway.* He was instantly aroused. Roxanne Hart was without a doubt the most gorgeous woman on the face of the earth. The fact that he knew her and she talked to him as if she liked him blew his mind without fail. While he'd sell his soul to have her, he didn't doubt she was as far from giving him that as the Earth was from Pluto.

Even above his own reaction, he noticed she sounded stressed out, hushed, like there was someone nearby listening and she didn't want him or her to overhear.

"What?"

"Mikey, you have to help me."

"Anything," he said instantly. He was barely breathing.

"Good. It's Diane. She just found out that creep of a boyfriend is married and has been all along. She's falling apart in degrees. Unfortunately, I've got this idiot fashion show coming up in Paris this weekend. I'm leaving tonight."

Diane. Sweet, beautiful, girl-next-door Diane…mistress to a married man. That's not even possible. She would never, ever knowingly do something like that. Her heart and her head and her body are so connected, she can't give one without the other. Love made her easy. Nothing else makes sense. "Okay. What do I do?"

"This guy is *not* gonna let her go easily. You know that, don't you?"

Mike didn't know anything like that. He'd never even met the dude. But Diane... *Diane's so perfect. What idiot would let her go if he had her?* "I guess."

"Mikey, you know how much she loves him."

"'Course."

"That's right. You understand, babe. You really know her. She honestly had no clue this jerk was married, even though we all suspected it from the start."

Mike had to admit he had wondered a time or two. Diane was the type who thought *I'm in love; everyone I know has to meet and love him as much as I do* when it came to her relationships. *One relationship actually. Just one in a decade.* Yet none of them, her closest friends, had met the guy.

"She believed he loved her as much as she loves him, that they'd marry and have children together someday. That he was already married and had kids with his wife never occurred to her. She's too sweet and naïve."

"Definitely. But what can I do?"

"She's devastated and blind in love. I don't know if she can trust herself. I won't be here to save her if the jerk calls and tries to charm her into his arms with lies. I won't be back for a while. Darlene and the kids are going to Buffalo and they'll be gone most of the time I am. Brett and Savvy are going there for a week or as long as he can stand, too. Mikey, you're the *only* person who can be there for her."

If he'd spoken out loud, he would have spluttered like someone with a lisp. He felt weak. When had *he* become the only person who could be there for Diane? Why him? Why would Rox assume for one second he could do anything? Besides, Diane would never agree to anything like that. "I don't know…"

"Mikey, you have to do this," Rox said in that no-nonsense, *don't you dare refuse me* tone that rendered him completely helpless every time she used it.

"What exactly is it you want me to do?" he asked, wondering if he was as pale as he felt.

"I've already talked to Diane about this, and I've set her cell phone to speed dial *you* if that SOB shows up on our doorstep. If she gets in trouble, all she has to do is speed-dial you. When you see her number on your phone, you have to go to her. You'll do that, right?"

"What…what about Doobs?" Mike asked listlessly.

"You can't be serious. I can't believe you'd even suggest it," she scolded impatiently. "You know she's got that weird, star-struck crush on your other friend."

Ever since Rox and Doobs had broken up…violently…years ago—because the dude had predictably cheated on her, Mike suspected—she refused to acknowledge him beyond calling him *their* friend, not hers. Not her *anything*, thank you very much.

"You are the only one who can do this, Mikey. It's just you or no one."

"How will I know where she is?"

"She'll tell you, of course. You'll ask her. Either way."

"And she knows about this?" Mike confirmed.

"Yes. I'm trying to talk her out of staying at the company she works. If she goes back there and sees him, she'll be lost. I told her Brett wants to hire a secretary at the body shop."

"What? When'd that happen?" Brett had his own system of

organization. Nobody, maybe not even the dude himself, understood it, but somehow he managed to make it all work. Mike couldn't imagine he'd hire someone to figure out the business end of Foxx Body Shop.

"It didn't, but you know he needs someone to get that place organized. So...you can talk him into hiring Diane, can't you?"

Mike stood in place, his mouth open at least a foot. He had no idea how she expected him to do that. But how could he say no he wouldn't do it? Nobody said no to Roxanne Hart, least of all him. And Diane... Shoot, she was the most emotional person in the world. If she had her heart set on a job here, well, Mike couldn't imagine even Brett would be indifferent to her. Somehow, he'd have to talk his boss into hiring her. *And I have to be on call if she needs me. She'll collapse without someone to help her. She's not a strong person like Rox, Darlene or even Savvy.*

"I know you can do this, babe," Rox said with such warmth, Mike felt himself viscerally heating up again in response. "Besides, this is our Diane. We have to pull together for her. So you'll do it? Be her emergency backup as long as she needs to forget Robert Drake even exists?"

Mike took a deep breath. "Yeah. But you're sure she knows about this?"

"Yes. She knows. You need to save her from herself, even if she resists you. You're prepared for that, aren't you?"

His mind rebelled. Resistant females... Not his style. He couldn't shake the feeling Rox hadn't told Diane a thing and he'd be running in there cold. Confrontations were what he'd dreaded most in the past three months. He wasn't sure he could handle Diane rejecting him, even when he'd gotten orders from headquarters as his legit pass in.

"Sure," he managed weakly.

"I knew I could count on you, babe. Only you can do this. I owe you one, okay? You just tell me if you ever need anything, and I'm there for you. Okay?"

The mere thought of Roxanne Hart doing anything he wanted made him shudder so she asked, "You okay, babe?"

"Yeah…yeah." He wasn't entirely sure he was.

"Love you."

If only. But that's a dream. Reality is, I'm supposed to be some knight in shining armor for Diane, who'll never see me as anything but Porky the Drunk Pig. What have I gotten myself into now because 'no' isn't in my vocabulary when it comes to beautiful women?

Doobs and Brett both stood at attention as soon as Mike walked back into the converted gym apartment. The last three months, keeping everything bottled up inside of him, had made him crazy. He'd never been very good about shutting himself off. Generally his "s#*t", as his friends called it, didn't come out unless he was drunk and no was listening let alone taking him seriously.

Without an outlet, no force on earth could have held him back from blurting everything about Diane's boyfriend predictably being married with kids all this time and she'd just wised up about it.

"Rox is worried 'cause she's a mess and Rox's got some fashion show in *gay Paree* for who knows how long. Plus Diane doesn't wanna go to work in case she sees the jerkoff there. So Rox thinks you should hire her, Brett, since you need a secretary organizin' all this crap at the shop."

Brett snorted a laugh. "She thinks that, does she? We've done without anything resemblin' organization since I opened this place."

"I hate answerin' the phone," Mike interjected violently. "It rings constantly. I get settled in under the hood and now I gotta be up, fillin' out paperwork, fieldin' all the calls." The phone rang non-stop, especially because the shop did such brisk business by word of mouth.

"You have only been working part-time since Savvy had the little munchkin," Doobs said to Brett. "Why not hire someone so you can pick and choose the days you work? Diane is a master at organization. She'll have every paper filed neatly and correctly in a week or less."

"Maybe. I think I could afford her. I'll have to look at some numbers, but I don't see why not. That all Rox said?"

Mike faced them both sheepishly. "Nah. I'm supposed to be somethin' like an emergency backup if that dog shows up at her door, growlin' for a bone. Rox thinks he'll trick her into takin' him back if she gives him any opening."

"She probably would," Brett agreed.

Doobs grinned. "Well, it's a good role for you, Mikey my man."

Mike snorted at the claim. "I don't know what Rox expects me to do. I don't think she told Diane anything about it, and she'll get the surprise of her life when I come barrelin' in."

"Just like Rox to make a decision and expect everybody to fall in with her plans." Doobs didn't look at them when he spoke.

"What do I do when I get there and after Diane gets over her shock?"

"You'll know when the time comes," Doobs assured him, going back to the weight bench and lying down beneath the bar. Mike automatically moved behind him to spot.

"I don't have a clue what to do."

"She'll let you know what she wants of you. If she wants you there at all."

"How?" And how would he know one way or another if she didn't say the words? He'd never understood how to read women.

"You just will. That's all. She wants you to save her from herself. So do that."

Mike groaned.

Brett laughed at him. "Wouldn't wanna be in your position."

"Thanks a lot."

"You could-a said no."

"No. I couldn't've. Nobody says no to Roxanne Hart. Nobody." Mike never said no to a woman period. The inclination wasn't in him. If Diane called him, needing him, he wouldn't have a choice. He'd run to her at the speed of light, for whatever, even if she ultimately told him to get out and leave her alone.

Mike sighed heavily. Diane hadn't bothered to see or talk to him in three months. Yet he was supposed to be there for her when she needed him. Maybe it was stupid for him to feel hurt about that, but he didn't doubt for a second she hadn't noticed his absence during this time, not for one instant.

What've I been doing with my life? Before, I was drifting along, wasted and worthless. Now...what am I now? How am I any different? I got motivated to jump out of the rut I've been in all my life. I've been watching this movie from the sidelines. I've been nothing more than a glutton, a drunk, so desperate for affection, I've slept with women too drunk to have a clue what they're doing and, if they did know, they acted out of pure pity.*

Whenever Mike thought about those times, he cringed. He didn't remember any of their names. Not even one. He barely remembered their faces anymore. Because the only way to get past the self-disgust was to turn his back on the memories while he'd focused himself entirely on becoming a different person, shifting himself into places his life could change.

The next step had been to convince himself beyond a shadow of a doubt he was never, ever going to hook up with Diane or Rox. Darlene had only been eliminated from the hope list altogether because she'd married Jace.

If he was going to learn a new way, he had to take Diane and Rox off that list, too, not simply dropping them to the bottom when he knew deep down they were both at the very top. Even that wasn't a lot of help because they were the *only* women on the list beyond nameless checkout females or shop employees from the places in New York City he frequented and thought were cute.

Fact: Women are never attracted to me. Never have been. I don't say or do the right things. I sure don't look appealing to them. Besides, I've learned only the lonely are desperate enough to lower their standards and make choices that take away pride and dignity. I don't wanna be desperate anymore. I sure as shooting don't wanna be lonely. I can't let loneliness rule my life from now on.

That meant, of course, changing the compass of his life. Finding women who didn't pity him or hang around because his friends asked them to.

Mike grimaced as he reached down to help Doobs replace the barbell back on the bar. After losing all the weight and letting his hair do what was natural, he found himself no closer to finding a woman who could like him for him. Roxanne's decree only made things worse for him. He was putting himself back in the position he never wanted to be in again. Being there for Diane until Rox, Darlene and Savvy got back and could serve as her emergency rescue was definitely a step backward on his new heading coordinates.

What can I do though? I gotta go through with this. I made a promise. Besides, Diane... Sweet, soft, adorable, sexy Diane is the only girl in the group who's always seemed accessible to me. No, definitely not in the sense that his wildest dreams could come true and he might someday be with a goddess like her. But she wasn't untouchable or already spoken for. Even after her decade-long relationship with this phantom married dude, Diane Hoffman had never seemed "taken" and her beauty was real, not of some other ethereal world he'd never hope to visit. Doobs was right, though—the role of rescuer fit him. If he was really lucky, Diane would learn to appreciate him and maybe she'd become a close friend instead of a love interest. That was just as good, right?

Mike told the guys, his friends, he had to get back to work. Their send-off made him feel strangely warm and glad for the uncomfortable confrontation that'd brought him back into their elite circle. As he descended the stairs into the garage, he warned himself not to get his hopes up about Diane. He'd done that for too long, clutching recklessly at intangible longings he'd never fulfill.

His biggest worry: He didn't know how to go into the role of a knight in shining armor without falling hopelessly in love with his charge.

Chapter 3

Since the combined forces of Roxanne's agent and bodyguard had shown up at their building in a limo so they could head to the airport and ultimately Paris, Diane had been eating fudge. And mashed potatoes loaded with enough butter to choke a horse. And pizza. Hot wings. More fudge. She recalled her best friend's worried face as she left because she'd had no other choice. *This endless eating probably wasn't what she was worried about though.*

Diane rolled her bloated body off the couch and lay for several minutes trying to pep-talk herself into moving for the first time in hours. Rox had tried futilely to talk her into going with her, playing up the amount of fun they'd have and the shopping they'd be doing. Diane knew the opposite would be the case. Diane would work non-stop.

A fashion show was the last place Diane needed to be. She'd cried off her makeup and she didn't fit into anything but the same, stained slob clothes she'd put on...*when?* Since she hadn't bothered to shower, she'd been in the same clothes since long before she could remember.

After dragging her heavy body to the bathroom, she discovered what she'd dreaded. She had her period. Somehow tears renewed. Every month, this was the reminder that she wasn't living the life she'd always imagined for herself. A good girl didn't worry about getting pregnant because she was in love and what she was doing was right. *But I worried each time Robert dropped in for such a short time or I visited him wherever he was for even shorter. The visual reminder that I wasn't pregnant would convince me I was fine again for another month.*

What happened to me? I used to be the good girl my parents raised me to be, the one who believed that sleeping with any guy who wasn't her husband and wore his ring with a marriage certificate safely stored was wrong. I never went too far with any of my boyfriends. I wanted to give my husband my virginity on my wedding night. Now I'll never live that beautiful dream.

She couldn't imagine now what she'd given it up for either. She'd sunk so far from her own ideal all because she'd fallen in love and Robert had uttered the magical words "I love *you*". Her Prince Charming had turned into a toad overnight. Over and over she imagined him leaving the hotel bed they'd made love in, getting in his stupid car and driving home to his wife…making love to *her* and saying the very same words he'd uttered only hours before to a woman he wasn't married to.

His wife isn't *The Other Woman, no matter how it feels to me. I'm not the one he married and had precious children with. Robert and I will never have a big June wedding, never have kids together. I'll be alone the rest of my life because how could I ever trust another man? I can't. I'm done.*

She couldn't imagine a time she'd more wanted to be surrounded with her friends. But they were all gone, and she couldn't call them and sob in their ears either. She hated that she'd become a zombie, but, even after a shower and squeezing her body into tight clothes, she didn't feel human.

She desperately didn't want to be alone right now because she longed to talk with Robert so badly, she could hardly keep her finger from dialing the memorized number. She'd been carrying her cell phone around with her just as she'd promised Rox she would. Mikey had been set up as #1 on the speed dial.

Mikey Lund. Of course he was a friend. But Mikey...he was such a big, sweet, goofy, adorable teddy bear. She couldn't imagine opening her heart to him any more than she could, say, Brett or, worse, Jamie. Her silly, star-struck crush on Jamie Dubois affected her even after ten years of being in love with Robert. Jamie was so good looking, she'd almost puked in panic the first time Rox introduced them.

To add to her already guilt-ridden conscience, she recalled the incident that'd happened a few years ago. Robert had been unavailable for months, as he had been recently. The last time they were together prior to this, they'd fought about getting married. She'd been weak. Only that could explain what'd happened. Roxanne and Jamie had had a weird relationship, having known each other since they were kids. In college, they'd been best friends and something more, but not really romantic. Out of nowhere, Jamie and Rox had been hot and heavy. Exclusive. No one could believe it.

Abruptly a few months after the relationship started, Jamie

showed up here at Roxanne's apartment. Diane had assumed he was coming to see Rox, but he'd revealed they'd broken it off. And he'd come on to *her*. Diane had been mortified—and too easily seduced once he'd turned on the charm. She'd never believed he noticed her before. Besides, Roxanne was having fun with the relationship—she wouldn't get serious with anyone, especially Jamie. Right?

While Diane told herself now she never would have gone along with anything back then, doubt had always lingered in her mind. Roxanne had walked in on them at exactly the wrong moment. Though nothing intimate beyond a kiss had happened, Diane could see the scene from her best friend's point of view. She couldn't have failed to believe Diane had been about to give in to *her* boyfriend's seduction. The damage had been done.

Rox told her later they hadn't broken up at all. From her side, she'd believed things were better than ever between them. Maybe it could have lasted and become something special. She claimed Jamie hadn't wanted anything special with her or anyone else. He'd wanted to break up with her and chose this way to end it. Diane had been a mere pawn. Rox insisted she didn't believe Diane betrayed her—only Jamie—but deep down Diane worried and had ever since that Rox blamed her for what might have happened.

The role of The Other Woman seems to suit me. I almost became another one with my best friend's boyfriend. But I didn't, not voluntarily. Maybe I never would have. But how will I ever know for sure? Jamie tried to seduce me just as surely as Robert did. He put me in the position without ever giving me a chance to make an informed choice all because he wasn't honest any more than Jamie had been that one time. If Robert had told me he was married first, I wouldn't have gotten involved, period. I wouldn't have with Jamie either. I believe that. I have that to salve my conscience, at least, don't I? So why am I wavering about this whole, idiot thing? I know what I have to do.

With quailing determination, Diane moved through the apartment, removing and throwing away anything associated with her relationship with Robert Drake. As she worked, the memories overwhelmed her, but she saw them with a new perspective—the one of *mistress*, not *the only woman he loves*. The taint was irrefutable. In retrospect, she had to admit her friends were right. And that led to another irrefutable conclusion: She was an idiot. She had to be because she'd never realized the truth. While she'd buried her head in the sand, she equally never stopped to consider the prospect of what was happening on the surface. *Because I was so much in love? When did I become one of those women?*

She turned all the framed photographs over so she wouldn't have to look at them. Robert's few love letters—always typed and then signed with only an "R"—went in the trash. She worried she'd take them out later. Had he always burned all her messages, emails, notes and cards so his wife wouldn't see them?

The doorbell rang, and she instantly panicked. Who would be visiting her? All her friends were gone. She all but choked when she approached the front door and used the peep hole.

Oh, no, no, no! Robert stood where he'd never come before. Almost without thinking, her finger depressed the #1 button on her phone still in her pocket. With the same lack of consideration, she unlocked the door and slowly opened it, using the wood as a shield. Foolishly, her first thought was, though she'd showered, she hadn't put on makeup, her eyes were red and raw, she was unbelievably fat and bloated with her period. She looked worse than sick, worse than dead.

Where is my protection from him? I've never had any defenses with this man.

Yet, when he took a step toward her, his expression one of regret and sorrow, she instantly took several steps back from him. He pushed open the door and entered. With one hand out, she warded him off. Surprising her, she realized tears were slipping down her cheeks. "Don't. Don't you dare," she insisted.

"Diane, please, you have to listen to me. I know what this looks like."

"*Looks like*? I know the truth. Are you going to try to deny you're married with children, all living in New Rochelle suburbia..."

His sigh was heavy. She saw him through new eyes. Saw how short he was—she was five-five. He couldn't have been a single inch taller than that. And he was bald. At the beginning of their relationship, he'd had a headful of brown hair. Now the male pattern baldness had set in so there was only hair in a friar's ring around his head. His nose was hooked. Deep dimples surrounded his unsmiling mouth. He wore the pinstripe business suit that was her favorite with his Italian loafers. She suddenly felt so young looking at him. Why had she never seen how old he was? His forty-five years felt much older than her thirty-one. Or had he lied about his age, too?

For a long moment, he simply looked at her in frustration as if he was incapable of lying now. "You don't understand, darling."

"No, you're right. I don't. You're married. Your children are young. Five, six, seven? You have a family, Robert! You have a wife. You used me. You lied to me. You carried me along on this massive delusion for ten years!" She was screaming the words at the top of her voice, never once considering her neighbors might hear.

He looked around self-consciously yet turned back to whisper, "I *love* you."

"How dare you say that? Don't!"

"It's absolutely true. I have to say it. My heart won't allow anything else."

"Do you love her?"

Even as she asked this question, she realized it didn't matter. It shouldn't matter. Who cared if he loved his wife when he was betraying her...with another woman he claimed he loved? All that mattered were the lies he'd told.

But his long pause was so revealing, Diane was forced to factor the obvious reality in. She understood in his pause that he did love his wife...which meant he was here to try to convince her to be content with their life as it was. He'd string her along for the rest of her life. Never marry her. Never have children with her. While he went home to his wife and children whenever he wasn't with her.

What did I ever see in this man? I had a terrible dream, it's over now, and...

At the end of the hall, the elevator opened, and Mikey Lund ran out of the box. Literally, *ran* almost at top speed. But Diane noticed instantly that this wasn't the same Mikey she'd seen...what? a few months ago? She couldn't quite remember. He looked so radically different, at his approach she forgot about Robert entirely.

Another thought entered her befuddled brain. Mikey had come. She'd pressed her speed dial and he'd—by the looks of it—run all the way here. Where did he even live? Or had he been close by when her call came in?

Mikey had come just as Rox asked him to. He was here to rescue her from Robert, and she'd never been more grateful for anything or anyone in her life. She threw her arms around her old friend, seeing Robert's upset expression. Without a word, he walked away and entered the open elevator doors.

Diane pulled a panting Mikey into her apartment, noticing for the first time he was gasping for air. She locked her door, asking, "How in the world did you get here so fast?"

"Live…two…blocks…away," he managed over the next minute and a half.

Mikey lived two blocks from her? She'd had no idea. She'd never been to his apartment, never even wondered where he lived. She only saw him when their friends got together as a group.

"But the doorman," Rox started in surprise.

"Rox…gave…key."

Diane had given Robert one years ago, just in case he ever stopped by, which explained how *he'd* gotten past the doorman. He'd never used it before. *I should have taken it back.* She hadn't been in her right mind to consider it.

"Let me get you water… Or would you rather have beer?"

"Water."

Mikey Lund had never refused a beer in all the time she'd known him. When she returned from the kitchen with the bottled water, she noticed again how different he looked and studied him while he guzzled the water like he always guzzled beer—in one draught. "My goodness, Mikey, how long has it been since we last saw each other? You've lost like two hundred pounds! And your hair… What did you do?"

She reached over to touch his soft, brown, well-trimmed hair. Mikey hadn't always had this color of hair. *I think he did the first time we ever met though. After that, it was always blond and poufy, greasy... Has he been dying it all this time? Why?*

"This color and style look really good on you." Nothing like the weird bird's nest he'd sported for so long. Now that she was looking closely, she saw radical differences. His weight loss had affected his face, too. Instead of doughy, pasty white, it was tan, thin and his cheekbones were amazing. This was how his face was meant to look.

The unbidden thought, *No wonder Rox thinks he's so cute. He really is* strayed through her mind and made her flush.

He wasn't speaking, just looking incredibly nervous. For once, he was being the old Mikey she knew and loved. His breathing had returned to normal. If he lived two blocks from her...well, it would have still taken a good ten minutes. He had to be full-out *running* at top speed from his apartment to hers to get here in less than five. Why in the world would he do that? Had Roxanne put the fear of God in him if he wasn't where he needed to be instantly?

Warmth filled Diane. While Roxanne could be intimidating, she suspected Mikey had come here for no other reason but because *she'd* needed him—not because he'd been ordered in no uncertain terms to head here at the first sign of trouble. From the first time she'd met the shy guy, she'd believed he was sweeter than Willy Wonka.

He'd just proven her right.

Mike had never seen Diane look at him like this before—look at him strangely, almost in awe. He felt his entire body heat like lava, then the burning shot straight to his face. He couldn't meet her eyes. In her mind, he knew she thought he'd lost hundreds of pounds. *Hell and damnation, she must've seen me as the ultimate porker—probably all she ever saw in me.*

But she'd also noticed the changes in his hair—altered in the first place because of a stray comment she'd made the first time they met. She'd all but run her fingers through it a moment ago, which was little more than torture for him. Almost no one touched him willingly. He could hardly breathe during that suspended time, afraid he'd explode if he didn't hold himself rigidly under her crazy-good touch.

Just as abruptly as she'd thrown her arms around him in front of her idiot boyfriend, she now flung herself on the couch next to him. It was then he noticed a few things about her: Diane always looked incredible. Pretty and sweet and sexy all at once. Today...well, today she looked sad, depressed, and maybe even sick. Her eyes were dark and red from obvious crying. She wasn't dressed the way she usually was either. Even still, wearing stained and ill-fitting sweats, she remained his gorgeous Diane Hoffman.

You came to rescue her. You can't sit here like a lump and say nothing now. "So...that was the jer—guy? That was the guy?"

"Jerk? Is that what you were going to say? Yes, the jerk."

She was being more polite than he would have been if he

hadn't thought better of calling the monkey-suited loser "a jerkoff" at the last second.

"I'm sorry, Mikey. I just freaked out when I saw him. I pressed the speed-dial before I could even consider what I was doing."

"Before or after you let him in?"

She glanced at him, her expression collapsing. "I shouldn't have opened the door. I know that now. He's not... Oh, Lord, I'm such a fool! He doesn't want to change. He actually said that. That nothing had to change. How could it not?"

Just like that, she was sobbing and talking a mile a minute. Mike could only fathom she'd done both, a lot, since he couldn't understand her very well. Feeling helpless to console her, he said nothing. Just looked at her off-center to prevent himself from turning into a tomato again.

"He said he's married—yes, admitted it! Admitted to having a family with his wife but said he didn't see that anything needed to change between us! I can't believe I've spent all these years dreaming of the day when we'd get married and start having children together. While he wanted nothing to change, ever."

In the past, when Diane broke down with him, the most courage he could summon amounted to putting his hand on hers lightly. More like his fingertips on the back of her hand. He'd been worried she'd reject him and scream not to touch her. *Also worried my sweaty meats on her would offend her.*

He touched her lightly now, not expecting her to have much reaction since he'd done this much before. In the past, she'd barely noticed while his entire universe had come down to five barely-there contact points between them. Instead of that this time, she threw herself in his arms full-body this time. Jumping in shock,

Mike's wits scattered like random stinger missiles. He'd spent a lifetime dreaming of this very woman in his arms like this—for any reason at all. Hell, no reason. He'd take it. She was so small and soft, and she smelled like chocolate fudge and marshmallows.

Almost like a distant memory, he recalled how they'd shared fudge so many times, when he was fat and she was depressed, which was often because her dude never showed up to any of the parties their friends threw. Sometimes the jerkoff promised he'd come, but he never did. No one believed he would, no one but Diane herself.

Feeling awed that she wanted to be close to him, Mike murmured awkwardly, "It's not your fault."

"How can you say that?" she wailed. "Roxanne and Darlene tell me they always knew he was married."

"'Cause none of us ever met him?"

"I don't get that. How does *that* tell everyone a man is married? How is that a telltale sign of anything but the truth? He traveled a lot. Constantly. Most of the year, he was off, covering his region, trying to sell our products. It's his job. I work for the same company. He wasn't making any of that up. Those were legitimate travels."

She really believed herself, Mike realized. Maybe she was right. But that was just one of many red flags Mike and their friends had seen. They didn't need to meet the guy to know what was downwind.

"None of you understand. I mean, I knew something had happened in Robert's life. Something that explained everything. His parents...if they were dead or alive, I don't know, but I know they hurt him and he was so scarred from his childhood. He couldn't rush into marriage or having a family because of what they'd done to him. He couldn't trust that everything would work out like a fairytale. He didn't like to talk about his family…"

Mike felt so sorry for her as she spoke because he could see the truth dawning in her eyes the more she said. Weaving some sob childhood story had all been part of the elaborate deception to hide reality from her—that he was already married with kids, so any relatives he actually had would know she wasn't his wife. That was why the dude didn't want to talk about his private life. She'd fallen for his "fake past pain" fabrication hook, line and sinker. "Ah, Diane, you're so sweet."

"I'm dumb," she choked out. "Oh, Lord, I'm so dumb."

He shook his head. "You're innocent. Trusting. You never would've believed someone could be so evil to you."

She looked at him with her eyes red and scoured. He couldn't look into those velvet eyes without wanting to do things he couldn't, ever. "Do you truly believe that, Mikey?"

"Everybody who knows you, really *knows* you, understands you'd never knowingly get involved with a married dude."

She shook her head, her long, messy ponytail flying. "I didn't question anything. I never considered what he told me and implied wasn't real. I never had a clue he was lying to me. I believed everything he told me."

"You don't have to defend yourself to me. I know it. You wouldn't, end of story."

Sinking back again, still so close to him she was practically sitting on his lap, she closed her eyes. "That means…" She swallowed hard, like there was a whole corn chip in her throat. "I know. And now that I know, I can't continue. I have to end it. No matter how I feel, how bad it hurts, I would rather die than willingly be some married man's *mistress*."

Diane wasn't like other women. All of their friends…Rox, Darlene, Savvy…they were so strong, few men dared to stand up to them. Diane wasn't like that. She wasn't strong. She was soft and sweet, loving, pliable, and every inch the nice girl mothers talked about longingly.

"I'd like to kill him. For takin' advantage of you like that. For puttin' you in that position."

He was talking out loud, not considering that she was sitting there listening to him watching his hands clench into fists. When he'd seen the bald stub of a guy advancing on her in her doorway, all he'd thought about was getting blood all over the cretin's pristine suit and shiny shoes. If Diane hadn't thrown herself at him the way she did, he would have, too. She might have hated him for it later.

Leaning closer so one hand was on his chest, she asked plaintively, "Mikey, will you help me? I know I'm not strong enough to do this alone. Roxanne is right about me. I'll cave in right away. I would have if you hadn't come when you did. Roxanne has always looked out for me. I don't know what I'd be now without her. But she's not here. It scares me that I believe I might have let Robert charm me into going on the way we have been, even with his wife always between us."

"What do you need me to do?" he asked, his throat suddenly so dry, he could hardly shove the words out.

"I have to stay away from him. I can't let him get to me. I can't give him the chance to…to work his magic over me. I have to stay away, can't be anywhere he is or he might be."

Aware that he wanted to be there for this woman more than he wanted his next breath, aware she was sprawled over him with her tiny body all breasts and hips, his head felt cottony. Somehow he managed, "Brett says you can work at the body shop. In the office. That place has never seen organization. Don't know if he can pay you as much as you're makin' now..."

"I don't care. They're downsizing left and right anyway. I've taken a pay-cut already when they gave me less hours and more responsibility. It was only a matter of time before they took away even more or eliminated my position altogether. And it's not like the job at the garage is permanent, right? Once it's all organized there, I can always look for a job somewhere else."

"Sure. Yeah. You can start at the garage whenever you're ready and leave when you're done."

With her face marked with tears and redness, the hope she wore appeared strange, but it gave him a surge all the same. Was he actually *helping* here?

"First I have to call and quit my job." Turning her head, she laid against his chest, murmuring, "I'm scared. It's all happening so fast."

Mike's hand was inadvertently filled with her long, thick, silky hair. He didn't even have to move to stroke the ponytail. "You don't have to do anything right now," he insisted, sounding half scared himself with the words.

"But I do, Mikey. I have to. Now. Or I won't."

Her words sounded determined, almost as determined as her body language. She nestled tighter against him, and his whole body reacted to having her full breasts pushed up against his side, soft as pillows. He didn't feel anything like comfort though. He felt strangled with the need not to move, not to breathe because he didn't want this to end, or end in his embarrassment. Limply, he uttered, "Sure. Yeah."

"Will you help me stay away from Robert?"

"I'm on speed-dial," he said, his accompanying chuckle choked.

"But that won't be enough, especially if something happens and you're at work or can't get here. I really appreciate that you're willing to do this, do whatever you can, Mikey. I don't know if I can be strong. Not on my own."

"Whatever you need."

Aw, dude, what're you doin'? You're in a bad place. You're tryin' to get yourself as far as you can from bad habits, temptation...like hopeless crushes on women who'll never see you as anything more than fat, sweet, loser Mikey. Never as a boyfriend. Never as a potential anything.

I want a real girlfriend, a real relationship. That's the one thing motivating me. I lost all the weight, got rid of the booze. I don't wanna be alone all my life, don't wanna die alone, never having a single love of my life ever. Not even for a day. I'm not gonna get that here. Diane's never gonna see me as a man she can love, like her precious Robert. So what am I doing?

Even with his pep talk, Mike knew he couldn't deny her anything. Not when she was asking him for help, snuggled up to him like a kitten, soft as one.

She sighed, sounding half asleep as she nestling deeper against him. He thought he might implode with need. "You're such a good friend, Mikey. I don't know what I'd do without my friends. I wish now that I'd called you earlier today. I've been so miserable—"

Her cell phone went off, loud and insistent, and she jumped.

When she fumbled to see the screen, Mike also recognized the caller. *The stub.*

Diane's eyes met his and he saw the plea in them. "I have to talk to him. I have to tell him not to call me ever again. He won't accept that from anyone but me."

"Won't accept it from *anyone*," he told her softly.

Like he knew she wouldn't, she didn't listen to him. She swallowed and brought the phone up to her ear, pushing herself to her feet as she did. A second later, she listened, then said, "That was Mikey. Mikey Lund."

Dude had the nerve to ask who I was. From her expression and the guy's loud voice coming from the phone, Old Robert was jealous. Mike had never been in the position to make any man jealous of him. He could only enjoy the sensation that wasn't exactly grounded in reality. He wasn't with this woman, no matter what the creep thought. Not the *way* Mike wanted to be.

"Robert, stop. I can date anyone I want. I can do whatever I want. You've lost any right to be jealous. You never had any right… No. I won't see you anymore. Everything had changed between us. It's over. Now stop calling me."

She was shaking when she pressed a button and threw her phone into the chair like it'd become a snake in her hand. Laughing, Mike said, "Good for you."

But she was shaking and sobbing again. "You have to do something, Mikey. Can you? You're a mechanic. You can block his calls, right? On my phone?"

He glanced at it. "I don't know. We can give him a distinctive ringtone so you know it's him when he does call and can shut your phone off. Or you can get a new phone with a new number. If there's some way to block his calls altogether, I don't know it." His mechanical skills didn't carry over to cell phones unfortunately. He only owned one because it was cheaper than having a landline.

Would she do either of his suggestions? She had to know one or other would be the best thing for her.

"I thought I could do it. But what if I can't? If I see him ever again, I'll..."

Mike reached up and touched her hand with his fingertips again. She looked down at him. "I'll help ya. Don't give up so easy."

She half swallowed, half sighed, her expression pure chaos. Sinking down, she grabbed the collar of his shirt. "Help me convince Robert you're my boyfriend. It's the only way. The only way to get him to leave me alone."

Did she have the slightest idea how unfair she was being to him? Asking him to pretend a dream he'd longed for endlessly was coming true? To convince one guy she was over him, she would playact being in love with him and assume Mike would go along with this just to help her. Every second with her, even the ones filled with her misery over some jerkoff, made him want to really be with her. The line between make believe and reality was too fine for him.

Knowing he'd regret this, probably more than anything he'd ever regretted in his lifetime, he told her exactly what she wanted to hear.

Chapter 4

"What?" Diane laughed, sure she'd heard Mikey wrong. Though she hadn't eaten anything since before he showed up, she was starting to get hungry around nine that evening. "You don't want fudge?"

He shook his head again.

"But we always have fudge together!" That'd been one of the few constants in her life. When no one else wanted to descend into misery, Mikey Lund would join her. Now he was refusing. *Mikey! Mikey Lund!*

At only five foot five, she'd always struggled with her weight. Mike was taller than her, but, when she looked at him for the *countless* time since he got here, she noticed he looked shockingly taller than ever before. *Can you lose a drastic amount of weight like this and grow taller as a result? Or does it just seem like it because he's so much taller than he is wide now?*

Why had she never noticed his eyes before? They were forest green—a compelling green with tiny flecks of brown. *Why haven't I ever seen his face in general?* No matter how often he shaved, he always seemed to have five o'clock shadow. Now she realized how soft the hair looked on his tan face. Without all the layers of bloat, he had a pointed chin and lean cheekbones with subtle dimples. His lips were full and beautifully shaped. The one thing that saved him from being breathtakingly gorgeous was his too straight, almost pointed nose that was slightly large. *A Sean Penn nose—one that doesn't hurt his good looks but doesn't help either. I like that. I don't think I can be with a man who's too handsome, like Jamie...*

The direction of her thoughts made her gasp, and Mikey's tentative fingers on her hand brought her back to reality—the reality that the relationship she'd invested herself in had ruined her. She slammed the freezer and sulked against the sink. "I'm so fat. I let him do this to me. Well, no, I did it to myself because I'm pathetic. I'm hideous."

"You could never be," Mikey defended without a pause after her words.

He wouldn't look at her, not surprisingly. He almost never looked into her eyes. He was too shy around women to do that. But the fervency in his words soothed her aching heart. Mikey was so sweet. If any man could believe she was beautiful, even looking as bad as she did at the moment, it was Mikey Lund.

Since he wasn't facing her, she let herself look at his tall, lean body. He was wearing jeans that showed off his new, appealing shape with an almost new t-shirt that stretched across his muscular chest. His arms bulged with muscle, not fat. It'd only been a few months since she'd last seen him. She could hardly believe he was the same man he'd been then. "How did you lose all that weight, Mikey? It's just shocking!"

"Half the man I was?" he teased himself, his grin adorable enough for her to want to coo. "I cleaned out my apartment. Threw out all the junk food and booze. Stopped drivin' past all the places I knew I couldn't resist. I walk almost everywhere now, too."

"You mean, you didn't keep any fudge in your freezer just in case you hit rock bottom?"

"Well, fudge isn't my downfall. Pizza and beer are my killers. But that's the strategy I used to overcome."

"It's hard to believe you stopped drinking," she said gently. "I've never seen anyone drink the way you always have."

He nodded. "I think the liquor store I always bought from went outta business after I quit cold turkey. I've been drinkin' heavy since I was eleven."

Diane gaped at him. "What? Didn't your parents notice?"

"No. I was just another mouth to feed."

She turned. "Oh, Mikey, that's so sad." *Why didn't I know this about him? I've known him for a decade! But then I always talked about myself when he was around.*

He shrugged it off, the way she expected him to. "I got more money than I ever had before, now that I'm not spendin' most of it on booze and junk food."

"What will you do with the money?" she asked, wanting to hear more about this man she was only beginning to realize was an acquaintance at best.

"Save it. Never did that before."

His willpower inspired her. If Mikey could do it, maybe she could, too. She opened the freezer again, took out the container of fudge she'd plowed through in the last few days and dumped it in the garbage. Admitted, it was mostly empty, but her intention was good. Mikey beamed at her. Then she marched into the living room with a bottle of water and plunked down on the couch. Mikey followed her but didn't sit too close. "I've never done much saving for the future either. I honestly don't even know what I do with my money. Roxanne pays more than her share of rent for this place. I could never afford it myself, but she insists she hates living alone so she should pay more. She can afford to." She sighed, screwing open the bottle. "This isn't the life I imagined for myself."

"What'd you imagine?"

"I bet you can guess. I would finish college, work for five-ten years, then get married and have at least three kids. I would stay home to raise them while my husband was the breadwinner. Robert was the only man I ever imagined in the role of my husband."

"Other than the *who*, it sounds nice."

"Does it? What about you?" *I never ask him that. Why have I never asked him about his life? Why have I always been so selfish with this sweetheart who's only been good to me?*

"Other than bein' a stay-at-home mom, yours sounds like a pretty sweet setup. Not that it'll ever happen for me."

"What do you mean? Why won't it ever happen?"

"I'm not exactly Prince Charmin'. Or Jamie Dubois, for that matter."

Diane flushed deeply—all of her friends knew of her girlish crush on Jamie. She hated that. She hated that Jamie himself must have seen how silly-starstruck she'd always been around him. She couldn't string two sentences together when he was in the same room. "You're some woman's Prince Charming, Mikey. Look at yourself. You look amazing. And I..." She abruptly sniffed and got a cringing whiff of herself. "Oh my gosh, I stink. And I'm so tired." But she'd never sleep. Not wondering how far Robert would go to continue their immoral relationship. She still couldn't believe how insanely jealous he'd been, believing she was dating Mikey.

I'm using Mikey again. I've always used him and never realized I was doing it. But he's a crutch for me. When I'm low, he makes me feel better—regardless of how it makes him *feel. He's too nice to me. I'm so unfair to him.*

"You should sleep," he said quietly, so gentle she wanted to put herself in his strong arms again, where she'd felt safe and cared for in the turbulent storm that blew in with Robert.

"I need a bath."

"Take one."

Hating herself for her inadvertent cruelty to him for so many years, she tried and failed to prevent herself from admitting, "I don't want you to leave."

Why did he seem so surprised at her words? That made her feel worse.

"I won't leave."

"Will you come in and talk to me while I take a bath in Roxanne's big old Jacuzzi tub?"

His face turned so red, she couldn't help giggling. "I mean, after I'm in. You won't see anything. Roxanne's tub is so huge, and she loves six-inch-deep bubbles in her bath. Everything will be covered."

His embarrassment didn't really lessen. His eyes averted, he nodded.

"I'll call when I'm ready for you to come in."

Though she giggled a few more times as she gathered fresh

pajamas and supplies from her room, she couldn't help wondering if Mikey was picturing her naked.

Now it was her turn to be embarrassed. Her body had become a horror to her in the last, dreadful months since she'd last seen Robert. She'd struggled all her life to keep her weight down. Sometimes she could make her waist smaller, but her hips and bust were always too big for her petite figure. She couldn't bear the thought of any man seeing her naked. *Maybe I'll never feel comfortable like that again. I was blind over exactly the wrong man.*

After the tub was filled with hot water and a thick layer of fragrant bubbles, she opened the medicine cabinet in her friend's private bathroom to look for something she could take for her cramping, maybe something that could also make her sleepy—to sleep without dreams. She could hardly believe the number of prescription bottles lining the shelves. What were they all for? While Diane had no doubt her friend had indulged in more than a few illegal drugs when she was younger, she'd never seen Roxanne take prescription drugs.

Frowning, she pulled one bottle off the shelf and saw a sleep aid. Roxanne had advised her to take these the night she found out the truth about her boyfriend. Diane wanted to sleep soundly tonight because tomorrow she had to quit her job at Global Pharmaceuticals. They wouldn't like that she wasn't planning to give them any notice, but maybe they were already considering cutting her position and it wouldn't matter anyway.

She couldn't risk going back for even a day. She knew for a fact Robert would be in tomorrow and every day afterward if she gave two weeks' notice. She'd probably have to go in to get her final paycheck though. *Maybe Mikey will go with me. He's such a nice guy.*

And I'm not the nice girl I've spent my life telling myself I am.

She swallowed two of the Ambien, opened the bathroom door, then rushed to slip out of her robe and into the hot water. Then she called out to Mikey. By the time he came shuffling in, his face averted and radish red, she was completely covered with bubbles from neck to tippy-toes. He maneuvered Roxanne's foreign Mademoiselle chair closer to the tub but still wouldn't look at her once he was sitting.

He's such a sweetheart. Not a pig at all like most men. Like Robert Drake. And he's so darn cute. How could I not have noticed how adorable he is? How is it Roxanne noticed and I didn't? She even said she might go after him, he's so cute. But Mikey and Rox? No way. She'd decimate him with her aggression. Mikey couldn't handle a tough woman like Roxanne. Jamie is perfect for her in that regard. He can take her ruthless hardness, her ups and downs, her violence and her rare child-like moments of vulnerability. Not Mikey. Never Mikey.

Diane swallowed, feeling weird thinking about him in a "boyfriend" light. But she had to admit, she didn't like the idea of Roxanne pursuing Mikey at all. She couldn't explain even to herself why the thought bothered her so much.

She shifted in the tub, aware suddenly of the discomfort rolling off Mikey. It made her palpably sensitive to how ridiculous and fat she felt. "Mikey, do you believe it's possible to love two people? I mean, to be completely in love with two people at the same time?"

He shrugged. "What do I know?"

"I can't get over how Robert claimed to love me. He didn't say the words, but when I mentioned his wife I just knew by his expression that he loves her, too. How is that possible? Are passion and desire and love *common*? I mean, wouldn't they have to be if you can love two people with the same amount of passion and love? Doesn't one passion negate the other and prove love false?"

"I guess. Sounds right to me."

Diane frowned. "Have you ever been in love?"

The noise he made was strange. "I don't even know how to tell if you're really in love. How is it any different than lust or a crush?"

Diane's throat ached when she looked at Mikey and saw how uncomfortable he obviously felt with this topic. Had he ever been in love? She realized he probably hadn't. They all knew of his crushes—on Darlene, Roxanne. *Me. I think he even had a crush on Savvy at some point.* But has he ever been in a real relationship? The only women she'd ever seen him with were her friends and that'd never been anything but friendship, as well as drunk bimbos in love with Brett, Jamie or both. The times those women had been all over him, he'd seemed humiliated and powerless to stop them. *No, Mikey's never been in love and he wouldn't know whether it was merely lust or a crush or true love. Poor Mikey. It's not fair. He's such a good guy.*

She wanted to cry again, and for once it wasn't for herself. But she only said, "So Robert never loved me. Or he never loved his wife. He used me either way. It's the only thing that makes sense. He doesn't want to give up free sex with a woman blind in love with him."

Mikey didn't say a word, but he looked as miserable as she felt. *Why am I talking about this? I'm not in the least bit comforted by it, and he certainly can't be. I need to shut up.* Luckily, she could feel the pills working, making her sleepy and woozy, pitifully drunk on depression and grief.

One minute, Diane was talking nonstop about things Mike didn't want to hear because they made him feel every inch of his worthlessness and his inability to make a woman really like him. Besides, she'd never get over that classy stub and see Mike as anything but the drunk lardo he'd been all his life. The next minute, she stopped running off at the mouth—dead stop. Out of the corner of his eye, Mike saw she was slumped down in the tub, obviously not wanting him to see anything even if there were more bubbles than water covering her. He forced himself to glance her way. Frowning, he said, "Diane, you okay?"

She didn't say anything. Was she asleep? In the bathtub?

"Diane, do you think maybe you should get out..."

She didn't move, didn't respond at all. He stood and leaned over the tub, tentatively touching her barely emerged shoulder. Though he'd hardly nudged her, her head slumped to the side and forward at the same time. "Diane?"

What was going on? She was tired, sure. He could tell earlier she hadn't slept much since she found out about her creepy boyfriend. But this wasn't just sleep. She seemed dead to the world. He shook her bare shoulder now. She didn't stir at all.

Not knowing what to do, Mike turned and saw a hand mirror on the double sink. He grabbed it and brought the glass close to Diane's mouth. Then he leaned in and saw her breath had steamed the mirror. She was alive...so why was she so out of it?

When he set down the mirror again, he saw an open prescription bottle and picked it up. *Ambien? Sleeping pills? Okay, so maybe she took these and they hit her harder than she expected. But I can't leave her in the tub when she's knocked out like this. If she wakes up and finds out I had to see her naked to get her out of there, hell and damnation, she'll freak out. Truthfully, so will I.*

For the next minute, he squatted by the side of the tub and tried to wake her by shaking her and saying her name loudly. Nothing he did brought her out of her swoon. Biting his lip, he looked around and saw the large stack of colorful pastel towels on a rack. *Okay. What else can I do?*

After making sure she was sitting up far enough not to slide down with her head under the water, he grabbed half of the towels and all but ran to the bedroom connected to the bathroom. He tore the satin comforter off the top, then laid the towels out on one side from the pillows all the way down to the bottom of the king-size bed. Then he ran back to the bathroom, pulling his t-shirt over his head. He draped one of the extra-large towels over top of her in the tub. It was then he acknowledged that, one way or another, he would have to touch her in places he'd only fantasized about. He didn't have a choice because he couldn't leave her in the water where she could drown, or at the very least turn into a prune.

Taking a deep breath, he plunged his bare arms into the tub on the side closest to him. Closing his eyes at intimate contact with her skin, he slid both his arms under her body—one under her back, the other under her legs. Then he lifted. With his awkward pushoff, he ended up submerging her and soaking the towel instead, which plastered itself to her upper half. In the wave of water plunging over her, the modesty towel he'd draped respectfully over her front slid off and revealed most of her lower body.

He stopped breathing, tried to avert his eyes, but he wanted to look at her naked so badly, he hated himself; wanted to see the shape of her perfect breasts with the wet towel molded tightly over them. She was completely out of it, completely vulnerable to him…

He wouldn't take advantage of her. Even with his vow to protect her, there was absolutely no way to avoid seeing more than he should.

As fast as he dared, he carried her to the towels he'd laid out on the bed and laid her on top of them. Turning away as soon as he did, he rushed to the bathroom and got another dry towel. He brought it back, knowing his mind had already burned the sexy image of her sprawled, wet and half uncovered on the bed, into his memory.

Nothing was working the way he intended. He was nervous and repulsed with himself for the arousal he couldn't control, especially after he covered the wet towel over her with the dry one. He knew she'd be uncomfortable with the wet one on her all night, so he tried to do a magician's trick and take the wet one off while the dry one was on top. Only pulling on the wet one—fast like a band-aid—also yanked the dry one off. He saw everything.

He'd never forget a single inch either. While the only fully naked women he'd ever seen were in magazines (the women he had sex with never took off more than a few articles of clothing), the picture Diane painted before him made him forget every one of them.

Swearing at himself, he worked quickly after that, his gaze averted, getting her fully covered with the dry towel and then the blanket. He was sweating, panting, groaning in regret that his intention to safeguard her modesty had failed so completely when she suddenly turned her head and murmured, "So ashamed."

Mike blushed, a second from racing out of the room in case she woke up. But she didn't. She didn't seem conscious at all. She'd spoken in her sleep. *She doesn't know what just happened. She doesn't know I saw her naked. She's not talking about me or to me.*

He swallowed, overwhelmed with sympathy for her. The jerkoff had tricked her so completely, yet *she* felt bad about herself over something not even her fault.

Wiping his arms and upper body with the wet towel he'd taken off her, he left her in the bedroom by herself and went to drain the tub. Flashes of curvy hips, legs, killer breasts went through his mind as he worked. *Never understood guys who rush past foreplay. I could spend six hours on breasts alone. With Diane's...man, I'd never wanna stop, even knowing now what other treasures she has in store. I may not be a stud, but that's one thing I can do right. Twenty-four hours wouldn't be enough for everything I'd wanna do to that gorgeous body...*

He'd never been more excited, not even those humiliations with Doobs' and Brett's castoffs. In truth, he'd spent a lifetime ill-satisfying his own sexual needs, and that was another thing he'd vowed three months ago to quit cold turkey.

He wasn't sure how to control himself now, but the thought that Diane would die of shame and he'd kill himself as a consequence if she discovered him actually yanking on himself, or found out what he'd done in reaction to accidentally seeing her kept him in line.

For the next hour, he sat without daring to move in the bathroom in the ridiculous chair he'd pulled up next to the tub when Diane was inside it. The slightest memory of her nudity set him off again. But he fought himself every single time, filled with the kind of self-disgust that'd changed his life overnight a few months ago.

When he'd finally cooled off in sheer determination and stopped panting raggedly, he studied the prescription bottle. Should he try to wake her? Diane had once told him she couldn't handle any drugs. She worked for a pharmaceutical company, yet ibuprofen made her woozy.

Swallowing his self-revulsion, he forced himself to think of the woman lying in the next room unconscious. Maybe he'd screwed up in his attempt to rescue her this time, but he couldn't have left her in that tub while she was knocked out like that. He had to make sure she was okay. She was Diane. His friend.

He stood and worked his cell phone out of his pocket. With a few touches, he called up Rox from his contact list and dialed. He had her number mostly because she'd taken his phone and put it in there the last time they were together. She'd also made him take a picture of her—wearing that spandex stuff that couldn't hide anything. If not for that picture, Mike was sure he wouldn't have remembered how hot she'd looked dressed like that. Not after seeing Diane the way he shouldn't have.

Until Rox answered, sounding half asleep, he didn't think about what the time difference was in Paris. "Mikey, what's up, babe?"

He found himself burning with shame again at the hoarse tone of his voice when he said, "Hey". Somehow he felt like she knew exactly what had happened recently and, just like Rox, instead of thinking he was dirty, she was amused.

"Diane called me. She took some pills. The bottle says they were prescribed to you. Ambien."

"She didn't really? Is the bottle full?"

"Yeah. Well, except what she must have taken. Maybe two."

"It's completely full?"

"I don't think she meant to try to kill herself. She wanted to sleep, but she knew she wouldn't be able to. 'Cause of that stub."

"Okay. So the jerk called her?"

"He showed up here."

"And Diane speed-dialed you?"

"Yeah."

"Good for you, Mr. Lund. You've done very well. And you're with her now?"

Why did he feel like such a creep precisely because Rox was saying nice things about him? He was no hero. He'd...well, he'd never live down what he'd done, lusting after her like some kind of perv while she was unconscious.

"She told him to go away, Diane. And then she was depressed. Didn't wanna be alone. Decided to take a bath, and she must've taken these pills just before getting in."

"Let me guess, she was in the tub, wearing bubbles in a head-to-toe body suit, when she called you into the room?"

"She all but passed out in there. I couldn't wake her up. So..." *Maybe if I tell someone—not Diane—I won't feel like I'm depraved.*

"Oh, Mikey, you adorable thing. You saw her naked and of course it got you hot. But you were trying to rescue her. I'm sure you didn't do it on purpose. *I* don't have any doubt you had her draped with a thousand towels. It's not the end of the world."

"Would be for her if she found out."

"So she doesn't need to know. You didn't do anything but look and react. As you should have. She'd be more upset if you didn't react—trust me. That's all she needs to know. You were a hero."

"I didn't mean to even look..."

"You don't need to defend yourself to me. I know you, Mikey Lund. You're a good guy. And I'm not at all worried about our friend because you're there. You're her Prince Charming."

"I'm not."

"You are. If you're so worried, you can always show her yours."

Mike gaped as if she could see him. Was she suggesting he get naked in front of Diane? Fair's fair? For a long moment, he cringed at the thought of such an angel seeing his fat, disgusting body. He'd never let a woman see any part of him but one and that only to facilitate the dirty dive.

"I wish I was there now. That's a show I'd hate to miss," Rox said and chuckled in the throaty way that set him on fire.

Was Roxanne Hart, Supermodel, now implying *she* wanted to see him naked? Catching a glimpse of himself in the mirror, sans shirt, he suddenly realized he wasn't the barrel he'd been all his life anymore. He was trim and muscular. He had the body he'd spent a lifetime wishing for and believing he could never have. No one in his family was thin. He'd assumed his dough-boy shape was hereditary.

"Oh, Mike, how can you not see the truth for yourself? If not for social convention and other factors, I'd be all over you in a heartbeat. You don't know how hard it was not to drag you into the broom closet of the gym that day we last saw each other and have my way with you. Can't you see how gorgeous you are now?"

Who is she talking about? Me? No way. Roxanne Hart isn't coming on to me for any reason but pity. A woman like her never looks at guys like me. Sure as shootin' doesn't drag a loser into a closet for a quickie.

"Well, good, because your humility is part of your charm. You'll stay with Diane until she wakes up?"

She hung up with another throaty chuckle when he croaked he would. He was standing in front of the mirror that filled most of the wall above the sink, still without his t-shirt on. Humility aside, whenever he looked at himself in the mirror lately, he had to reintroduce himself to the person staring back. He barely recognized himself. He was in good shape. He really was. He'd combined diet with exercise. There wasn't an inch of fat on him anymore.

Despite the radical changes right in front of his own eyes, he couldn't get himself to believe an attractive woman like Diane would ever see him as anything but a friend. *Someone to help her convince her creep of a boyfriend she's over him.*

Mike yanked his still wet shirt on and reluctantly walked into the bedroom while he pulled it down. Diane hadn't moved since he left her. She slept so deeply, he could see her vulnerability and he felt even worse about his earlier behavior. She was so pretty and fragile. *I can't trust myself with her. I'll fall in love with her…or whatever it is that makes me stupid over all the girls I know and those who are only nice to me because I'm a customer or something. Diane will never see me as anything but her last resort. Her fudge buddy. Maybe I don't know what real love is myself, and I wouldn't know the difference in this case. But, no matter what happens, just like always, I'm gonna hurt when she makes it clear I'm not good enough for her and all the kissy-lovey stuff she wants for us while convincing her boyfriend it's over is fake. How do I wise-up and keep myself distant?*

How?

Chapter 5

Diane woke in an unfamiliar bed, becoming conscience of her location and situation slowly. Her head was fuzzy and she didn't feel in the least bit well-rested. *The drugs. Ugh. I feel drugged. I didn't sleep off the effects.*

As yucky as she felt, she remembered strange dreams that'd become reality. Tears. She remembered Robert getting further and further away from her and wanting that as much as she didn't. She recalled flashes of Mikey, and she felt strangely embarrassed as she tried to sit up but felt like she had no coordination at all under the influence of the sleeping pills she'd taken.

What happened? Pieces of a puzzle came to her in reverse order. She was in Roxanne's bed, surrounded with towels—above and below—that felt slightly damp. She was absolutely naked. She'd taken a bath. Mikey had been here—been with her in the bathroom.

Throwing off the blanket, she looked down to see blood,

luckily not much, on the towels beneath her. She'd gotten her period yesterday. So how was it she was sleeping in Roxanne's bed *naked*? Had the drugs knocked her out so completely, she had no memory of ever getting out of the tub?

She rushed into the adjoining bathroom, clutching the top towel to her, and put on the panties and pad she'd brought in with her. She slipped into her robe, tying it tightly as if making up for a "loose" night she couldn't remember, not daring to look herself in the mirror. The fancy clock in the room told her it was barely six in the morning.

Feeling like she might pass out any minute, she tentatively went out to the living room. Mikey was passed out on the couch, his shoes kicked off. He was sound asleep and she wondered again what had happened last night. *Did the sleeping pills kick in while I was in the tub? Did I pass out? What he must have thought! But I woke up bare naked, asleep in my roommate's bedroom. How did I get there?*

She felt almost too sick to allow herself to think past that question, but her face burned hot at the implications. Mikey must have thought she fainted or something—from grief? He'd rescued her. He must have. And then he'd come out here to watch over her all night.

Though her head was light enough to float off like a balloon, she couldn't help sinking onto the coffee table in front of her old friend. He looked so different! She couldn't get over the changes. Surely the pills made her soft and gooey when she watched him for an undefined amount of time, marveling at the changes and how adorable he was. Rox had been right about that. He was good looking almost beyond bearing. Strangely, her recollection of some of the things he'd said was sharp—private things about his parents not realizing he was an alcoholic from the time he was pre-teen; that he'd never been in love and didn't know what the emotion even felt like.

What a lonely life he must have led. Are all his friendships like ours—superficial, one-sided, completely selfish? He's such a nice guy. How often has he been there for me when I most needed a friend, and he asked for nothing in return—not even acknowledgement of his own existence. He doesn't deserve to be overlooked or used. Especially by me. Because I've done that too much already with him. I don't want to do that again. Starting today, I'm going to be a real friend to him, too. Somehow. Maybe I can help him get a girlfriend, someone who'll be as nice and sweet to him as he deserves.

He woke with a start, surprising both of them as he all but leapt to a sitting position and demanded, "Are you okay?"

She blushed again. "I'm sorry. I...I don't remember much. I must have passed right out. I took some..."

"Sleeping pills. Yeah, Rox's prescription. Didn't you say you can barely tolerate ibuprofen?" He rubbed his eyes.

She frowned. "You remember that?"

He nodded as if the retained memory was of no interest, but it was just another thing that made him so wonderful while she'd been anything but to him. "What happened?" she asked. "I'm actually not sure I want to know."

Just like that, his face turned the color of a beet. She knew the basics simply from that.

He scrubbed his hands over his face, then leaned over his knees. "I'm sorry. I just...I couldn't wake you up. I saw that prescription bottle on the counter. I called Rox 'cause I thought she might know what was goin' on. I couldn't leave you there, but there was no way..."

He'd seen her naked or nearly so.

Okay. Diane took a deep breath and let it out. Even as she realized that, her mind assured her the Mikey she knew and loved would never take advantage of her. Never. He would have tried to respect her privacy as much as he possibly could, but she couldn't imagine how much that would have been possible. She'd passed out cold in a tub full of thick bubbles, buck naked.

She slid over to the sofa and put her arms around him. He looked at her with his eyes wide, like he could hardly believe her reaction. "I know you, Mikey. I trust you. I'm sorry you were put in that position. You must have been so embarrassed. But thank you. For being there for me. For rescuing me yet again. You always take care of me. I don't even know why..." Tears of fatigue and medication-fuzz filled her eyes. "I've never been a good friend to you, Mikey Lund. I know that. I've been so selfish, and I'll never do that again. I'll try not to anyway. I seem to do it without even realizing I am."

"Don't worry about it," he said, sounding even more humiliated.

"I am worrying about it. You know, my memories of my lowest points for so many years, you were always there."

He laughed, and she realized she'd made it sound like he was the *cause* of her low points. "I mean, you were the bright spot. You're the one who lifted me out of my misery. Anyone else would have told me to shut up and *wise* up. Do you think it's possible that deep down in a place inside me, I somehow knew about Robert all this time and just didn't want to face it? Because the truth seems so obvious now, so in-my-face blatantly clear. But it wasn't before."

"I think you're too sweet to've ever considered what a creep he was. You're a nice girl. You're innocent. You love with your whole heart, and that kind of love...well, sometimes it blinds us to what's really goin' on. Not that I've got any personal experience."

The drugs were messing with her entire being. She couldn't stand to hear Mikey say such a thing, and she hugged him harder, wishing he would tell her that all the high points of his life had been spent with her. That she'd been such a good friend to him, he barely noticed his loneliness. *But that's not true at all.*

While she hugged him, feeling more comfort than she expected she was bestowing on him, she randomly thought again that Mikey had seen her naked. When she was so fat and bloated, he'd seen her naked. For once, she was the cow. She didn't like that thought, but it wasn't any more comfortable for her to acknowledge she *wanted* Mikey to have thought she looked sexy when he saw her bare. But how could he? "I never want to eat again," she murmured.

"Don't do that. That's the worst thing you can do."

"What do you mean?" Her "diet" consisted of gorging and then starving to make up for her lack of discipline. She'd done that her whole life.

"If you stop eating in reaction to eating too much, you'll overeat the next time and you probably won't choose anything healthy or low calorie. Besides, you do know when you fast, your body compensates by storing fat, right? In other words, as soon as you eat, your body converts the food to fat just in case it goes without again. That way it'll have fat stores to rely on when you fast the next time."

"Great. Are you serious? So when I'm good and don't gorge, I'm getting fatter?"

"You're not fat. Not at all."

Diane didn't look at him, but she could feel the fervency inside him when he spoke, and her mind took her to another place she'd never imagined it would go: Mikey had always had a crush on her, sure. What girl didn't he have a crush on? But he liked her. Despite her selfishness, he still liked her, and he'd seen her naked last night. He didn't think she was fat, "not at all", so that meant... *He thinks I'm sexy. He liked what he saw. He might've gotten aroused, seeing me.*

That kind of thinking should have made her worried or disgusted, but she felt neither. She became warm and almost uncomfortable in her own skin at the thought of Mikey's reaction to seeing her in the nude. *Because I know he was a perfect gentleman, even if he didn't want to be. Because he saved me from my own stupidity.*

He went on, and Diane was grateful he couldn't read her mind. "But, yeah, that's how it works. Best thing you can do is eat something healthy now. And don't let yourself get too hungry between meals."

I want him to see me when I look good for once. "What should I eat?"

"For breakfast? Fruit. Whole-grain toast. Something like that."

She wasn't in the least bit hungry, but she believed Mikey. The only way to get herself in shape was to change her way of thinking. He'd transformed almost completely and he'd obviously done it the smart way. "Will you help me get in shape? You seem to know just what to do."

"Easier said than done, but sure."

"Let's start today."

"Okay."

"I have to get ready so I can go in to work and quit. Will you go in with me? And then we could go to the body shop and see what's in store for me?"

"While you get ready, I'll go pick up some fresh fruit. Are you sure you're okay?"

Diane chuckled, hugging him a little a tighter around his big, strong shoulders. "I admit, I don't feel great, but I'll be okay as soon as I get some coffee in me and take a long shower. I must smell offensive." Yet she couldn't get herself to back away from him or let go.

For the rarest of moments, Mikey actually looked her in the eyes—up close and personal. "You do know that's not possible, don't you?"

She smiled at his sweetness. "Do you forgive me, Mikey? For being so unfair to you for so long? You've been such a good friend and I haven't been to you. I never, ever want to hurt you. Will you tell me if I do?"

He did this shrug-headshake thing, and she knew he was rebelling not against the idea that she could hurt him but that he could open himself up enough to admit he'd been wounded.

"Friends are honest with each. I want you to be honest with me. I want us to get to know each other. Everything. Okay?"

"Why?"

His question bothered her and she wasn't sure why. "Because we're friends. We have been for a long time, but not... I don't feel like I know you very well. I've been selfish, but you're not someone who talks about his feelings often."

"Why would anyone want me to?"

"Of course I want you to!"

"Why 'of course'?"

"Are you being deliberately difficult? I want to be your friend like you've been to me. I like you, Mikey. I love you! You're such a good friend. So get used to it. Okay?" She jumped up.

He didn't look convinced, and she knew she'd have to prove herself. She wanted to. "I'm going shower. I'll see you at seven o'clock?"

He reached for his shoes. "Okay. Call me if... Anything."

She smiled. "You're on speed-dial."

After a long, hot shower with enough soap to make everyone around her allergic, she dressed in one of her loosest, layered business pant suits. With makeup on and her long hair in a stylish twist, she felt better mostly because she looked better than she had in days. She made coffee in Roxanne's expensive machine and a large mug of the caffeine dissipated the last side effects of the sleeping pills. Before Mikey arrived, she quickly tossed all the towels and sheets in the washing machine, then remade Roxanne's bed.

Surprising her, she started to feel hungry on her second cup of black coffee. She decided to call in to work to distract her until Mikey came with the fruit. The human resources department secretary she was mildly friends with picked up. "Feeling better?" Nancy asked.

"Yes. But I'm actually calling because...well, I'm quitting, Nancy. I'm sorry I can't give any notice. I can't go back."

"Wow! Didn't expect that."

"I'm sorry."

"You know, Mr. Drake has been asking about you in the past few days. A lot. Does that by chance have anything to do with why you're quitting?"

Does everyone know about me and Robert at work? We were careful to keep it quiet. Robert was so adamant because it's supposedly a no-no for co-workers to fraternize romantically. But I spend a lot of time in his office, the door locked, when he's in town. Has someone noticed that?

Diane found she couldn't speak, and she knew she didn't need to when Nancy said, "Well, I guess it doesn't matter anyway. We've all heard talk of more downsizing. The axe is falling all over the place here. If you're sure, I'll rush the paperwork through this morning if you want to pick up your final paycheck later."

"I can pick it up this morning."

"Then I'll get going now. We'll miss you around here, Diane. It would have been nice to throw you a going-away party."

Robert would be there. I couldn't bear it. "Thanks, Nancy."

She hung up first, then sat at the breakfast bar with her coffee, realizing abruptly that Nancy was single. Mikey was single. She didn't really have to wonder what his type was. He would find Nancy attractive. Should she try to set them up?

A vague disquiet settled over her at the thought of playing matchmaker with Mikey. She didn't know him much better than she did Nancy, but somehow she felt the woman wasn't right for him.

Her cell phone buzzed, and she saw Roxanne's photo come up. She pressed the button to put it on speakerphone. "How's Paris?" she asked.

"Well, you sound perky, Samantha Stephens," Roxanne said on a laugh. Her friend sometimes called her that because her nose was slightly upturned and made her look like the spirited witch on *Bewitched*. "Especially after drugging yourself and passing out in the bathtub."

"Okay, what do you know?" Diane demanded.

"What do you know? Did he tell you he saw you *naked*?" Roxanne sing-songed the last word, obviously relishing the development.

"Not in so many words. I figured it out myself based on…well, I can't remember much of anything between the time I got in the bathtub and when I woke up naked in your bed."

"Alone?"

"Roxanne! Yes, alone! Of course alone."

"Why 'of course'? I wouldn't cringe at waking up naked next to that hunk."

Diane's face burned. *Because I half-thought about the same thing at least once this morning?* "He's really changed. I barely recognize him."

"There was a stud fighting to get out of him before."

"Well, you sound really taken with our Mikey Lund." Diane said the words irritably, sipping her coffee.

"Who wouldn't be?"

Fighting her annoyance, Diane found herself taking a deep breath because she felt like all the air had been sucked out of the room. Why did it bother her if Rox planned to chase Mikey? She'd catch him easily—without a fight. But then what? *She'll take her fun, then chew him up and spit him out. It's what she does to men. Every man but Jamie Dubois.* She spit nails at him because he *wouldn't let her make mincemeat out of him.*

Her own violent thoughts shocked her. She loved Roxanne. She'd always secretly envied her because she almost never got involved—not with her heart anyway. No man could hurt her because she wouldn't let them.

"Seriously, are you...well, are you going to get involved with Mikey?" Diane asked, trying to get herself on-board with the concept.

"Are you kidding?"

"What does that mean?"

"It means, I would absolutely love to have my way with him, a dozen times at least. But that's all it'd be. He'd get all invested in it and I'd end up hurting him. I wouldn't do that to Mikey. I thought about it, before and after his weight transformation. I considered it a lot. But he's too much of a teddy bear and I like to hug him too much to squeeze the life out of him just for sex. Incredible sex. He'd be so good. I've seen him with other women. He'd be life-altering."

Diane was sitting rigidly, unable to move or speak or even breathe. Abruptly, her friend gave a verbal shrug. "Eh. But I can get sex anywhere, incredible or otherwise. I can't get my teddy bear just anywhere. I love Mikey. I genuinely love him, and I can't say that for too many other guys. I won't soil him by touching him that way."

The unexpected sweetness of Roxanne's words made Diane feel just as sweet toward Mikey. *I love him, too. Maybe I've been unfair to him, inadvertently cruel to him, and I don't know him as well as I'd like to or should. But I love him, too. I genuinely love him. I want only good for him. So I have to be careful that I don't accidentally use him because I'm selfish again.*

"So where does that leave you, my sweet?" Roxanne purred, sounded like a seductive vampire wanting to feed.

"What? What do you mean?" Diane asked warily.

"He saw you naked, and he liked what he saw. Oh yes he did!"

"He told you that?"

"Oh, he felt all guilty about it. Mr. Noble. He's adorable. But I guarantee the beast had to be locked in its cage last night to prevent a violent escape."

The colorful way her friend described Mikey's state of...*cough*...mind after seeing her *au naturel* embarrassed Diane to no end, but she couldn't help wishing she could ask him about it. Any attempt in that direction wouldn't be wise or appropriate, but denying she liked the idea of Mikey Lund becoming aroused over her was impossible. *More unfairness to him, but I'm a woman.*

That was nice, too. She'd convinced herself she never wanted to fall in love or feel sexy or get caught up in any man's seduction again. Even as it felt too soon, she wondered for the first time if she'd spent most of her time as Robert Drake's girlfriend grieving the loss of what could have been. Her behavior for years could be described as grief. Up and down, falling into patterns of denial and desperation. She'd been getting over him instead of having a relationship that was going in the direction she'd hoped for. *Now all that's left is to leave him and my elaborate, cart-before-the-horse plans behind.*

When her doorbell rang, Roxanne heard it and said, "Don't tell me..."

"It's Mikey. He went out to get breakfast."

"So what are you two doing today?"

"I quit my job and I'm starting at Foxx Body Shop soon."

"Good for you, babe. Call me and tell me everything when you get a chance. Love ya."

"You, too."

"Give Mikey my love."

"I will."

Diane realized as she hung up and ran to the door, stretching to the peep hole to see Mikey there, that she hadn't found out how Roxanne was doing in Paris. *I am selfish so often. But mostly because my friends never seem to need me to be there for them.*

She opened the door to find Mikey juggling two bags and a bouquet of yellow roses, blue irises, and deep pink gerberas. "For me?" she asked in pleased astonishment.

He nodded, and she took the flowers from his hand, standing back with her face buried in them so he could come inside with the bags. "Thank you. They're so beautiful."

Robert never brought me flowers. He probably didn't want to spend any money on me that his wife could find out about. How often did he say that birthdays and holidays and romance in general were overrated? All because he didn't want to create a paper trail? Did he pamper his wife?

Diane fervently thought, *I hope he did. I hope his wife never finds out how horrible he is. She doesn't deserve to be hurt by all this. He's the one who deserves to suffer.*

She followed Mikey to the kitchen, where he set down the bags and looked at her. "You look great."

"Thanks. So do you. Did you have time to run home and shower *and* get all this stuff?"

His hair was wet and brushed the collar of the sport shirt he wore not tucked in. She'd never seen him in anything but ragged t-shirts and jeans that were baggy, fitting right under his huge gut. Now he looked so trim and his jeans fit his lean legs perfectly. *And his cute butt... Wow, is it ever cute.*

Quickly, her face hot, she turned and reached under the sink to get a vase.

"Why did you take sleeping pills last night?" he asked.

"I wasn't trying to hurt myself. Honestly. I just wanted to sleep. I promise I'll never take those again."

"Good."

"Did you worry I was trying to commit suicide?"

"Well..."

She shook her head, popping the flowers in the vase of water and setting them on the breakfast bar. "I like living too much to ever consider that. I'm going to make changes in my life though. I already called work and quit. My paycheck will be waiting when I get there to pick it up."

"This morning?"

"If you don't mind."

"Nope. We have time. Breakfast won't take long. We'll take my car. Too far to walk to your workplace."

"The body shop seems far from here, too."

"I can get there in fifteen in my car. Takes more or less an hour to walk, but it's worth it."

She nodded. "It is. You look great. I need to start walking, too. We could walk to the garage together every morning and after work."

He smiled, looking happy and a little embarrassed because he was obviously pleased with the idea. So was she. She helped him cut up the fruit, then they toasted nine-grain bread she expected not to taste good, especially with the sugar-free, fat-free fruit spread.

Sitting side by side, shoulders touching at the breakfast bar, she ate the healthy breakfast with true appetite and enjoyment. "I can't believe this is good for me. It tastes good—not like cardboard." And she loved the fruit so much more than she did all the sweets and junk she'd inhaled yesterday. "I've never eaten enough fruit. My mom and sister always put sugar on it or put it in some kind of too-rich dessert. We rarely ate it like this—fresh and natural."

"Same when I was a kid. I think fruits and vegetables were officially banned from the Lund household when I was growin' up. We ate nothing healthy, ever, that I can remember."

"Your family is overweight?"

"Everyone. Every single last one, down to grandparents and nieces and nephews."

"Your parents and your... How many brothers and sisters *do* you have?"

"Yeah, both my mom and dad are tubs. I have two brothers and four sisters and they all have a ton of fat kids. I was the runt of the litter in my family. We were all huge. Always. There was no chance of anything else with the things we ate. Deep fried five times a week was the norm. I always told myself I couldn't be thin 'cause bein' fat is a genetic thing. It's not true. It's all about smart choices, exercise. What about your parents and sister? Are they overweight?"

Mikey knows about my family. He's asked me about them. He remembers everything I told him over the years. Why didn't I ever ask him before? "Well, plump. We're all so short, it's practically a given that a single extra pound shows. But we're farmers, so we work hard all day. I suppose that's why our weight's rarely out of control."

"It doesn't show. Not on you." He was holding his coffee cup in the middle, not looking at her. His gaze was fixed on the onyx marble.

"I can't believe you don't think I'm fat. I've gained so much weight in the last few months. I've let myself go."

"You could be healthier, but you're not fat. You're definitely not fat."

Scolding herself in her mind, Diane pushed the words out: "I guess you'd know." She sneaked a peek at him.

Instantly, he went radish red and wouldn't look at her.

Diane leaned against him. "Don't apologize. You didn't do anything wrong. Seriously, Mikey, you don't think I'm fat after seeing me like that?"

His lean jaw went taut. "You're perfect," he said softly. Surprising her, he closed his eyes and all but whispered, "Absolutely perfect in every way."

If every woman had a meter inside that got filled with compliments that came her way, Diane's was overflowing—shooting up in the air like fireworks. She suddenly felt beautiful in a way she hadn't since she was in college, when guys had come on her constantly and were always trying to get her to go out with them and more. Mikey's veiled compliments gave her a confidence she'd lost. "You don't sound like you're just being nice."

"Seriously, I'm sorry. I didn't mean to see you that way." As if by force, he looked at her but didn't quite meet her eyes when he said, "Honey, I don't know if I'm ever gonna be able to sleep again without rememberin'."

Diane laughed but not loudly—happily. She hugged him, and he seemed embarrassed but he was grinning, too. "Roxanne said I should return the favor. Maybe you wouldn't be so upset, knowin' I saw you that way."

"That sounds like her."

"Yeah."

Diane sipped her coffee again. "You look so fantastic, Mikey. You really do. Any woman would be happy to see you naked."

He laughed sheepishly.

"You know what I mean. Roxanne told me she wants you and has for years."

"What?" he said in utter disbelief.

"She told me that, and I believe her. She saw you with other women and wanted to step in."

"You're lying."

"I'm not! Oh, Mikey, I know it must be hard for you to see yourself the way you are now. To stop believing you're the person *you* see yourself as but no one else does, at least not anymore."

"A big, fat cow. Yeah, I don't know that I'll ever get used to not being that huge. I look in the mirror, and I turn away 'cause I think someone else is in front of me. Someone I don't know. So if somebody looks at me, a woman, I just assume she's disgusted."

"You shouldn't." Feeling bad for him, she slipped her arms around his waist and hugged him. She loved hugging him—but then that hadn't really changed. She'd liked to hug him before, too. Mikey was someone women hugged as much as they could. She couldn't explain why, but she felt safe and beautiful and consoled whenever she was near him. "You seem taller, too. Have you noticed that?"

"Probably weird, but yeah."

"Maybe I'll seem taller if I lose weight."

"Don't lose too much," he said so fast, she couldn't help laughing and asking why.

"'Cause you're perfect. You don't wanna lose..."

Warm and overflowing, Diane smiled. "My chest? Don't be embarrassed. God made men breast-obsessed. But I never lose that. My hips and my chest are always like this, no matter how much weight I lose. When I slim down, it's my waist that gets smaller. Nothing else."

Her boyfriends as a teenager and in college had always been crazy about her breasts, and she'd loved that. *I like the idea of Mikey loving my breasts. He's seen them. How embarrassing. But he liked what he saw.*

Recalling Roxanne's earlier comments about seeing Mikey with various women over the years, Diane remembered an instance just after college, when her and her friends had seemed to have parties every single weekend. Parties that involved a lot of things she couldn't imagine now: Countless strangers, a few friends. Kegs and kegs of beer, smoke, ear-drum splitting music, drugs, and, yes, sex. Diane had avoided that part, ever faithful to the absent Robert, but she'd seen most of her friends in intimate situations she wished she could forget. More than once, she'd seen Mikey in a dark, back corner with some sexy woman who'd at one time or another been the girlfriend of Jamie or Brett. She had no doubt about how much he liked breasts. He spent an inordinate amount of time on them, pleasuring them endlessly so the woman he was with had no inhibitions whatsoever. *I also remembered how...aware...I was of my* own breasts when I saw that. Aware and ultrasensitive. So sensitive, that the next time I saw Robert, I couldn't get enough of his attention, remembering Mikey...

"We better get going," Mikey said.

Diane was grateful to be torn from the memories, especially because her breasts felt excruciatingly, painfully tight and hard. "Let me go to the bathroom first, then I'll get my purse."

"I'll clean up."

Diane all but fled to her bedroom, recalling more than she cared to about the past with Mikey. She'd felt so guilty back then, she'd tried hard to block from her mind—felt like she was being unfaithful to Robert because she'd wanted Mikey to touch and kiss her like that. Endlessly. Thoroughly. Obsessively. Odd but now she felt guilty that she'd dismissed the possibility based on his weight. Even in that regard, she hadn't been fair to him. But she'd known even then that she was overcompensating because she'd felt disloyal to the man she loved for wanting something so base with another man who was nothing more than a friend.

She fought the urge to burst into loud sobs. Her frustration was equally sexual and emotional. She hated feeling like this. Never had she been a woman who cared much about sex—certainly not without the crucial ingredient of love. *But I was dissatisfied in that regard. Because Robert was never around, and I'm young. I'm healthy. I enjoy lovemaking immensely. And when Robert did come around, the first time was always over way too quickly and he rarely had the same energy I did for another round...or ten—even when I did everything possible to seduce him into agreeing.*

Bitterness settled in her mouth and made her throat clench. *I'm a slut. I hate him. I hate Robert for putting me in that position!*

It's okay to be a sex-fiend when you're married, as long as your spouse is the sole focus of your attention. But I wasn't Robert's focus except temporarily. He was mine though. I denied myself because of him. I didn't look for another man to love in the only way I can—in an exclusive relationship leading to marriage. I gave up that because I believed he loved me and needed more time, because of his troubled past and frequent travel, to put a ring on my finger.

"Diane?"

She gasped at the sound of Mikey's voice and realized she'd been standing at the sink not moving, so filled with fury at all she'd lost and given up for the wrong man, she had no idea how long she'd been there. "Coming," she called shakily and turned on the water just to make some noise.

She wasn't out of love with Robert yet, but she would be. She didn't want to love him for another second. She didn't want to waste her life on him. She wanted to be free to fall in love again with a man she could trust. *But no sex. No matter what, no sex until I'm married. It's the only way to stop this shame I feel. I have to be moral. It's all I have left to keep myself from dissolving.*

She couldn't do any of it alone. Her confidence soared at the mere sight of Mikey. He would help her. Just being with him gave her the strength she never seemed to have otherwise.

They got in the car and she talked nonstop all the way to Global Pharmaceuticals, asking him questions about himself and his life and his past. She wanted to know everything there was to know about her friend Mikey Lund.

At her repeated request, he came inside the building with her, carrying a box she'd brought along to clear out her desk. Nancy had her check ready when she stopped at human resources first, and the woman stood and hugged her, wishing her well. There was a moment when Diane considered saying she'd call her—with the unspoken thought of playing matchmaker with Nancy and Mikey—but she let the moment pass. She didn't even introduce him and he didn't speak a word. Nancy looked at him more than once though.

They continued on to Diane's office in the sales department. The area was central to all the sales managers' offices'. She barely looked at the things she threw into the box. There wasn't much. She didn't expect Robert's office door to open, yet she knew once he appeared that this was why she was moving so fast. Just that quickly, her mouth felt parched-dry, she recognized the headache in her temples, and she felt both queasy and woozy.

"Diane," Robert said, starting toward her. "Please, come into my office. Let's talk."

"No."

"You're taking all this the wrong way. You're overreacting. I want you to stop being so belligerent. You love me. I love you. Now let's talk. Don't refuse me. We both know that you'll give in eventually so there's no reason for all this childishness."

He thinks if he's not silent here at work—brazenly admitting our personal relationship here—I'll capitulate. More than that, a part of her recognized his harshness as if from some distant dream. He'd used that tone when she was asking too many questions, making too many demands. She'd ascribed it to a defense mechanism he'd developed to protect himself from his parents' abuse. *It's probably a lie. All of it. I assumed and he let me assume, even encouraged it. He probably has parents like the Bradys, brothers and sisters he's close to, and a housekeeper like Alice he recalls fondly. None of it was true.*

Diane couldn't get herself to speak, in part because she felt so sick. The rest of her was filled to the brim with fury at his nerve warring with her own stupidity. Robert flicked a dismissive glance at Mikey, walked past him to her at her desk, and he grabbed her arm. "Talk to me. Now."

As if in slow motion, Diane saw a large, tanned hand appear on Robert's shoulder, then Mikey was there, towering over Robert like some superhero in a movie. Diane responded like a simpering female, too. She couldn't help it. Compared to Robert, Mikey looked huge—powerful, muscular, so tall and masculine, she became utterly breathless watching him. She remembered years ago, Mikey had gotten into fist fights *a lot* when he was drunk. She'd heard Brett say something about how, when he was wasted he got mean, and he'd take on guys twice his size—and win. He'd even gotten into a few legal scraps because of those violent incidents. He'd put men in the hospital, claiming later he hadn't realized his own strength.

"Dude, take your hand off her. Now. I won't tell you again." Mikey's voice was deep, even scary in its chilling calmness.

"Who are you to tell me what to do? You mean nothing to her. I'm..."

With the hand on Robert's shoulder, Mikey spun him around like he was a toy, put his other hand on Robert's throat and shoved him backward so he was all but bent backwards over Diane's desk. "The lady said it was over. It's over for her. You either back off or you get hurt. Take your pick."

The doors of the offices all around started opening, and the sales managers were appearing in them. Letting Robert lay there all but trembling, Mikey grabbed the box she'd filled, then put his arm around her—gently, as if he was afraid he was confining her after his effortless show of strength. Diane leaned close to him and let him lead her out of the building. All the while, she worried she would collapse in shock at what was happening—happening to her life. She was scared, mildly sorry for Robert's humiliation, and oddly exhilarated.

When they got to his car, Mikey opened the back door, put the box in, then opened the passenger door. Diane didn't slide inside. She threw her arms around him and hugged him tight enough to choke him.

"Was that okay?"

Diane laughed out loud at the one-eighty he'd done from Superman to awkward Clark Kent. Deep down, Mikey Lund was a teddy bear. But he could be a grizzly bear. She could hardly wait to tell Roxanne what he'd done. Rox would have him knighted in a heartbeat. "You were so convincing. I was terrified."

"I didn't mean to scare *you*." He sounded worried...and strangled.

She let up on her hold, pulling back to look him in the face. "Not that way. I mean, you were larger than life! I was in awe. You do intimidating very, very well, Mikey Lund. Or should I call you Superman?"

Now he laughed, sounding embarrassed. "I don't know what came over me. He grabbed your arm and I *freaked*."

He hadn't been acting. It wasn't part of the convince-Robert-I'm-over-him role she'd asked him to play and he'd agreed to. He'd genuinely run—flatout *run*—to her rescue again, the way he had last night. "Thank you. I wasn't ready to stand on my own two feet. Until I am, I'm glad you saved me from myself."

His expression softened, and he shrugged like it was no big deal. But his face looked twisted in emotional knots. *I feel that way inside.*

Even as she hugged him again, gentler this time, and he held her like she was fine china, she realized she didn't want a mere hug right now. Not from Mikey. She wanted him to do what he had inside the building. She wanted a visceral reaction. She wanted him to sweep her off her feet and kiss her until her legs gave out and he was the only thing in the world holding her upright and in one piece.

Teddy bear. Mike had spent a lifetime hearing women call him that. He couldn't take it as any great compliment. In his mind, the term was synonymous with *whale-sized porker who holds no attraction whatsoever for me.* Even still, Diane's reaction to his off-the-handle near-mauling of the creep who'd used her had felt good. He'd probably never forget the way she'd looked at him during the whole thing, and after, when she threw herself in his arms, and she'd held those incredible breasts all but flattened against his chest. He'd fought the insane desire to kiss her because he knew she'd reject him. Even the women he'd had sex with never kissed him at first. Like that disgusted them. Letting him fondle their breasts had seemed like nothing to them, but it'd never taken long for them to surrender to him completely once he got going there, and even kiss him like they were drunk out of their skulls from his consummate caresses. He was good at that. But sooner or later they all sobered up and saw him for what he was.

He wouldn't take that chance with Diane. She meant too much. And her opinion of *him* mattered more than anything to him. Was she merely happy that he'd made their fake relationship look real with his macho behavior? Was that all she saw in him? She'd claimed she didn't want to hurt or be selfish with him, but every second of their time together he wondered how much of it was real to her. She was reeling from the stub's deception. She wanted to forget all the damage done to her, distract herself from the whole fiasco. Asking him questions about his life, acting interested in him—all an act? A means to occupy her mind from reality? *Even still, I'm half in love. I'd sell my soul for this to be real. For her to be happy because she's with me.*

He drove them to Foxx Body Shop, tired and not sure he had the defenses to protect himself from wanting too much with this woman. He hadn't slept much, most of his time spent in one of those weird chairs in Roxanne's bedroom, watching over her. His mind had never been far from the memory of Diane's incredibly gorgeous nude body. Every time he slipped into overtired sleep, he was kissing those beauties he'd glimpsed for all of two of the most vivid seconds in his life. He'd fought a hard-on ninety-nine percent of the time through the night. *Most of today, too.*

He let out a pent-up breath. Diane was a touchy-feely person. She always had been, and he suffered for it. She liked to hug, liked to be close and touching someone at all times. Made her feel less alone in the world, he suspected. But he'd never been touched much in his life. His first memory was of holding onto the bars of his crib like those of a jail cell and crying for hours. Screaming for attention. Alone. Until he collapsed in fatigue.

He hadn't been held or hugged much, if at all. He didn't have any memories of those sorts of things growing up. He'd been smacked across the head, swatted on the bottom here and there, beat the crap out of by his older brothers *and* sisters. But mostly he was left alone without any physical contact. How often had he marveled that his parents and siblings never noticed him stealing from the countless booze bottles in their living room? He could down a whole bottle of that cheap crap his old man bought in a day. The dude never noticed, never said a word. Mike had taken beer from the fridge anytime he wanted—more than food even. Most nights, he fell asleep drunk off his ass and no one came in his room to notice the empty cans and bottles littered all around, some forming pyramids.

He grunted in shock, jolted from his memories, when Diane slipped closer to him and put her head on his shoulder. "So how bad is the office at the garage?"

He swallowed. "Well, there are file cabinets. But I think Brett puts his cigarettes in 'em."

"Seriously?"

"Yeah. He makes it all work somehow. Don't ask me how. I kind-a made my own system after a while. The only way to keep things organized for myself and not piss off customers so they never come back and tell their friends to avoid us."

He wasn't sure why he felt so withdrawn, his words pushed out ruthlessly, but he suspected it was that she touched him so freely and made him wish he could do the same with her. What would she do if he did? It brought to his mind the times he'd needed human contact so bad, he'd turned to Roxanne. He still couldn't believe he had the nerve back then, rarely, but he supposed the booze gave him false courage. She'd always wrapped her arms around him and called him "honey" and "babe" in that way she had that made him feel like the center of the world even when he was far from hers. Oddly enough, Roxanne Hart had a motherly way about her. Sure, he'd pushed for sex more than once with her—as far as she'd let him before thrusting him away, laughing and letting him down easy, for his own good—but that was instinct with a gorgeous woman.

Diane...Diane was so different from Roxanne. While he could easily imagine Diane getting married and having a passel of kids she'd be a good mother to, she *wasn't* motherly. Roxanne considered other people's feelings before her own, natural as breathing. Diane was almost always in her own world and had to be jolted out of it to think about someone else.

She'll never realize I'm a real person, with feelings and desires and not-so-noble moments. She's...well, she is selfish. She said it herself. She needs to realize I'm a man. I'm not a loser or a creep—someday I might believe that myself. But I'm nothing like that jerkoff she wasted most of her life on. Wasted her love on. I'd be faithful to her. Worship her. I'd love her senseless. Maybe I'd be as good for *her as good* to *her.*

"Hey," she said softly, lifting her head to look at him.

"What?"

"I don't know. You seemed to go into yourself a minute there. Where did you go?"

A place maybe you'll never see, lady. A place where I've been in love with you as long as I've known you and you love me, too. Really love me.

He shook his head. "Nowhere. I'm okay."

"You know, someday I'm not going to let you get away with that, Mikey Lund. You can't spend your life closing up as tight a prison. You'll go crazy if you don't talk to someone."

Careful what you wish for, honey. You might regret it if I ever learn to open up. Probably as much as I will.

They arrived at the garage, and Mike drove into the old parking spot he hadn't used in months. Forcing himself to cheer up because the happiness she'd displayed before was waning, he gave her an official tour and introduced her to the other mechanics. On the way upstairs to the office, she asked, "Are you sure Brett said it was okay for me to work here and run the office?"

"You wanna call him yourself?"

She got a shy look on her face. She'd always been hyper-nervous around Brett and Jamie. Mike had noticed that. But she hadn't been that way with him, and he'd believed it was because he wasn't sexy or even intimidating when it came to good looks. Not even close. He'd always wanted her to act with him the way she did with the cool guys. "Maybe later," she managed.

Mike opened the office door, and she gasped out loud. He wasn't surprised. The place was piled with mechanical books and ledgers and loose papers and files. "There's no rhyme or reason," she murmured, shocked, as she picked up a few things here and there.

"Brett's got his own system, like I told ya."

"Really?"

"Must. Business ain't in the toilet yet. Opposite, in fact."

"What did he say when you asked him if I could work here?"

"Doobs said you'd have the place whipped into shape in a

week, and Brett agreed you probably would. Then he said, 'I think I could afford her. I'll have to look at some numbers, but I don't see why not'."

"Not exactly thrilled. But I can't imagine Brett getting thrilled about much of anything."

Brett was always calm, unruffled. "Except Savvy and Harley. I've never seen him the way he is with his two girls."

"Love does that to you," she agreed without any sentiment. Mike didn't blame her, after what she'd been through. She rolled up the sleeves of her fancy jacket. "Well, I think I can do some good here. Stand back."

Mike laughed out loud, seeing the determined motivation on her face.

He didn't forget she was upstairs, so close to him he could call out to her and hear her voice at any moment, even once that whole morning.

Chapter 6

Her jacket off, shoes long ago discarded, Diane was surrounded in piles. On the left side, she'd organized every scrap of paper. On the right, the mountain loomed, years of accumulation awaiting its final resting place. She lost track of time, in total efficiency mode, and didn't look up until Mikey was suddenly in the open doorway, looking around in shock. She noticed for the first time that hours had passed and the emptiness of her stomach called attention to itself.

"Doesn't look like I did anything. The mountain is still winning," she said, struggling to her feet. Mikey came to help her, making her realize how stiff and sore she was. "But this is a good start—although it might take weeks to actually go through all this stuff. It's a miracle Brett made this work so long."

Mikey laughed. "He stopped by. Dropped off this check for you before they headed to Syracuse."

He handed it over and Diane saw that he'd signed it but there were no numbers written on it. Frowning, she looked up. "Didn't he say what my budget is?"

"No. Just said you should get what you need."

She sighed. "I don't know exactly what I need because I can't find anything. I went through all the file cabinets and drawers, looking for file folders…"

Mikey was shaking his head. "Never bothered with them."

"Okay. Then that's definitely on the top of my shopping list. What are these pink things?"

She reached over to the immense pile of them. She could barely read most of them they were so old, grease-stained and sloppy, but since they were all written on the same blank pink scraps of paper, she'd put them together.

"Work orders. Calls come in, and I jot down all the info on those pink pads Brett got in bulk about ten years ago."

"So do you actually need all of these? I mean, some of them are dated 2000."

"Probably not, unless you wanna start a client list or somethin'."

"So, when the phone rings, you write these down…"

"Put 'em on the skewer near the phone downstairs—usually. Sometimes they get moved and I can't find 'em. When they're old, I toss 'em up here on the desk."

Diane took a deep breath. "That explains a lot. So all those phone calls this morning are people calling, wanting you to work on their cars?"

"Most."

"Who took all those calls?"

"I did."

"How did you get any work done? The phone rings about every eight minutes! I timed it a couple times."

"I know. Another reason we need a secretary. But you probably wanna get it organized up here before you start that part of the job."

"I think you'll also need me to get you organized *downstairs*, too, if you're having trouble finding things."

"So long as you don't touch my tools or anybody else's, do whatever you want."

He was grinning, and she couldn't resist adding her own. She went over to hug him, glad to see him again after all her hours of sneezing and feeling frenzied at how much work she'd gotten herself into. Fortunately, she was good at this kind of thing.

"I'm probably a mess—don't know if you wanna get too close," he warned once she reached him through the piles she'd carefully sorted out.

He was wearing a pair of coveralls with his name on them, and they were absolutely huge on him. "I think you need to replace those."

"Suppose I do. I always expect myself to fall back into the old habits. Haven't thrown out any of my fat clothes yet either."

Mikey was looking at her a little strangely and she realized why when he reached his hand over and wiped something off her cheek. "Pretty dirty up here, I guess. You got it all over you."

"What?"

"Dust, dirt, spiderwebs…"

"You're kidding?"

She looked down at her pant suit and saw he was right. She was filthy. She started brushing herself off anxiously, twisting and ending up turning in a circle as Mikey directed her on where she was dirty. He was pointing—right at her rear end—and no matter how much she rubbed and wiped, he didn't seem satisfied. "What is it? Can you get it off?"

He raised an eyebrow. "You sure?"

"Yes! I don't want to walk around like this all day. I guess I better not dress like this tomorrow."

She turned so he could brush her off. Tentatively, as if waiting for her to swat him away, he brought his hand to her behind and, after a moment, he leaned closer, prompting her to say, "What? What is it?"

"Gum, I think... Hold on."

His fingers were trying to work it off her lower left cheek, and she stood, feeling strangely caressed by his palpable assistance.

Whatever it was went in the trash several, long, lingering, thoroughly enjoyable moments later.

"Did you get it?"

He nodded, his face looking flushed, his eyes averted. "Tomorrow you better wear old jeans and a t-shirt. It's pretty dirty up here. The whole shop's like this."

"Including the bathroom. Have you guys *ever* cleaned it?"

"Not in recent memory."

"I felt like I had to call in the CDC after I went earlier." She'd only stopped her work once. Seeing the unisex restroom had almost made her ask for clean coveralls and gloves, not to mention an entire roll of toilet paper laid out in strips on the toilet seat.

"Sorry. We're guys. Guess we don't think about those things."

"I think you need more than a mere secretary can provide."

"Maybe. So you wanna get some lunch? I usually bring

something I made the night before but…"

"I bet that helps you control your calorie intake a lot." At her office, one of the underlings frequently made a lunch run at one restaurant or another nearby—none of them especially healthy, and she ordered off the menu like the rest of the employees.

"Yeah. If I get too hungry, I'll scarf whatever's closest."

"You have to teach me everything about being healthy, Mikey. I need help. I'm so bad at self-discipline, especially when I'm hungry or depressed. Speaking of which, I could eat half a cow about now."

"What about this? There's a sandwich shop with a low-calorie menu about two blocks from here. The office supply store's not far from there. We'll walk. We've got an hour. We can get lunch and what you need to get organized here, and be back by one."

"The office supply order could be pretty large. How will we get everything back with us?"

"They'll probably deliver. If not, we'll run over there after work and pick it up."

"Okay."

He shucked off his coverall, hanging it on the coat tree near the door, collecting dust. Just in case she had stains, she slipped back into her jacket and shoes, then stuffed the blank check from Brett into her purse, which she looped around her shoulder like a bandoleer. On the way to lunch, she said, "I haven't had a job where I'm busy every second, behind in work, for a long time. My job at the office isn't difficult. I have to admit, I like being busy. I've always hated being the office assistant who's doing her nails when someone shows up—really, there's not much to do once I finish my daily work. Even when they cut my hours and I became the secretary to all the districts, I never had any work piling up. It'll be nice to be busy again."

"Are you sayin' you actually enjoyed the dusty job in Brett's office?"

"I really did," she said happily. She'd organized compulsively, filling her head with ideas on how to separate everything and keep the system methodical. And she'd thought about Mikey—thought about him from the day she met him until today. She marveled at how little she knew him. Recalling his actions with Robert, maybe she should have been frightened or wished he hadn't been so aggressive. But she found herself so detached from the man she loved now. She felt sick to her stomach about the role she'd been thrust into unwillingly. She'd accepted that she'd been stupid, but at the same time she believed she'd done all she had blindly.

She hadn't known he was married and finding out or merely suspecting *would* have made her abandon the relationship immediately. But it wasn't Robert she'd dwelt on this morning while she worked steadily. It'd been Mikey and the things he'd said and done of late that made her aware again and again how unfair she'd been to him all this time. *How much I want to get to know him through and through. Be a friend to him—a real friend.*

"How was your day?" she asked, trying to match her stride with his long one. She knew he was deliberately walking slowly for her. She'd taken his hand almost as soon as they got out on the sidewalk. After spending her entire childhood having her hand held whenever she went anywhere or did anything outside the farm, she supposed holding someone's hand while walking down the busy sidewalks in New York City was a given for someone like her. She wondered if Mikey minded her constant need for human contact.

"Busy. It's always busy there. I like that though. I barely look up until I get hungry. Today…"

He stopped talking abruptly, and she nudged him. "What? What was different today?"

"You. Up there. I thought I should check on you and realized it was already lunch time."

"It would be nice to have lunch with you every day. I usually eat at my desk. Alone. I never worked with a lot of people I was friends with. I mean, friends outside of work."

"Yeah."

"Is it like that for you, too? Other than Brett?"

"I like all the other mechanics. Don't socialize with them outside the body shop. Most of 'em got wives, families, grandkids. We got nothin' in common except cars."

"That was me, too. I feel like I'm starting all over again today. It's kind of exciting."

"You really over that jerkoff?" His tone was non-confrontational but surprised.

She looked up at him quickly. "That probably sounds bad. I just know I could never stay with him now that I know the truth. If I'd the slightest idea he was married at any point in the last ten years, I know I would have broken it off immediately. You probably don't believe that…"

"I do."

"Really?"

"Yeah. You're not the kind of woman who could be a guy's mistress. You're too pure."

She wrapped her other arm around his as they walked. "I don't feel that way at all. I don't feel I deserve anyone thinking so nicely of me."

"None of it was your fault. Okay? It wasn't. It's all his fault. He went out of his way to dupe you. You didn't have the street smarts to see his type for what he is."

"I'm dumb."

"Sweet and innocent," he corrected.

The rush of tenderness she felt for him made her hug him to her harder. Even if she didn't deserve his good opinion of her, she desperately needed it. "Thank you for respecting me even when I'm having a hard time respecting myself."

He obviously didn't know what to say and so pointed out the sandwich shop. When they went inside the crowded place, she said, "Where's the restroom? I'd like to wash up first. Will you order me whatever you have? I'll pay you back later."

"Are you sure you don't wanna choose yourself?"

"Yes. I'm sure I'll love whatever you suggest."

After relieving herself, she stood in front of the mirror aghast that Mikey hadn't tried to brush off more than he had from her opposing cheeks. Her face was filthy with grime, the elegant twist in her hair a tangled mess. Getting herself fixed took more than ten minutes. Mikey had already gotten them a table and their food was delivered as she sat down. She pointed at him in mock menacing. "From now on, if I look like a witch, you'll tell me, Mikey Lund. All right? If I have hairs sticking up, lipstick on my teeth or dirt all over my face, you'll tell me before I go out in public."

He laughed, and she couldn't help joining him. What else was there to do?

"You were adorable," he claimed innocently. "Nowhere near a witch."

"You had the guts to walk down the street with me anyway. I'm grateful for that."

They dug in, and she couldn't believe the sandwich was anything like low-cal. "This is so delicious. It can't be good for me. Are you sure they didn't mess up our order? This has mayonnaise on it. It has to be full of fat."

"Not much. Just enough." He showed her the menu and she read it in shock. She didn't usually read the ingredients or nutritional aspects of anything she ordered from a menu. She automatically assumed anything healthy wouldn't taste good.

The grain bread similar to what they'd had for breakfast was lightly toasted and the chicken on the sandwich was incredible. Even the vegetarian vegetable soup tasted like heaven. They both plowed through the meal as if they were starving. When she was done, she realized she was full but didn't feel like she'd overeaten for once.

"What else?" she asked as they finished up their bottled waters and she compulsively cleaned the table. "Other than walking to work, what kind of exercise do you do?"

"Usually jog on the weekends."

"Okay. I'm not much of a jogger, but I want to try all of this. I actually feel good today! I haven't felt this way in a long time."

She looked away to locate the trash bin. When she glanced back, she caught Mikey staring at her chest. He averted his gaze so quickly, she might not have realized what he was doing any other time. Now that she knew how he felt about her breasts...

She swallowed, unable to feel anything but grateful that he found her attractive when she was as far from her ideal weight as she'd ever been. Since he was looking away, she took the time to study him again. His face was so handsome, she couldn't think anything but that he was breathtaking. *Maybe even cuter than Jamie Dubois—hands down the most attractive man I've ever known or merely seen. Mikey's so accessible. Jamie* isn't. *I prefer Mikey's new good looks.*

"What? Now do I have something on my face?"

She laughed. "No. You're just so darn good looking. I can't stop staring at you, Mikey. I can't help it."

"Mike."

"What?"

"My mom and sisters call me Mikey."

"Everybody calls you Mikey. You've always been Mikey to me. I can't imagine calling you anything else. I mean it affectionately."

"I know. Whatever."

"Does it bother you?"

He shrugged. "No. Not really."

"If your family wasn't affectionate, I suppose you don't like to be called Mikey because of them."

"I don't know." He looked like he regretted saying anything now.

"Tell me the truth, Mike…" Somehow she managed to say the name without the "y". "Does it bother you when all of us call you Mikey?"

"No. Just makes me feel like a big, dumb, fat kid."

"We don't say it that way."

He nodded.

"Well, I'll try to call you 'Mike' but it won't be easy."

"You said your sister calls you 'Diany' a lot and you hate it."

Diane marveled that he remembered her telling him that. Did

he remember everything she'd ever told him? She suspected he did despite how wasted he'd been all those times. "In part because we've always competed. Who got kissed first, had the first boyfriend, graduated, got married, had the first kid. She always wins in love. I've won the academic race."

"Does it bother you?"

"It shouldn't. It's pretty silly. I tell myself I'm the lucky one, but, at the end of the day, I just want to be kissed and held by a man I love who loves me. I want to be married and have lots of children. For all my nose-in-the-air stuff about my education and career, I wish I had her domestic life."

She stood up and Mike took the trash from the table, leading the way to tossing it out before she took his hand and they headed for the office store.

"What about you?" she asked. "How do you get along with your family?"

He shrugged. "I'm the screw-up. Always have been. I hated school. Shop was the only class I did well in. I was drunk most of the time, so somehow I got through it. I think my teachers hated me so much, they just wanted me out. I graduated without bein' held back. Don't know what I would've done if Brett hadn't hired me right outta high school. Right from the start, he trusted me and left me in charge a lot. It was when he was still in that rock band and only started the body shop to have somethin' to fall back on—must've known the music career wouldn't last long, and it didn't. Maybe I was a screw-up, but Brett's faith in me made me wanna be worthy of his trust. So at the garage, if nowhere else, I did everything right."

"Where does your family live?" she asked.

"New Rochelle."

The words immediately reminded her that Robert's family lived in the same city. He'd called her cell phone all morning and she'd ignored it, turning the volume so low, the constant buzzing didn't bother her—not even as much as the phone ringing in the shop had. She couldn't understand how he wanted to continue pursuing her after Mikey had humiliated him so thoroughly. He had a lot of nerve thinking he could call the shots in her life after his façade of lies had been unveiled so completely. *Did I really give him that much power over me before? Maybe I did. But I won't ever again. It's over, and amazingly it doesn't feel like the end of the world it did at first. I always assumed I'd feel dead without him instead of realizing the truth. I was too in love to see how wrong our relationship was.*

Mike saw the exact moment when Diane lost interest in him once the dude at the office supply store latched onto her like a fawn and followed her around while she shopped. *I actually thought she wanted to be real friends with me after all her questions.* For once, she hadn't simply wanted to unload on him. She'd never seen him as a real person, someone she could care about and not lean on.

During the lunch break, she'd seemed to forget all about herself and gave him her full attention. Even on the couple-blocks walk to the office supply store, she'd been engaged, asking him to help her clean her apartment out of junk food the next day. They'd go jogging first in the morning—she'd probably collapse. She'd asked jokingly if he would carry her home over his shoulder if she did, and he'd laughed and agreed wholeheartedly. In the afternoon they could get groceries. She would make him dinner... On second thought, since he knew as well as she did that everything she cooked had at least two full sticks of butter, she'd buy the groceries and help him cook something healthy. Tomorrow had felt like a date to him, even as he told himself not to look at it that way.

Now she was all female vixen, flirting almost unconsciously with the dude with a nametag that said "Isaac" wearing fancy slacks, his hair looking like he'd spent over a hundred bucks on the cut. Mike trailed behind, handling the cart, infuriated because of all he'd been thinking as they'd laughed and talked together earlier. She touched him so often—holding his hand, hugging him, squeezing his arm—he couldn't help thinking he wanted to hold her close and never let her go. But none of that meant anything to her. He was just some guy to him, not one she'd ever flirt with the way she was with Isaac.

You see why you can't fall for her? You're nothin' to her. A crutch. Somethin' to hold her up while she's fallin' apart.

With her cart full of boxes of file folders, labels, pens and stuff organized people used, she made her way beside the clerk to the cashier. Mike pushed the heavy cart, growing more and more withdrawn. *She likes rich guys. Snazzy dressers. She's not likely to fall for a mechanic who owns a single thing—a car. Not even a very good one.*

By the time they were out and she was gloating about how "Isaac" had offered to deliver all her supplies to the shop personally, Mike was in a thoroughly bad mood. "I'll bring 'em up to the office when they arrive," he said in a clipped voice, not bothering to make his strides shorter and slower for her. Since she'd taken his hand almost as soon as they were outside, she was all but running to keep up.

"Thanks," she said, looking slightly confused when his gaze skirted over her. "We'll be late, won't we? I'm sorry. I just..."

Got to flirtin' and lost track of time. I get it.

"Mikey, you shouldn't have to worry about those things. I know how busy you are. Why don't you let Isaac bring them up? He agreed to deliver them. That way you won't be bothered."

Why? So you can give him your phone number? "Whatever," he said. He had no doubt by the time her beloved Isaac left the office at the shop, she'd cancel their plans tomorrow so she could go out on the date with the creep who would ask her out while he was up there.

They made it back to the garage in half the time, and, panting with the exertion, Diane had asked how to take a phone order. He told her and showed her when they got back, then, without another word, he left her to return to work. If she sensed his mood, he didn't notice and didn't care. He wanted nothing more than to do what he had all his life—slink into a corner and disappear from the world, a hundred percent sure no one would even notice whether he came out of hiding or not.

Chapter 7

That afternoon. Diane didn't work with nearly as much focus. She couldn't get over how withdrawn and sullen Mikey had become after lunch. The worst part was that she'd only noticed his temperament on the rush back from the office supply store. Before that, she'd been on cloud nine, and she felt completely foolish about her reaction to having a successful, sophisticated man come on to her so obviously. For many years, she'd noticed that men no longer flirted with her the way they did when she was in her early twenties. She'd always assumed, like someone who was married, she sent out "taken" signals to other men.

Isaac Ravi, the supply store manager, had been so blatant about his attraction to her. After all she'd been through, knowing she hadn't lost her appeal had given her a rush that carried her through the time with hardly any real memory of what'd happened. He'd flirted, she'd flirted. It'd been no surprise when he'd agreed to hand-deliver her order that afternoon at no extra charge.

Because her head had been so light, she hadn't noticed Mikey's bad mood until they almost reached the body shop, where he'd unceremoniously dumped her on her head and went back to work without so much as a "see you later". She couldn't fathom what had happened to put him in such a state. Whatever it was, she was so upset that, when Isaac asked her out after delivering the supplies directly to the office, she was too deflated to offer him the slightest encouragement. She'd simply said she'd recently ended a long-term relationship and she wasn't capable of anything at the moment. Isaac acted all understanding but nevertheless asked for her phone number in case she changed her mind later. Because she no longer had any nimble female skills, she gave it in an effort to get him to leave.

She quickly went to work labeling folders and getting what she'd already organized into piles inside them and into the all but empty cabinets in the office. She'd set her production line up on the table that overlooked the garage below and she had a clear view of Mikey working below. He'd never come up to get his coveralls and he was working in his regular clothes—all but his shirt which he'd taken off because he was obviously too hot. *Too hot is right. He's not only adorable. He's sexy as all get out. And he's furious. I can tell just by the way he moves, his face stone-like. Is he mad at me? Why?*

The answer came. She didn't like to consider it, but his reaction had been like jealousy. He'd obviously noticed her flirting with Isaac and vice versa, and he hadn't liked it. While it was true that Mikey seemed to have a crush on all women and she'd never been excluded from that, she couldn't help wondering if he was developing feelings for her—not the friendship ones she'd been encouraging. In small part because of his weight and heavy drinking, she'd always been very careful not to give him too much attention or make anything personal with him. Mikey was the kind of guy who read too much into the slightest look, a stray word, a touch. *And I've been all over him—as a friend—since he ran to my rescue yesterday. I've always been afraid he'd fall in love with me if I gave him an inch. But it's only been a day, less than twenty-four hours, and he knows I'm still reeling from Robert's betrayal. It wouldn't be fair of him to expect anything of me, to want more than I can give him.*

She'd been unfair to the man for as long as she'd known him, and the sad fact was she'd never been attracted to him. He didn't take care of himself. Yet she wondered now at her own double standard. She hadn't been taking care of herself at all for a long time. Diet and exercise had meant nothing to her. She'd been too depressed about her dwindling romance to take care of herself, then, when Robert finally came around, she'd crash diet and exercise to make sure she looked good for her man. She was still so out of shape, and she supposed the fact that both Mikey and Isaac found her sexy had gone straight to her head.

Though the details of her flirtatious encounter with the store manager were fuzzy, she nevertheless felt guilty about what an airhead she'd been. True, Isaac was the picture of rich sophistication—something that attracted her—but all things considered, Mikey was the hunkier of the two.

Did Mikey want me to flirt with him? But he would have wanted more than I can give him—so unfair to him. I was trying hard to make our friendship mutual instead of one-sided. I didn't flirt with him because it would hurt him and I don't want to hurt Mikey. He's important to me. Isaac is nothing, less than nothing to me.

Diane swallowed hard, jolting when Mikey abruptly turned and looked up at her. He was obviously still so pissed, he turned away with a scathing look. She knew then what she had to do. The longer she continued even friendship with Mikey, the bigger chance he'd get hurt. He'd fall in love with her. He'd want things she couldn't give him. *None of this is fair to him. I have to stop this—this whole 'rescue mission' thing. I have to stop it now because it's not worth what it'll do to him when I have to insist we'll never be together that way, any way but as friends. I'm not capable of anything he wants, especially not so soon.*

She continued to work long after all the mechanics but Mikey left, and then until he came to get her. He was clearly not happy and only grunted words about 'leaving something for Monday'. He grabbed his coveralls, saying he'd see her in the car. The door they'd come in in the morning was already locked—she could go out and it would lock behind her.

Diane could hardly believe his behavior. It forced her to view the situation with Robert in her office at Global in a different light. Mikey had done that because he was jealous, too—not simply to rescue her and force Robert to stop pursuing her. They'd only spent a few hours together, and already he was in so deep! The part that bothered her most was that Mikey seemed to have no desire to talk about his feelings. He was going to sulk and stay silent. That worried her because she knew she had to stop the friendship she'd been intent on expanding, and what would he do? Start drinking again? Gorge himself until he was a huge once more? That was the last thing she wanted.

He took off as soon as she was inside the passenger's seat. "Mike..." *I'll never get used to not calling him 'Mikey'.* "I know you're upset, and I want to know why."

"Nothin'."

She looked at him. He stared out the window at the road, his face completely impassive even while his eyes seemed to burn everything in his sights. "No, not nothing. Not this time. You can't keep bottling everything up inside you. You have to talk to your friends. If you don't, you'll turn to the same destructive patterns you've been in all your life. Now tell me. I know you're mad, and I want to know why. I won't let up until you tell me, so you might as well get it over with."

"You sure you wanna know?" he asked in a low, menacing growl so unlike the Mikey she knew and loved.

"Yes, I'm sure. Let's have it."

"Okay. What the hell was that back in the office supply store? You and that dude...hell, you were all over each other."

"What? We were not."

He turned to her, his gaze piercing.

"Okay. I admit I was flirting back. I'm embarrassed now. I guess the attention went to my head."

"Yeah. *His* attention."

"What does that mean?"

"Nothin'," he all but spit.

"Don't do that. Tell me what you mean, Mike."

He sneered. "He's rich. Sophisticated. Just your type."

He's mad because he's not my type. It's true. I've always gone for successful, sophisticated men. Mikey...well, he's a mechanic. A grease monkey. He dresses like... I can't even imagine him in a suit. "Nothing happened with Isaac, Mike. It was harmless. It's over."

"Yeah. You're gonna tell me the dude didn't ask you out while he was up there in the office forever?"

Diane's cheeks flushed at the harshness in his tone, so unlike the gentle teddy bear she'd always known. "You're right. He asked me out. I didn't accept. I refused."

"Why? 'Cause you're still cryin' over the married jerkoff?"

She'd never felt so stung in her life. Tears flood her eyes. She turned to see they were almost to her apartment building. Defensively, starting to snivel, she managed, "Why I refused has nothing to do with Robert."

He snorted. "Then why'd you say no?"

"Because…because he asked me to go out tomorrow and I already have plans."

"What plans?"

She swallowed. "*We* made plans, didn't we? I want to be with you."

She hadn't planned the response. In fact, once the words were out, she knew she'd said exactly the wrong thing—the thing that would lead Mikey down a path she was sure she couldn't follow. She'd wanted friendship with him. She'd asked him to help her convince Robert she was over him, but she couldn't go through with it now. "Mikey, honey, the more I think about this, the more I know it wasn't fair for Roxanne to ask you to run to my rescue any more than it was for me to ask you to make Robert think we were dating so he'd leave me alone. You have your own life. You weren't put on this earth to rescue me or anyone else. I can't expect you to come running to save me every second. I'm sorry we dragged you into this. You should go out tomorrow. You're so attractive, any woman would want to be with you. Go for it. I promise you, no one will reject you."

He'd parked on the curb in front of her building. Because she knew she'd burst into tears in a second, she leaned over and kissed his cheek, noticing how withdrawn and shocked, even sorry, he looked. She hugged him lightly, wishing she could hug him harder and have him hold her against him again. *Not fair to him.* "I'll always be grateful for all you've done for me, Mike. You're the greatest."

She forced herself to jump out of the car and rush inside her building. All the way to the top floor, tears streaked down her face. *This means I'm spending tomorrow alone. I want to be with him. Mikey. I still do as much as I did when we made the plans. But this is for him. Canceling will protect him. Halting this 'friendship' is the very best thing I can do for him.*

Even accepting her own logic, she wished she'd never said any of it. She wished she'd jumped out on the words, "See you tomorrow—bright and early!" Maybe Mikey wasn't the only one rushing into things headlong here. She could hardly believe how much she'd come to need him in a few short hours.

He hated himself the second she was gone. He'd done everything to bring about her reaction, and now he regretted his short-sighted jealousy. She'd dumped him, albeit as a friend. Somehow that felt just as bad as if there'd been something more between them.

He drove to his parking garage and walked home, remembering things he told himself to forget. All her hugs. Her compliments. Her pride in him. Her sadness over his childhood. *That sweet mouth, pressed to my cheek. Those beauties I would give my right arm to touch for the next twenty-four hours.*

After he was shut up inside, pacing across the length of his small apartment, Mike sighed. Damn, he wanted a bottle of whiskey right about now. A *case* of it. He didn't turn on any lights, didn't do anything but consider his options. He'd half fallen in love with Diane already, and she'd wanted nothing more than friendship. Maybe even genuine friendship—something new between them. "We made plans, didn't we? I want to be with you."

Ah, I'm an idiot! Maybe the best thing for me is not to spend another second with her. It'll only make my feelings for her worse when she's not feelin' anything for me but like. *I don't want like. I want love, passion. I want her to get as jealous over the thought of me with some other woman as I get at the idea of her with any other dude. I want her so bad, I can't think straight anymore. She's every thought. Every prayer. Every fantasy.*

He threw himself on the couch in the dark, putting his hand over his eyes. As soon as he shut out everything, she was there, soft, sweet, warm and beautiful. *Naked. God, burn my eyes out. Please. I don't wanna remember any part of her, especially not those parts.*

Abruptly, as he fought an arousal that felt so wrong his throat closed up completely, a thought popped into his head: *What if I just show up at her apartment tomorrow morning like nothing happened?*

The idea forced away all else for him. Pretending they hadn't fought, she hadn't dumped him, that they still had plans... What would she do?

Hell, you don't got any pride at all, do you? She let you down easy. She could've ripped you to shreds, but instead she was gentle and sweet. She put you first for once. She was crying when she did it, who knows why when you're not worth cryin' over...

He sat up, certain that the one thing he couldn't do was go over there and act like nothing ever happened. But that left him wondering what to do. His apartment felt empty. He didn't want to do anything—eat, watch TV, read a book (a new thing for him since he'd been trying to find new interests), work out. He remembered how Diane had said he needed to talk when something was bothering him; if he didn't, he'd lash out and do self-destructive things. She couldn't have been more on the mark. He'd never doubted that one day he'd lose all his willpower and then he'd end up fatter and drunker than ever before.

What mattered anyway? That was the part that kept tripping him up. He didn't have a life outside of his job. He didn't have many interests—the idea of going to a bar or nightclub, an art gallery, concerts...none of those things were *him*. He hadn't really figured out anything that fit him. His family had never given a damn about him. He would have said the same about his friends if they hadn't reacted the way they had that day in the apartment above the body shop. More than anything, he wanted to be somewhere he could meet women like Diane, only ones who might actually be interested in having a relationship with him. He just didn't know where to go or what to do when he got there.

Maybe I should call Doobs. At the very least, maybe it'll keep me from fallin' back on those old habits. Or maybe I'll fall back in. Eh, he probably has a date anyway.

Frustrated, he got up and went to shower—something he did

every night after he got home, since he usually stopped at the gym after work. Not wanting to go back up to the office to get his coveralls, he'd worked in his street clothes and stained them good in the process.

Although he sickened himself by hoping for what he didn't believe would happen, he put his cell phone in his pocket once he was out and dressed, his hair still wet, planning to take a walk to clear his head. He went in the opposite direction of Diane's building and made sure he avoided restaurants and liquor stores along the way that could tempt him.

He'd barely gone four blocks when his cell phone rang. Abhorring his own eagerness, he pulled it out and his mind all but exploded when he saw Diane's number on the screen. Not breathing, he connected and brought it to his ear.

Her voice came on the line. "Mikey, it's Robert..."

He didn't stop to think. He turned around and started in her direction at a dead run.

Chapter 8

After her brutal tears, she'd done nothing but change her clothes—decent shorts and a top that didn't feel quite as tight as everything else she owned had lately—and avoid the fridge. There was nothing in there that could be deemed healthy. She was serious about losing weight.

But how can I do it without Mikey? When I'm with him, eating healthy is fun. I didn't slip into my old habits. Tomorrow we would have cleaned out my fridge and cupboards and started all over again. Since Roxanne rarely shops, there's nothing she'll miss. I bought all the bad stuff. She eats healthy most of the time and when she doesn't she ends up with the perfect figure anyway because she only falls off the wagon occasionally.

Diane paced the immense apartment with her phone in her hand, wondering if she should call Rox or even Darlene. She knew Rox would lecture her for hurting Mikey, and she deserved it. Why had she been so stupid? Flirting with Isaac had been stupid and fun—she'd done it effortlessly, the way she used to. She'd known it was just as fun for Isaac, and there'd been no chance of either of them getting hurt. Garnering his attention simply made her feel good.

Flirting with Mikey...no, she wouldn't do that. It would hurt him too much. *Yet I felt genuinely beautiful with him. There was no silly flirting, no deception to get the attention and praise I needed. He'd simply given it. So shyly. Even sweetly. He'd been mad at himself for seeing me naked...*

If only he hadn't fallen in love so quickly and become possessive. She asked herself why it bothered her that he'd done that. Because his behavior when he'd effortlessly subdued Robert had done the exact opposite. She'd been awe-struck, even aroused, witnessing that. Afterward, she'd desperately wanted to be close to *Mikey*—not Robert, the man she'd spent ten years of her life believing was the love of her life. *He's not. He's not anymore because he did the one thing I absolutely can't tolerate. That ruthless, selfish act shattered my love for him, a love I know now has been encased in glass for a decade.*

Though she was stunned at her own conclusions, she felt utterly certain of them. It wouldn't be easy to get over the little things—no love, no romance, no sex, no marriage, no babies, no forever after. But she'd changed her entire life overnight and she'd started fresh. That would help her adapt. *It's being alone doing that I can't get over. Because it's Mikey I want to be with. His friendship was healing me. And I genuinely wanted to heal all the jagged scars he's reluctantly revealed to me just recently.*

With a bottle of water she'd snagged from the fridge and run with to prevent herself from lingering too close to the freezer,

Diane sat down on the sofa Mikey had slept on. She wondered why she was so afraid of the fridge now. She'd thrown that fudge out. *Mikey cheered me on like I was a champion. He made me feel like I was one.* But she didn't know what was buried in there. Could she ever eat the endless supply of fudge her Mom and sister made for her?

How do I get him back?

The thought was abrupt and overwhelming. She couldn't do that, though, could she? She'd let him off the hook. She couldn't lead him on inadvertently anymore because he must have been thinking their friendship would lead to romance. Or maybe he didn't mean to get so upset. It just happened because they'd been spending so much time together. Even as Diane considering that, she knew they hadn't spent that much time together, and he wasn't the only one who'd been...well, *enjoying* their companionship. She'd loved being with Mikey, talking, hugging him, really getting to know him, and being so completely distracted from Robert the way she had been with the new and improved Mikey.

He is adorable, sexy.

Her doorbell rang and her heart flew up into her throat. Her hands still holding the phone and the bottle of water, she raced to the door. At the last second, she held herself back and looked in the peep hole. Then her excitement crashed. *Not Mikey. Robert. And I have no backup. No, I don't believe I'm going to fall into Robert's arms, but he won't accept that this is over. He won't let go. With Mikey here, he has no choice but to back off. Mikey's gone though. I sent him away. Let him off the hook.*

Diane had no conscious thought—her finger went to the number to speed dial Mikey and, with a mind of its own, that finger pressed the button. *He won't answer. I don't deserve him to.*

But she lifted the phone to her ear, heard as the connection was made, and she said, "Mikey, it's Robert…"

There were no sounds, no words. She had no way of knowing whether Mikey had heard her or hung up on her. She was on her own. *I have to do this myself.*

Her courage proved itself to be mere bravado when she opened the door with flourish and demanded, "How dare you come here?"

After looking over her shoulder and around her, he pushed his way inside the apartment and closed the door. Diane quickly set her phone and the bottle on the apothecary cupboard just inside the door. Robert held his hands up in a gesture of surrender. "You have to talk to me, Diane, honey. Listen to me. I love you. I can't let you go. Why would you think I'd allow that? You mean everything to me. I know you love me, too. You can't just let this die. We're destined to be together. What about all our plans?"

She made a noise of shocked disbelief. How could he be saying these idiot things? "You're married! That destroys *everything* between us. Everything. Including those foolish plans you never intended to come to pass in the first place."

"What is it you want? Just tell me, Diane."

Can he be serious? Is he actually considering…?

"Diane, are we alone?"

"It's none of your business whether or not I'm alone."

He seemed to take this as proof that she was alone. He advanced a few steps closer and she ended up with her back against the wall, her hands up, warding him off.

"Tell me what you want, darling. Do you want me to leave her?

Is that it? Okay. Fine. I'll leave her if you'll come back to me and forgive me."

Diane shook her head, flabbergasted because she'd never expected this. Certainly never expected him to offer it without her demanding it first. Would that change anything for her? Could she go on with their life together, always remembering that he'd left the woman he'd loved enough to marry for her, left his own children as if none of them mattered to him? *No, that would be worse. My respect for him would become subterranean. I would be even more ashamed for the destruction I caused to ensure my own happiness, even as I could never, ever be happy again.* Why would he suggest such a ludicrous thing?

The answer came and proved she wasn't as naïve and dumb as she'd assumed, at least not in retrospect, in self-defensiveness. *Because he's sure he has time to dupe me again. He believes if he offers it, I'll run back into his arms, give myself to him completely...until the wool is firmly back over my eyes. He'll take years pretending he's leaving and divorcing her. But then his children will be grown and maybe he'll really want to leave the wife of his youth.*

Standing up straight, Diane demanded, "When?"

He clearly hadn't expected that, and she almost laughed at how thrown he looked. "When? What do you mean when?"

"When will you tell her you're leaving her? Now?"

He instantly became mute. She knew then he'd assumed saying those words would weave a magic spell over her, providing him with exactly what he wanted.

"Let's do it right now, Robert. Let's call her and tell her you're divorcing her for me. I want to hear. I want to be here when you do it. Put it on speakerphone. It's the only way I'll ever trust you again."

She was lying from start to finish, curious how far he'd take his gambit. In truth, even if he did leave his wife, she wouldn't want to be with him anymore. She couldn't let herself marry someone who'd already lied and cheated on her, lied and cheated on his wife—a poor innocent woman without the slightest clue what a cretin he was. He could do it again easily if given half a chance.

Making sure it's over and I never go back proves the truth of what I've been saying: That I didn't know he was married and if I had known I would have left him instantly. Anything else makes me Robert's whore, unworthy of any respect. The only moral thing I can do now is step away and never be so trusting again of a man who may well be a stranger after ten years.

"Sweetheart, let's not rush into anything," Robert said softly, cajoling as he stepped closer, reaching for her. "I will leave her. But it's complicated. You have to understand that. I can't just…"

Diane shoved him away with all her strength but only just managed to escape his clutches. "Do you really think I'm that stupid? You have no intention of leaving her tonight or in whatever slow degrees you think will pacify me. I don't want you so bad that I'd stay with you even knowing what you are, what you're doing to your poor wife and children, being with me. I'm not the person you thought I was, Robert. I don't love you enough to be that kind of sinner. I was wrong to sleep with you and believe your promises that we'd get married and have a family someday. I should never have let you seduce me in the first place. But I won't keep compounding the wrong of our relationship by staying with you now. Leaving her won't change what I know about you. You disgust me—that you could do such a thing to me and her, claiming you love us both…"

"I do love you, Diane. I love you so much."

Somehow he managed to get his arms around her, and Diane couldn't escape even as, in the back of her mind, she remembered that this was all she'd ever wanted. Robert holding her for the rest of her life, day and night, young and old, through every season. When she was in his arms, she felt like she knew who she was and what her life should be. But all of that from start to finish had been a lie, a deception with absolutely no basis in reality.

When she hit him with both fists on his chest, he backed off in shock and she ducked away. "I never knew you. You're a stranger. I don't love strangers. I'll never make that mistake again."

"How can you say that? If anyone knows me, it's you."

"No."

Someone pounded on the door, and Diane ran for her life to open it, half believing she'd see a mirage of Mikey there. But he was really was standing there, gasping for air, barely able to hold himself up. He must have run here again. Had he been at his apartment or somewhere further away to warrant the fact that he couldn't talk and couldn't do anything as he panted like he was close to dying? His hair was wet, shirt soaked.

Diane looked behind her to see Robert's expression of utter frustration at being interrupted like this again. She could see how annoyed he was. His jaw tightened and his fists did the same. Was he really going to take on Mikey? After what happened last time? Okay, so at the moment he wasn't up to a fight, but Diane knew once he got his wind back, he'd flatten Robert like a cockroach.

"I want you to leave, Robert. You used me and tricked me and made me believe lies that I based my present and future on. I want nothing to do with you. If your wife is smart, she'll leave you, too, and take your children from you. How can you look at any of them after all you've done? You don't deserve them, and you don't deserve me. Maybe she needs to know the truth about how you so cruelly deceived her all these years—"

"You know you can't do that," Robert said, his tone unyielding and filled with a threat.

"Why shouldn't I? You destroyed my life without blinking an eye, and you still have the nerve to think you have a say about what I do and who I do it with. Now, give me back my apartment key and get out of here. I don't want you to ever return."

Surprising her, Robert paused a moment, then shook his head. "No. You can't mean any of this. You're just reacting. You're hurt. You'll regret this soon and you'll want me back. I won't let you throw away the best thing we've both ever had. We'll talk when you feel better."

Though Mikey was still wheezing, he pushed into the apartment and gasped out, "Give her key back, dude. I mean *now*."

"Who are you? You're nothing. Just leave us alone, Goliath…"

Just like that, Mikey rushed at him and slammed him up against the wall so hard the drywall collapsed in around Robert's head. Diane cried out in shock. Robert floundered to stay upright and escape Mikey's steel hold over his throat.

"Listen, you little jerkoff, she just said don't call her, don't come around here ever again. You understand English? She doesn't want you. It's over for her. If you don't listen to her, listen to me. Give me a chance, asshole. Just give me one chance. I'll make ya bleed all over that nice, fancy suit of yours and those shiny shoes. Take that back to your wife and explain it, why don't ya?"

Diane stared, her hand over her mouth, not doing anything but watching this spectacle in utter shock. *I should stop this. Mike's put tough guys in the hospital.* Yet she couldn't move.

Holding Robert so he was gasping for breath with his arm across his throat, Mikey started going through Robert's pockets one by one until he found the key. As he pulled out the contents, he made embarrassing comments, belittling the man and his equipment. Then, with handfuls of his shirt, he yanked Robert out of the conclave he'd made in the wall, dragged him from the apartment, down the hall, toward the elevator at the far end. Robert was trying to fight now, but, though to Diane he'd once seemed strong, he was a fly compared to Mikey, who swatted him into the elevator so he fell to the floor in the back corner. Mikey reached inside the box and pressed the button to send the elevator to the ground floor. He ducked out as the doors started to close.

Diane was gaping, but, when Mikey turned around and their eyes met across the long hall, she could hardly breathe herself. How had she ever thought Robert was strong and masculine, that he could protect her and keep her safe? He was a pitiful weakling. *Or maybe Mikey's just a...a Goliath. A gorgeous, sexy Goliath who can protect his woman easily.*

Only Mikey's gaze wasn't self-confident and strong, the way she expected after his display of superiority over Robert. *Because he didn't do it to prove who was most worthy. He did it because he was protecting me and trying to keep me safe now and in the future. Mikey really cares about me. It's not about being macho.*

Diane rushed out to the hall and threw her arms around her hero. "I'm so sorry, Mikey...Mike."

"Call me Mikey."

"But you said..."

"I like the way *you* say my name."

Diane couldn't help giggling.

"Can we sit down somewhere? I was four blocks from my apartment and how many more from yours when you called. I just started runnin' full-out. My legs aren't steady yet after that."

Yet he'd shown no sign of weakness with Robert. Though doubtful she was much help, she put her arms around him to support his weight, then led the way back to her apartment. She closed and locked the door behind them. A moment later, Mikey sank onto the sofa. Diane rushed to bring him the water she'd gotten for herself, and he swilled it down in one drink. After it was gone, he gasped some more before managing, "Seemed like you were handlin' things fine on your own. Sorry about your wall."

"Roxanne will be thrilled," she offered honestly. She glanced at the Robert shaped "hole" near the door, then shrugged.

"Sorry if I went too far with the stub. I really had to hold myself back from doin' worse."

Why do I get so excited at seeing Mikey display his toughness? It's crazy. And when it's done, I just want to touch him, feel his rippling muscles. I want to know I'm safe in those deadly yet gentle arms. Lord, what's happening to me!

She'd suspected Mike was holding himself back from hurting Robert seriously. She'd seen him fight and often thought it was like watching a Steven Segal movie—you could hear bones breaking under Mikey's hulking grip. She shuddered, almost unconsciously leaning back on the sofa with him and wrapping both her arms around his heavily muscled arm closest to her. "I've seen what you can do in a fight. I know you controlled yourself both times with Robert. But I wasn't doing a very good job of 'handling things on my own' before you got here. No matter what I said to push him away, he kept convincing himself I didn't mean it, that if he promised to leave his wife eventually, I'd give in to him because it's what we both want. I convinced myself I'd cave if I was ever alone with him, but I'm sure, Mikey. I don't want anything to do with him anymore. It's like whatever *veil* was over my eyes has lifted completely. I see him for what he is. I'm disgusted that I ever loved him and wanted a future with such a selfish coward."

"See, you don't know yourself very well if you thought you'd cave."

"I know I'm stupid. I was about him, and I was stupid to say all that stuff earlier, Mikey. I'm sorry I flirted with Isaac. You don't have to believe me, but it was fun. There was nothing in it one way or another."

"Not for you, maybe. But, if there's nothin' in it for you, why not..." He looked away. "...with me?"

Diane couldn't imagine the courage it'd taken for him to ask such a question. "Oh, Mikey, you matter! That's why I didn't flirt with you. Isaac means nothing. Flirting with him was harmless. With you, I knew I'd hurt you eventually. You'd..."

"...assume somethin' that's absolutely true. You'll never see me that way."

Flushing slightly and easing herself away from physical contact with him, she forced herself to remember *she* was the one who'd encouraged him not to bottle his feelings up inside. "How can you even want me to flirt with you, Mikey? I was the mistress of a married man for ten years. I'm sure none of you believe me when

I tell you that I didn't know and would have left him if I'd had the slightest clue, but it's true—"

Mike leaned toward her and put his finger over her lips to stop her from talking. Every thought in her head dissipated at his nearness and his touch.

"I believe you. If there's anyone on the face of the earth I'd believe that of, it's you. You're not that kind of girl. Nothing could ever convince me you'd willingly, blindly or subconsciously deceive yourself into havin' an affair with a married man. So stop sayin' that. I believe you."

The need to tell him in a gush of overwhelmed emotions that she loved him came…and went. Mikey would never understand she meant as friends. He was the best kind of friend a girl could have. "Thank you. But that's just it, Mikey. I don't want you to feel obligated to me. To feel like you have to rescue me. I don't want to hurt you. You're not like other men that I can flirt with easily because they mean nothing to me and we're both just having fun. You matter to me too much."

For a long moment, he stared at her and his earlier comment seemed to write itself across the air between them: *You'll never see me that way.* Diane knew she should address the concern, get it off the table. Tell him straight out that, no, he wasn't the right man for her.

She couldn't do it. The words formed and broke up so fast, they never made it to the surface, where she could say them and save this sweet, wonderful man. She couldn't explain even to herself why she couldn't say them. Mikey had only ever been a friend to her the entire time they'd known each other. She'd had deep, shameful moments she'd hidden locked away inside her when she'd seen him pleasuring other women and wished to be each one. She hadn't understood her own longing and tried to forget it each time her desire surfaced. *I can't fall in love with Mikey Lund. I don't know why, but I can't. Maybe it's not a question of "can't" but "won't". I don't know why not either.*

"Do you wanna keep me on your speed-dial?" he asked softly, when he averted his gaze and focused on the empty bottle in his hand.

Diane sighed, aware she was hurting this man even as she was trying so hard not to. "Maybe you could put me on your speed-dial, too. You're not put on this earth to rescue me. I want us to be friends. Mutual friends who rescue each other. If you ever need rescuing, that is."

"Do you want me to rescue you?"

That was the question, she realized. That was the only one Mikey would allow to matter to him.

"Yes." It was the only answer she could give him. The truth. "Don't let me be selfish with you, Mikey. I know you're incapable of speaking up for yourself, but I want you to. I want to know what you think and what you feel. I want to know if I hurt you."

Unfortunately, he was much too complicated a man to say that he wore his heart on his sleeve. He did the opposite—he withdrew instead, turning the pain inward, but it came out in other ways whenever he did. In the past, he drank like a fish and ate like a bear after a long winter. And, today, he struck out at her in jealousy for one second, yet came running when she needed him and he was willing to continue being her rescuer whether she ever wanted more from him or not. *Maybe it would be better for me to end this. Or maybe I can be good for him. Maybe I can help him see how worthy he is, how wonderful and attractive. Maybe I can help him with his confidence.*

She stuck out her hand. "So, mutual friends and rescuers?"

He looked at her hand, and she wondered if he was second-guessing the wisdom of this just as she was. But he shook to seal the deal anyway. One way or another, she wanted their pact to work out.

After yesterday's power-run, Mike probably would have called off his Saturday morning jog if not for the fact that Diane Hoffman showed up at his apartment before seven a.m., just as they planned the night before, wearing satin shorts, a tanktop straining against the swell of those beauties he couldn't get himself to stop looking at as often as humanly possible, and jogging shoes. She'd pulled her long hair up into a high ponytail that bounced as much as her breasts did when she ran beside him. But she was even lazier than he was. They'd barely made it to the park before she wanted to give up, go home and have breakfast.

"Are you laughing at me, Mikey Lund?" she demanded when she bent over, clutching her side and gasping.

"You've never jogged before, have you?"

"Admit it, what you're really asking is whether I've ever *exercised* before!"

She was screeching and offended, and Mike couldn't help laughing harder. Just like that, she took off like a bat out of hell, streaking out ahead of him, leaving him far behind. Mike barely had to push himself to catch up with her again. Almost immediately, she diverted off the jogging path and collapsed on the grass facedown, panting and gasping. Laughing, Mike dropped down beside her, looking down at her and even lifting her ponytail hiding her face. "You okay?" he asked.

"No. It's official, Mikey. I'm not a jogger. I never want to jog again."

"You were kinda *running*, not jogging. Joggin's a lot easier than runnin'."

She still hadn't lifted her face from the grass and, on the pretense of looking around at the beautiful July morning, he saw again how sexy she was in her exercise gear. *Short shorts, tight tanktop, gorgeous legs.* She was petite and yet voluptuous. It was a combination he liked so much, he had a hard time not looking at her, not touching her. He blushed when she finally turned to look up at him. Before he could glance away, he noticed she was wearing makeup. *Makeup to jog? Who puts on makeup to get sweaty? Unless...*

No, he wasn't about to let himself complete that thought. The fact that Diane hadn't wanted to answer his question about why she couldn't feel romantic about him had told him all he needed to know. Though he was no longer a drunken slob, she'd always see him that way and therefore would never be attracted to him the way he'd always been to her. She didn't want to see him as a potential boyfriend. *She wants to be mutual friends. That's all. A friend who can't stop hugging me, touching me, making me want to do the kind of things to her that make it impossible for me to sleep lately. And when I do... Bye-bye, self-discipline.*

"What are you thinking?" he asked to get himself to *stop* thinking.

"When do we get to eat?"

Mikey laughed out loud, standing and pulling her to her feet. She put all her weight on him, and he didn't mind a bit. She was sweaty, sticky, and clingy. *It's how I like my women.* "Let's eat at my place. I'll make you an egg white omelet."

Diane looked up at him, making a face. "How can that be good? Wouldn't it be tasteless?"

"Trust me."

She smiled. "Okay, but only because you introduced me to the best chicken sandwich I've ever eaten in my life—low-cal or otherwise."

"After we're done, we'll go over to your apartment and clear out the junk."

"Can't we donate it somewhere? Some of those packages have never been opened. It's such a waste. I grew up on a farm, you know. Wasting goes against all my principles."

"Would we be doin' anyone a favor givin' 'em junk food like that?"

"I suppose not."

When they got back to his apartment, she walked inside first, complaining, "I'm so sweaty and stinky. I can't eat like this. Can I shower here and borrow one of your shirts?"

He couldn't say no. Not to this woman. He got out one of the brand new v-necked ones, knowing she'd looked sexiest in it. Then he pointed her into his bathroom, certain the sound of the shower would torture him. *She'll be naked, a fantasy come true. Diane Hoffmann, Goddess of Fantasy, naked in my apartment.* Even if it wasn't the way he'd always wanted her to be, it was probably the best he'd get.

"I'll start breakfast prep."

In the kitchen, he busied himself chopping green peppers, onions, mushrooms. He worked slowly and methodically, waiting anxiously for the moment when she'd come out with her hair wet, wearing his low-cut t-shirt and showing off those beauties without her sweat-soaked sports bra…

Lucky for him, she didn't opt for modesty. On her, his t-shirt, even one twice as small as he used to wear, was like a dress. One so tight over her breasts, she was all but popping out of it. To add to his agony, she kept pulling on it, revealing more each time instead of hiding, the way she intended.

"I'll shower fast. Then we can get these started. Do you wanna grate the cheese?" He nodded toward everything she needed to do that already on the counter.

"Sure. But isn't cheese bad for you?"

"As bad as a hamburger is, maybe, because it's full of fat. But it's got as much good as bad: protein, calcium, Vitamin A, folate. Substitute it for meat and it tastes just as good and it's just as satisfying. We shouldn't cut it out. We should just be careful how much we have." His nutrition advice covered his real thoughts about her wearing his t-shirt like lingerie.

She said, "Okay."

Now I get a cold shower. But he knew if he recovered at all under the icy spray, he'd be right back where he started when he came out and saw her again.

Only the Lonely by Karen Wiesner

Chapter 9

Shaking her head as Mikey disappeared into his bathroom, she tried to get the picture of him wearing those skintight latex compression shorts out of her mind. He'd told her when she arrived that he'd been embarrassed to wear them at first but then realized in the end he was less embarrassed than wearing anything else. Regular running shorts didn't keep anything...well, in place. Right away, Diane pictured him running through the park with his *equipment* bouncing as badly as her breasts did even wearing the tight exercise bra she'd put on. Even as she giggled softly and blushed, she was right back to picturing every muscular line of his lower body in the painted-on shorts.

When she forced herself to unwrap the sharp cheddar cheese and cut off a chunk to shred onto the plate, she wondered at the difference in Mikey's new, lean, toned body and Robert's. How had she ever seen Robert as attractive? Beyond his sophistication and sharp dressing, he was a flabby, forty-five year old man who'd lost the hair on his head and gained twice as much on the rest of his body. *Because of the stress involved in juggling two women and kids?*

Diane leaned against the counter after slicing off another formidable hunk of the cheese. She hadn't loved Robert's looks. She'd loved *him* and her love had made her see him as the most handsome man in the world. *I'm not shallow. I'm not. But Mikey has such thick, full, soft hair. He's so muscular and strong. The hair on his chest and legs is sexy. Not white and old-crinkly. Lord, I can remember how hard it was to do certain, sexual things Robert asked for occasionally. Because I was mildly disgusted with his pale, flabby, small...*

The image of Mikey in those shorts—every part of him big and strong and appealing—came again, thrusting into her mind with shocking force. Even as she tried to tell herself she was ashamed of having done those things with a man she wasn't married to—and that was true, she *was* deeply ashamed for her immoral behavior—she knew she wasn't feeling guilty so much as she was aroused now. *Over another man, not the man I was supposed to love to the ends of the earth.*

Mikey was attractive. Why couldn't she think it? He was breathtaking. Maybe it was wrong she found him so sexy now that he'd lost weight and hadn't before when he was fat. He was the same person he'd been then, wasn't he?

She wasn't entirely sure he was.

Why do I have to feel guilty for ending a relationship that was wrong? I'm guilty of carrying on the relationship at all, but not for ending it. That's the right thing to do. Robert's the one who sinned so horrifically. I'm not evil for letting go of my feelings for the wrong man. As long as his wife doesn't find out and she can be protected from Robert's deception all this time, I can move on. Move on to...

Mikey appeared suddenly in the room, dressed in well-fitting jeans and another t-shirt just like the one she was wearing, and she gasped because his gaze was on the cheese she was supposed to be shredding. Wrapped up in her thoughts, she'd unconsciously devoured all but the last chunk still in her hand and the little she'd grated. She threw the remainder down like it was a snake. "What... I don't... I didn't mean..."

Instead of scolding her, Mikey laughed. "Two days after I started my diet, I ate five Di Fara Specials in one sitting."

Diane opened her mouth in shock. "You did not! You're just saying that to make me feel better for eating two pounds of cheese all at once!"

He chuckled. "Oh, I ate that much all right. I haven't done it since 'cause I got so sick after I gorged on that much at once, I didn't eat anything but raw carrots for two days afterward."

"Is that to be my penance?" she asked, feeling better though she should have been horrified still. "Carrot sticks?"

"Have you actually ever tasted one—I mean without ranch dressing or without frying it in a stick of butter? It's actually really good raw."

"Mikey, is there any hope for me? I ate that much without even realizing I was! And, the worst part is, I'm still hungry."

His gaze over her body was warm, sweet, but she knew even then he was thinking about her naked breasts beneath the stretched cotton. *Just like I was thinking about him—not flabby, white and tiny but the exact, breathtaking opposite—beneath those shockingly tight shorts.*

"You're beyond beautiful. Nothin' could *ever* change that."

He believes that. He really doesn't believe I'm a chubby, busty stub.

Because she couldn't help herself, she laughed sheepishly, and Mikey joined her as if he was feeling just as awkward and embarrassed as she was about being unable to look away from her new best friend.

Diane made tiny, distressed noises with every package and container he threw away or emptied. He'd filled three thirteen gallon trash bags already. Her mother and sister sent her far too many "care packages"—he'd seen that pattern within minutes of undertaking this chore. There'd been enough fudge buried in the freezer to feed a small continent.

"Mom is always worried I'll get too skinny. She still thinks men of this generation find plump girls sexy, like past generations of men did. Maybe she's right because my sister's husband seems to love her shape. Neither of them ever worry I'll get *fat* eating all the stuff they send me. It's partly because my best friend is a supermodel and Mom thinks every movie star is too thin."

"Rox isn't like most supermodels. She's more like Cindy Crawford." Roxanne wasn't skinny and she was nowhere near fat. She had curves in all the right places. Yet Mike still liked Diane's shape better, maybe because, though Roxanne's breasts were large, they fit the rest of her body. She was tall and svelte, streamlined. Diane's breasts were closer to *huge*—some would say maybe *too* big for her tiny body. But in Mike's mind Diane was...

"Perfect. Perfect in every possible way," Diane agreed.

He didn't say, "Yeah" but he agreed silently that Diane's body was perfect in every possible way. "Maybe you should tell your sister and mom to stop all this bakin' and sendin' you stuff that's not good for you."

Diane swallowed reluctantly at the idea. "Technically, fudge *isn't* baked."

"Your family makes the best fudge I've ever tasted." *Chocolate nut, chocolate marshmallow, peanut butter.*

"It's my go-to drug. Whenever I'm depressed or unhappy, nothing cheers me up like fudge." She glanced at him, her face covered with longing and affection. "Except you. You cheer me up better than food. You're good for me. This stuff isn't. You're right. I have to stop, tell them to stop sending me *anything* food."

Mike tried not to let her words go straight to his heart and libido. Forcefully, he turned back to the fridge.

"They'll never believe I want them to stop. When Penny and I were kids, all hours of the day we'd be sneaking into the freezer to get fudge. Mom started making triple batches because, whenever she and Dad wanted a sweet treat, the fudge was gone. Even that didn't help. The more she made, the more we ate. How will I convince them now I suddenly don't want anymore?"

"So when they call on Tuesday, I'll be here. I'll tell 'em I lost weight after I stopped sneakin' fudge and you need to stop eatin' it, too."

She giggled, and Mike looked at her for a moment when she said, "That would work. Whenever I suggest Robert thinks I'm fat, she tells me to stop eating. She'll do anything in the world to see me get married. But then I have to tell them..."

She trailed off, and Mike filled in what she was thinking: *Tell them I was sleeping with a married man for ten years, thinking he would marry me at some point.* Diane wouldn't tell her parents the truth though: That none of it was her fault.

"How did you know?" she asked suddenly. "That my Mom and Penny call together on Tuesday?"

"Seven o'clock. Speakerphone. Dad chimin' in for about two seconds, enough to ask how his baby is, before he leaves his womenfolk to it. You told me before." He supposed she'd be stunned if she knew he remembered just about everything she told him all those times when they'd been together at a party, she got depressed, asked him to come home with her, and, with a chunk of fudge in her hand, her mouth kept going and going like the Energizer bunny, eating and talking nonstop. She'd told him anything, everything. He'd sobered up fast those times and he'd eaten the fudge, too, just to keep his hands occupied and as far from her as he could get them.

"How do you remember these things? *Why* would you remember them? They're not important to you."

"You're important to me," he muttered, sticking his head back in the freezer.

He was both surprised and unsurprised when she came up behind him and hugged him around the middle. "You're so good to me, Mikey. I don't deserve it."

More than anything else in the world, he wanted to turn around, pull her into the alcove of his arms, and kiss her until she knew she mattered more to him than any person alive.

That was exactly what he couldn't do.

Five bursting bags in the dumpster later, she asked, "Now what?"

"Now we go shopping."

Because it would be a trip that ensured she'd have healthy food on hand and not junk, they took his car. "What about dinner?" she asked as they filled a cart at the supermarket together.

"I'm gonna teach you a simple recipe. Chicken Marsala—the light version. Only two hundred twenty-five calories per serving."

"That's good?"

"You get a full skinless, boneless chicken breast and mushrooms—bursting with flavor along with roasted seasonal vegetables, which add another hundred and twenty-five calories per serving. To compare, there are about a hundred and twenty calories in a one-ounce serving of fudge with nuts. That's about a cubic inch."

Diane held up her fingers to that teeny-tiny size, and Mike nodded. "So I can have three bites of fudge or a full meal like the one you're making?"

"Yeah."

"I'm going for the full meal. You know, even that egg white omelet you made this morning was good. It was as full-flavored as the whole egg ones my mom used to make with butter and cheese and mushrooms and bacon. Not taking into account the brick of cheese I ate before, I was satisfied and felt good after I ate it. I do want to learn how to cook for myself again. Healthy. I've lost all my skills in that department. I used to like to cook."

"I cook for myself because it's the best way to be healthy, but I don't like doing it much. I had to figure out the best restaurants to offer low-calorie menus. That way, when I don't feel like cooking, I can still be healthy and not lose ground."

"Is it healthy to have lost as much weight as you have in such a short time?" she asked in concern, eying him closely not for the first time today.

"Why not? I exercise a lot. I put good things in. I'm not hungry most of the time. The junk cravings come only occasionally now and I don't feel as guilty when I have a little bit of bad."

She nodded with determination, hugging him easily. She was smiling big as the sun when she looked up at him. "I want to be like you when I grow up, Mikey Lund."

He chuckled, his heart hurting despite his vow to distance himself.

Cooking with Diane was fun. They laughed and talked and he felt like everything was mutual between them. Somehow that was worse. Before, he could fall back on the fact that she was disgusted by him romantically. That knowledge curbed his tendencies toward her eventually. She didn't seem turned off by him now, even when she wouldn't let herself entertain the idea of seeing him as a man she could be with as more than friends.

"Can we have dinner together Tuesday night, when my family calls?" Diane asked as she made up the table for dinner. Roxanne's assistant had apparently furnished the entire apartment after she moved in—just before Rox talked Diane into living with her. The expensive dining room table had probably never been used. Mike couldn't help noticing Diane had set their places right next to each other instead of on opposite ends, seven feet apart. Whether she admitted it to herself or not, she liked to be close to him. What reason did she give herself for that, or did she never bother to question it the way he had been constantly lately?

Mike swallowed, putting up a smile. "Sure. I can show you another recipe."

"Yes, please! And we can watch Roxanne's show on the Fashion Network afterward."

Blanching, he started to protest.

"I'm not a big fan of fashion shows either. The clothes are always so weird. I can't imagine normal women dressing like that. It's like a big costume show. But Christian Dior is supposed to be *all that*. I don't know one fashion designer from the next. Me, you'd have to pay me as much as Roxanne pulls in to put on those crazy get-ups they walk up and down the runway in."

"You seem fashionable to me."

"Roxanne always tells me the only true way to be fashionable is by finding your own style. The shows are all drama and diva-backbiting. I always assumed she was humoring me because I'm a farmer's daughter from the Midwest."

Mike nodded, setting the main dish they'd prepared on a platter on the table. "Dinner. I'm not sure about the whole fashion show thing, but I'll try."

"We'll just pretend we're watching football," Diane said.

"Never much cared for that either." His family watched football like it was the only entertainment in life. Brett, Jace and Doobs seemed to like it, too, though not nearly with the obsession. He'd put up with it all his life because the food and booze were guaranteed to flow.

"We might as well plan dinner together tomorrow night, too, and Monday," Diane said. "I'll cook. If you want me to? I mean, I really need to get my skills back. Do you mind, or will you be sick of seeing me so often?"

Did she really think that was possible? He'd sleep here if she asked him to…anywhere she asked him to, even in the bathtub. *Second thought, that might make the fantasies twice as hot.* "I'll be your guinea pig."

She giggled and filled their wine glasses with water. He was used to eating at the kitchen sink, but she'd insisted on doing it "right". He'd go along with anything. Anything at all she wanted of him. As long as she wanted him around, he'd be here, no questions asked. Maybe she'd realize he was nothing like the jerk who'd used her like a prostitute when she was an angel. Maybe someday she'd see him as a good guy, a guy she wanted to be with.

Maybe she never will. But I'll stick around no matter what. What other choice to I have? I'd rather dream of Diane in person instead of dreaming of her alone.

Chapter 10

Sunday evening, after a delicious, satisfying, healthy meal she'd cooked, she and Mikey went for a walk in the park. It would be night soon, and she rarely went anywhere alone in New York after dark, but she knew she couldn't be safer with anyone else. Mikey would protect her with his life, if need be. She squeezed his hand, her other arm wrapped around his biceps, and hugged him from the side as they strolled slowly. Her mind was nowhere but here, right where she wanted to be.

Surprising her, Mikey asked, "You havin' any trouble sleepin'? You know, because..."

"Of Robert? No. It's so weird. I feel like the slate of the past ten years has been wiped completely clean. He was my whole life, and now I don't want anything to do with that life. Nothing. I'm also not sad that my career is basically over. Both our jobs were in jeopardy. There was the constant threat that we'd be down-graded to part-time or eliminated altogether. Sales reps these days with the recession have it harder than most people. More so than even my job. I was reallocated within the company whenever the company started cutting costs. Instead of working for one district, I worked for all the sales reps in the company, regardless of district. Then they cut my hours a little bit. I think I wouldn't have been laid off for years. They'd just whittle my hours down an hour here and there. Robert...well, I know they considered firing him because his sales were way down for a long time. Sales reps have to sell more every year—not less or equal. If he hadn't gotten that big sale recently—the one he spent how many months working on—he would have been fired for sure. So I believed Robert when he said he didn't feel stable enough financially to get married and start a family. I mean, if he was fired, he would have to start all over again. Find another job in a field that's shrinking. It wouldn't have been the same for me. The thought of losing my job just made it seem like the possibility of being a wife and mother were *more* possible. Though I wanted to have a good career for at least five to ten years after I graduated college, I lived for the day when I could quit and become what I've always wanted to be."

"You know, you're talking about this dude like he's *dead*."

Though Mikey spoke the words gently, she felt as though she'd been struck by them. "Maybe it is like that. It's how I feel. I'm excited to start all over again. To bury the baggage of what was wrong for so many years. But I know I still have to face it. I have to face telling my family it's over with Robert. I spent ten years covering up the fact that I slept with him. My parents would be so ashamed of me. We tell each other everything, and they expect me to be a good girl."

"You are."

"How can you say that, Mikey? I wasn't married. I..."

"...let him seduce you. I know that's how it happened."

"I did though. I mean, we were together a long time before I finally gave in, but I made that choice to let it go too far."

Mikey stopped suddenly and all but forced her—gently—to look at him. "Listen to me. Good girls have sexual needs, too. You wanted to fulfill your need for love first. That's the only reason you gave in to him. Once he gave you the commitment in spoken words, you let yourself go. Because you were in love and you believed him when he told you he would marry you soon. I bet every time the guy came back to town to see you, he laid it on thick about how soon you two would get hitched. Only after he said that would you fall into bed with him."

Diane looked at him, her mouth open in shock that he would realize all of her and Robert's reunions started the same way. She would hold out, wanting to be convinced she was truly loved and the future would mean the legal commitment she needed. Once Robert gave her lavish promises... *We would fall into bed, just like Mikey said.*

"You wouldn't have done that if he hadn't convinced you it was all about love. I know you. But it's not wrong for you to have sexual needs—in love or not."

"But..."

"It's not wrong to *have* them. What you do with 'em...well, that's where bad things happen. There're a handful of ways to do it, only one of them ideal, 'cause there aren't too many people alive who don't have sexual needs. Some people get lucky: Fall in love, get married, have sex. Satisfied. Nice. Hardly anybody gets that fairytale. Some people deny themselves love and sex in any form—

somehow. I don't know how, but they keep themselves as lonely as they are pure. Then there are those who take sex in place of love whenever and wherever they can get it. Finally, others require a declaration of love before sex. You were lookin' for the fairytale and couldn't have it, Diane. You wanted love too bad to deny yourself. So you did the next best thing: You insisted on hearing 'I love you' before sex. Without the words, you wouldn't have had sex. See?"

"Is all this supposed to make me feel better?" she asked, realizing that in Mikey's view of the world, she came in second from the last in a list of bad options below ideal.

"It's supposed to make you see you're not at fault for giving in to sexual need. Good and bad alike, we all need sex. You insisted on love first. That wasn't wrong."

"It wasn't ideal. I should have insisted on *marriage* first. I should have deprived myself."

"Maybe. But sometimes it's hard to be noble. You did the best you could in a world of crappy options."

He turned, she held his arm and hand again, and they started walking. "What about you, Mikey? Where do you fall on that list of yours?"

"I took what I could get. What else is there to say? I couldn't get love, so I took sex."

She'd kind of guessed that, wasn't sure why she'd wanted him to confirm reality. "This is embarrassing, but I've seen you with women, Mikey. Different women. Many different. Those women were very satisfied."

He frowned, not quite looking at her but turning his head toward her. "You've *seen*..."

"I'm sorry. But we were at a party each time. In a roomful of partiers, there's a lot of...well, *sex*. I'm sure you've seen it happening, too."

"And you saw me?"

With countless women, all different, various times.

"I saw..." She cleared her throat. "...before you got to the point of going into a bedroom for privacy." Those women he'd been with would have done anything for him when he touched them the way he did. They hadn't need privacy to be fulfilled over and over again.

What in the world are we talking about here?

"I'm sorry. I don't know why we're talking about this. I guess it embarrasses me that you know I was intimate with Robert without being married to him. I wanted to feel like I wasn't the only one. I mean...that needed that. Needed *sex*. Even if I held out for love first, I..." She couldn't continue. The fact was, she'd enjoyed sex. She loved it. But the deeper truth was that Robert hadn't even gotten close to satisfying her sexual needs. Even as he'd requested what he wanted from her sexually, he'd rarely gave her the same and offered excuses when she'd gotten up the nerve to make her own requests.

"Women are taught to believe it's wrong for them to like what they're doing in that area," Mikey filled in.

"I guess that's what it is. I feel guilty for even admitting to myself that, if not for morality and love and all that stuff, well..."

"Well what? Just say it."

"I'd be a sex maniac!"

Mikey was grinning at her. She felt so ashamed she wanted to die, yet she was laughing and somehow felt better for having admitted the truth.

"He wasn't much of a stud, I guess?"

"I feel terrible!"

"Don't. Why should you? He used you. You didn't know what he was doin' behind your back. She probably didn't either."

"I shouldn't even be talking about this stuff. It just feels wrong. But, lately, I've been thinking that being in New York makes me less of the good girl I was back home. I mean, everyone is so free here. Even talking like this and saying what I shouldn't, I can't be that free. Eventually, I'll come to my senses and realize, if freedom means no morals, I can't do it. Anyway, it'd be easier to stand strong there—at home."

"What are you saying? You're gonna move back there?" He seemed genuinely concerned.

"I don't know. I haven't decided. I love it here. I love my friends."

"Can't see yourself workin' in a grease pit indefinitely?"

Knowing how sensitive he was about his job, the lack of sophistication involved, she insisted, "Not for the reason you're assuming. I want to get married and have children. I want to stop putting that off. But I don't trust men anymore. How could I ever believe a man if he told me he wasn't married?"

"You don't trust *any* men?"

"Here? No. Back home, I would."

"You don't trust Brett, Doobs, me?"

She glanced at him, realizing somehow that what he was really asking was him—just him. "Brett, no. I've never been in the position to trust him. I mean, I trust he'll be good to Savvy and his daughter. I trust he'll be a good employer to me. Romantically for me... There's no reason I need to trust him beyond what I know of him. Jamie, no. I definitely don't trust him. I do trust you though."

"Really? I mean, do you really? You know I'm not secretly married?"

She laughed. "I know you're not. I do trust you." *I trust Mikey completely. The only way I don't trust him is that I'm always afraid he's falling in love with me. That I'll hurt him and he'll let me.*

"Good. I want you to trust me. But maybe this is one of those things like they say after you end a long-term relationship. Maybe you shouldn't make a decision about moving back to Wisconsin right now. You're still on the rebound. You're reelin' from what's happened. It's not a good time to make life decisions. Give yourself some time. There's no reason to rush."

Though she suspected he just didn't want her to leave, she knew he was saying the best thing for her. "I hate feeling so lost and directionless."

"You think you're directionless and lost right now?"

"Aren't I? You said yourself I'm reeling from what happened."

"Okay, but if you are, I don't think you're lost. Do you know what to do about that dude?"

"I need to never, ever see him again."

"That doesn't sound like someone who's so lost she doesn't know the direction she's moving in. Should you go back to the pharm company to work?"

"No. I can't. There's no stability, even if Robert wasn't a factor."

"And your own health?"

This so-called diet she was on didn't feel like any of the starve-and-gorge ones she'd followed before. It felt like a way of life she wanted to embrace with both arms—thin, fit ones. "You're right. I'm not at all lost or directionless. I'm the opposite for the first time in my whole life."

"Then maybe now isn't the best time to go runnin' back to Wisconsin to be a dairy farmer. Or the wife of one."

Diane laughed out loud. His grin made her feel warm and content, as if she could do anything, be anything as long as he was at her side. She was starting all over, but she was doing it the right way for once. The problem she couldn't talk about was that she used to have dreams. Now she had nothing worth pursuing. The only thing that felt right and made her happy was Mikey Lund himself. Was that a direction to run toward? Was that a dream to pursue?

They looped around the park and back to the entrance. In the darkness just beginning to fall, she saw a bold red Town Car parked nearby. The license plate was clearly visible. *Drake 8.* "Oh my gosh, do you see that Town Car?"

Mike started to look, and she hissed, "Don't look! That's Robert's car. Is he following me?"

Until this moment, she'd never considered the possibility. She'd been lost in this blissful life she was sharing with Mikey. How long had Robert been following her? The troubling answer was one she didn't question: Robert had been doing this all along. Since Mikey had impressed upon Robert the seriousness of discontinuing his pursuit of her, divested him of her key, then bodily threw him into her elevator and sent him on his humiliated way.

As if realizing the truth for the first time, Diane murmured, "He's not going to let it go."

"Diane?"

She looked up at Mikey.

"Does it matter to you anymore what *he* does?"

She swallowed. "No. Not at all." She spoke firmly and no shadow of doubt entered the privacy of her mind.

"Then what do you care? Let him waste his time. Besides, the more he sees of you, of us, the more convinced he'll be you're over him. You've moved on with your life. That can only be good, right?"

"Yes, but...Mikey, I promised I wasn't going to...well..." He would be hurt if she pretended to be in love with him, acted like a woman in love to convince her old boyfriend she was taken. How could she risk that? Hurting Mikey was wrong and she wouldn't do it.

"Let's give this sorry SOB a show."

Mikey spoke with such determination. When he put his arms around her, drawing her into the alcove of his body, she couldn't think straight. She liked it here too much. Here, she was reminded of how he'd swatted Robert around like he was a pesky fly. He'd kept himself in control even then, and he'd done all of it for her.

Diane looked up at him, saw his handsome, adorable face, his incredible eyes meeting hers, and she couldn't help smiling like a simpering female.

"So, just how bad was he at satisfying you sexually?" he asked in husky voice.

Even as she gasped in shock, she couldn't help giggling, feeling ashamed and remembering how consummately Mikey used his hands, his mouth on those women he'd been with. She could never have conceived of herself wanting to be with him romantically, yet he'd forever made her conscious of her own breasts, her own needs, her own dissatisfaction with the choices she'd made in her life. *What does that say about me, about him? What does it mean?*

Not until they returned to her apartment did she realize they must have walked right in front of Robert's Town Car on their way home and she'd never noticed.

Work flew by on Monday with the silent reminder that he and Diane would be together yet again for most of the night. When his cell phone rang, he assumed it was her, calling down from the office to tell him it was time to go home or would be soon. Instead, it was Doobs, inviting him to an annual event Mike had all but forgotten about in his obsession. "Coming to watch the fireworks from the yacht?"

Doobs' old man owned a forty-two foot yacht that he used to give river tours and private charters around the city. It was the perfect job for a laidback, unpredictable, unstructured guy like Doobs. He helped his dad out when he felt like it and did whatever he wanted the rest of the time. One thing he never missed was the fireworks cruise.

"It's the fourth of July," Mike said in wonder that he'd been oblivious to the date. Doobs' always invited his friends and his old man didn't charge any of them the way he did his clients—who paid a pretty steep fare.

Doobs laughed at him. "So?"

"So when does it start again?"

"Boards at nine, departs at nine-thirty. Three-hour tour."

Mike calculated. They'd go home, make dinner, eat, talk to her family at seven, then watch Roxanne's fashion show. Mike couldn't fathom spending more than a half hour on that. "Diane might wanna go, too," he said, trying to sound casual, like he hadn't seen her and might run into her. He wasn't sure he wanted his friends to know anything right now. What was there to tell anyway? They'd probably guess in a heartbeat Diane had made the big break from the married dude, let Mike be her rescue from her grief, and now he was deeply in love with her.

"Sure. The more the merrier."

"I'll ask her." Mike wasn't sure she'd be comfortable about it, but if she said no on the basis of their friends seeing them together…

Don't go there. She's not readin' more than friendship into us spendin' so much time together. So don't you. "What about alcohol?"

"That's right. You said you quit, didn't you? Unimaginable."

Mike supposed it was. He'd guzzled gin for breakfast and chased it with gallons of whatever else was at hand for as long as Doobs had known him.

"Sorry, dude, but the full bar is part of the cruise package."

"No problem. I don't need or want it. Probably see ya later."

The clock had been slow as long as Mike could remember, so he figured quitting wasn't actually ducking out early when he went upstairs to the office. The door was open, and the scent of fresh lemon hit him instead of a ton of dust. Diane was humming along to the radio, slightly off-key, while she worked. The office had undergone a radical transformation. Though there was obviously still a lot to do, the endless, mile-high stacks of papers were mostly gone and it was possible to move around the room. It looked bigger than ever before.

She turned, saw him and gave him a smile that he felt from his head to his feet. "Well, I handled all those phone calls. None of them urgent, but these are coming in next week." She handed him the stack, and Mike leafed through them, not really caring. He always read his notes from the day before or talked to the car owner before he started work anyway.

"Still enjoyin' the organization?" he asked, looking around the room again.

"I am! I really am. This has been a challenge, but twenty years of accumulation doesn't scare me. Pretty soon this shop will run like a well-oiled machine…" She chuckled as if realizing she'd spoken of a mechanic's shop that way. "I guess it already does. But the office will match now. Is it time to go home?"

"Yeah. If you're ready."

"I am. I'm starving."

"Stirfry coming up."

"I'm cooking though, right?"

"Sure."

Until the garage was locked up and they were walking toward her apartment, Mike didn't dare bring up extra plans for the night. When he glanced back at one point and saw the red Town Car trailing slowly behind them—the way it had that morning on their walk to work—he decided it was a good time to distract her. "So Doobs called. He's havin' his annual fireworks cruise."

"Is it the Fourth of July? How could I have forgotten?"

"I did, too. You wanna go? The boat leaves dock at 9:30."

"Let's go. I haven't been on his boat for a long time. And the weather is perfect."

She snuggled against him, inadvertently giving the jerkoff another big show. Mike felt half crazed having her so close to him.

They'd been spending all but their sleeping hours together, but even then she filled his mind continuously. He thought about kissing her so often now, he wondered what would happen if he did. She loved affection. She seemed fine whenever he hugged her because she'd started it. She didn't mind being held longer than maybe she intended. Holding hands, smiling, sharing long looks. *I'm dead and buried. I wanna be her friend, real friend, and I wanna be her lover, her husband, heck, her lapdog. It all sounds good to me!*

Pathetic.

Unfortunately, she chose that moment, before he could figure out something else to say, to turn back. She saw the Town Car, and she huffed under her breath. "He's unbelievable! Why doesn't he go home to his wife? How long has it been since he was home with his family? That poor woman! His children."

"He may be easy to get over, but that doesn't mean you are."

Diane looked up at him, obviously stunned. "He…"

Maybe she needed to hear that the guy had fallen under her charms. Maybe that would break his hold on her for good. But Mikey knew he wouldn't be the one to say the words.

"I destroyed a family. I wish so bad I could beg this poor woman's forgiveness. I don't want her to be blindsided like I was. I don't want her to feel like less. *He's* less. He's worthless, not her."

"You're right. What are you gonna tell your mom and sister tomorrow?"

She sighed, somehow sinking deeper against him as she did. "I've thought about that. I know I don't want to lie. I'd feel like I was protecting Robert. I don't even want to protect myself."

"You did an unwillful wrong. Why shouldn't you protect yourself?"

"How can you still think so well of me, Mikey? You know on the list of ideal choices, I'm almost at the bottom."

"*I'm* at the bottom. You're a step above."

Almost against her will, she smiled at him, then leaned her forehead against his as she hugged him. Her sweet breath became his own.

"Do you want me to tell your mom and sister?" he asked, so aware of her full lips, he already knew he'd sleep tonight dreaming of them.

"It's sweet of you to offer, and I know you'd paint me with a rosy glow. I can't ask you to do that. But I was thinking of something else anyway."

"What?"

"I was thinking I should call them tonight. After dinner. Just get it over with. The longer I put it off, the harder it'll be."

"We've got until nine."

"You'll stay with me while I do it?" she asked, holding him tighter as they somehow walked while twisted together like a pretzel.

Mike spoke from his heart, only partially hoping she wouldn't recognized it for what it was. "I'll always be there for you, Diane."

Chapter 11

"Mom, everything's all right. I'm calling early because I wanted to tell you…" Diane took a deep breath, her hand all but squeezing the life out of Mikey's. He didn't even flinch. "I broke up with Robert."

"What? Why?" her mother screeched, just as she'd expected.

"Mom, he was married. This whole time. I had no idea."

She couldn't help noticing Mikey's expression. He looked like he might implode—because he wanted to defend her?

"Hold on. Your sister is here. I'll put it on speakerphone."

Over the next long, grueling minutes, Diane listened to her mother and sister defend her, ripping Robert to shreds in the process. Diane wanted to cry when her mother said, "Well, it's not as if you gave him anything anyway. You're not married to him. So you'll just start over again."

She knew her mother meant "give him your virginity". *Mama actually believes I stayed pure for ten years in a relationship that wasn't anywhere near as committed as I wanted.*

"You're thirty-one, Diany. You need to start having children soon or you won't be able to," her sister said without the slightest tact. "But you really sound okay. Are you sure you're okay? I mean, you were so in love with him, jerk that he was. Never even came home with you so we could meet him…"

Knowing as well as she did that Penny could go on and on, her mother broke in to ask when she was coming home.

"Mom, everything's so up in the air right now. I have a new job, and I just started. I can't leave already, even for a short visit. I don't know when I can get away."

"It's been since Christmas. We miss you."

"I know. I miss you, too. Soon. I'll let you know."

"Well, we'll send you some nice fudge…"

"No! Mom, please. Penny. No more junk food. I've turned into a balloon. How do you expect me to attract a man I can marry and have kids with if I'm so fat? No more care packages. Nothing with food. Promise me."

They both agreed and even promised, but Diane didn't believe them. She was just relieved to have the worst over with. Once she hung up, she sank into Mikey's arms, curling up in a ball, all but in his lap. He held her as if he thought she was sobbing her heart out. Yet she wasn't. She'd never felt better.

She couldn't help noticing that nothing about his hold was tentative or shy. In fact, his large, muscular hand was just inches shy of her breast, a fact that made her breathing more than a little irregular. Because being with him like this was so wonderful and she didn't want to move, she tried to talk about something that wouldn't make her so emotional: "When's the last time you went home, Mikey? To see your family?"

"It's been awhile. 'Bout the only time I go now is Christmas. But not last year."

She frowned, not liking this. "Why not last year?"

"I couldn't. I just started thinkin' about all the food—you can't even imagine. Even when I'm so full I could puke, my mom's pushin' more on me. I'm not jokin' when I tell you I gain twenty pounds the weeks I'm back home. And listenin' to my dad and brothers raggin' on me about what a loser I am..." He shook his head. "I decided to stay in my own apartment and drink myself into a stupor without someone force-feedin' me every second."

"How did they react when you told them you weren't coming home for the holidays?" Diane had gone home to Wisconsin at Christmas with Roxanne, missing Robert, miserable and overeating. But being with her family and best friend had pulled her out of her funk eventually.

"Don't know. I never picked up when they called. Eventually they stopped callin'."

"Have you talked to them since?"

"No," he admitted.

"Oh, Mikey. You're not a loser. You're such a good person. A good man. You're the best mechanic in the world."

His expression was teasing with a sort of grin in hiding. "That kinda like being the best garbage collector?"

"No!"

"You like rich, sophisticated men," he pointed out softly.

"I'm moving up from that riffraff," she claimed.

They both laughed, and she hugged him. "I'd like to meet your family."

"Why?"

"Because I just feel like they don't really know you and they don't really know how to show affection."

"Force-feedin' and insults sure ain't the way."

"No. I'm not denying or underplaying how they've obviously been awful to you. But they kept calling. Didn't they?"

"Weeks. Every one of 'em. Over and over. Each one worse than the last. Trust me, I never considered those calls affection. Not remotely. I don't have any desire to call or see 'em."

She was bothered, mostly because her family—for all their little annoyances—meant so much to her. Surely Mikey's family had to love him. He was too lovable not to love! She would make sure they realized it when she met them.

"Someday I want you to meet my family, Mikey. I don't know why you haven't yet."

He went silent and she wondered what he was thinking. That she'd barely noticed he was alive until she needed someone to unload on? It was true.

Feeling uncomfortable suddenly, she murmured, "Why don't we go early? Spend some time with Jamie before the boat starts filling up with his passengers?"

The thought of spending the night next to Mikey, watching the fireworks on a big boat sailing calm waters, made her take longer to get ready so she could look her best. She left her hair down, loose, and wore one of the short summer dresses she hadn't fit in for a long time with adorable, sexy sandals that she'd never been able to wear with Robert because they had heels. Mikey still towered over her.

"Better bring a jacket in case it gets cold on the water," he advised wisely, despite his boggled expression. Though he kept trying to turn away, she knew he liked looking at her in the dress that made her feel slimmer.

She was eagerly anticipating a wonderful night, certain nothing could ruin it—until Robert suddenly appeared on the boat just moments after Jamie announced they'd be setting sail in a few minutes.

"He can't stand losing, can he? Why else?" she whispered in fury directly in Mikey's ear.

"Forget him. Remember he's not here. We can do whatever we want. Anything. He doesn't matter."

Mikey put such a possessive arm around her, she should have worried. At the very least, she should have felt threatened.

She experienced neither. She hugged Mikey and let him lead her to the back side of the boat, open with wraparound seating. He sat down first, then surprised her when he pulled her down on his lap.

When she turned to glance down at him, slightly wary, she smelled the mint toothpaste on his breath. He must have ducked into Roxanne's bathroom back at the apartment while she was in her own. His eyes seemed intensely green as he looked up at her in the growing dusk. She found herself wrapping her arms around his shoulders, which pretty much put her breasts exactly where they wanted to be. *If not in his hands anyway.* She blushed at the instinctive thought.

Another one quickly followed: *I'm not playacting here. Where is Robert? Did he leave? Is he watching?*

I don't care. I couldn't care less. I'm exactly where I want to be, doing exactly what I please. The only thing that's not exactly as I want is that I'm not kissing Mikey Lund.

Maybe the thought should have shocked her, but she'd had it so often in the last few days the realization was mere fact to her now. She wanted to kiss Mikey. She wanted him to kiss her. Maybe that wasn't fair because she didn't know why she wanted the next level of intimacy with him. It was too soon for her to feel anything for another man.

Had she been in love with Robert all these years? Funny, but it'd felt more like grieving.

The fireworks had started, loud and sounding like a proper celebration all around as the others on the cruise oohed and ahhed. She couldn't fail to notice Mikey hadn't bothered to participate. His gaze hadn't left hers for even a moment. When his hand reached up and tenderly brushed her hair back so he could cradle her neck, she didn't think at all. She leaned forward and touched her mouth to his. Just that quickly, everything around them faded, making this reality, the only one she cared to acknowledge.

His mouth was firm, warm, soft and full. She loved the taste of him. Even his breath when he sighed, his lips parting under hers, made her happy. His tongue came shyly, and she met him halfway, opening deeper. It was the kind of kiss that made her completely unaware of things like right and wrong, proper and improper, stop or go. She was lost, and the way Mikey took charge didn't help at all. He cradled her face in his hands and kissed her as if he'd surrendered himself to her in every way a person could succumb to another person. He didn't seem to care about anyone around them either. He wanted her, only her, and she wanted to be wanted by him. Nothing else mattered.

Maybe it was a good thing they weren't alone, that they had a friend nearby, that the fireworks were the show everyone had come for. She lost herself in the endless kiss, only vaguely aware when Jamie had said something.

Abruptly, Diane sensed motion and pulled back to see that Jamie was propelling them off the deck and into a different part of the boat. Everyone else was watching the show from the back of the yacht. She let Mikey draw her into a private room. His mouth was close. She leaned closer. Though she was suddenly so embarrassed she could hardly function and protest rose to her lips, she didn't get the chance to say or do anything. Mikey pressed his body full-length against hers and claimed her mouth again and again. Her entire body felt the onslaught, and she stopped being concerned about anything as petty as embarrassment. She was panting almost as much as he was. Her hands wanted this. Her breasts. Her lips and her *mind*. And she was desired—so much, so amazingly, beautifully, she could feel the glorious tangible evidence of it.

He didn't touch anything but her face, didn't even shift restlessly against her. She wanted that. She wanted to *writhe*. Mikey only kissed her, deeper and deeper, until she felt his caress everywhere all at once and her entire body tightened, contradictorily hardening and softening, painfully pleasurable sensations assaulting her...

She sagged, shuddering violently, and his hands caught her, holding her with every ounce of the strength that leeched out of her. How, why, she didn't know but she was sobbing, and he sat down with her on his lap and held her so she really couldn't breathe. *Exactly what I need. Because that* didn't *just happened. It couldn't have. It was just a kiss...*

She pictured Mike's hands, his mouth, on another woman, and

she shuddered again, trying desperately not to think of that constant fantasy. Then he started talking quietly, again exactly what she needed.

"Guys are born that way. Sexist. Once you give yourself to one of us, you belong to us. We think that way. Can't stand the thought of any other man touchin' ya. Ever. No matter what. Even if you tell us it's over."

Mikey didn't touch me, and yet I've never been more satisfied, sexually, in my life. I want more. I want everything now.

"So he doesn't love me?" she asked with a throat so dry, the words crackled.

"Maybe. Maybe as much as he loves his wife. Women can only love one man at a time. Men…"

Diane shuddered again, this time in horror. "I can't. I can't be a woman who can live with bigamy." Tears stung her eyes.

"You don't need to."

She pressed her face into the intoxicating cove of his neck. "Could you ever be like one of those guys, Mikey?"

He chuckled against her hair. "I'd settled for one woman who actually likes me and thinks I'm attractive. Wants me."

Even as her heart bled for him, she found herself pressing her hands across his chest, palms down. She wished he would do the same to her—press his hands across her chest, palms down. "Any woman would, Mikey. How can you not know that? Ask any single woman out, and she'd accept in a heartbeat."

For a long minute, he stared at her so intensely, she thought he would ask *her* out. She was the lucky woman he wanted to want him. *Oh, Lord!*

"Any woman?" he asked softly.

"Any woman. You have to start seeing yourself the way you really are. You're quite a catch. You should be asking women out every day."

He shook his head, clearly convinced in his own mind she was just being nice. "Don't meet a lot of women. Any."

"You will." *And I don't want you to choose any of them.*

"We better get out there."

Even as she reluctantly agreed, she wondered if everyone was thinking she and Mikey had...*well*...there in the cabin while they enjoyed the fireworks.

Robert was the first one she saw when she stepped out ahead of Mikey, mostly because he was the only one who remained sitting. Everyone else stood staring up at the light show in the velvety sky. A shower of loud sparks burst over the yacht, illuminating the murderous expression on Robert's face. She blushed, wondering if he'd seen anything beyond the glass in the cabin door.

Seen what? Mikey kissed me. That was all. He kissed me, and I went up in flames like a roman candle! From a kiss.

Even now, she wanted him to kiss her again, and he did. After they joined the others near the railing, standing side by side together, he looked down at her, she looked up at him. Instinctively, she reached up. He leaned down the rest of the way and kissed her so sweetly, she was lost hopelessly...*no, not hopelessly—hopefully*...in seconds.

Though she saw some of the firework displays, every few minutes Mikey would say something, she'd smile with what she knew had to be lovesick cow eyes at him, incline her lips toward him, and he'd kiss her again, deeply enough for her to remember, every single time, just how far one kiss had gone earlier.

Robert was the first one off the boat, but it was an observation that didn't impact Diane more than to simply note it. Those who'd paid wandered off the yacht in groups, leaving her and Mikey alone with Captain Jamie. Even then, Mikey kept his arm around her, and she didn't want to move an inch from him. She had the feeling his inhibitions would return the second they left this little paradise they'd found where kisses deep enough to cause explosions were A-okay.

Mikey and Jaime talked a little, and Jamie clasped his shoulder, saying, "Call me, dude."

Mikey agreed, but his friend said again as they were leaving, "Seriously, call me."

It was almost midnight, and she was sleepy. In truth, she was drunk on Mikey Lund's kisses, but she didn't want this to end. She wanted him to kiss her again and again. *And when I wake up, I'll still be in his arms. Because it's fine for us to do this. We can do anything we want together. Anything.*

When he didn't kiss her, instead said his goodnights at her door, she put her arms around him and hugged him, hoping he would ask her... *To spend the night? Yes. I want that. I want that more than anything else in the world. What's happening to me? Did Mikey drug me? How? When?*

"See you in the morning," he said, making a move she couldn't have anticipated. He was shifting away from her.

"Mikey..."

He whipped back eagerly.

"Early?" She swallowed, embarrassed at being so needy with the request, but she couldn't have taken her plea back for anything in the world.

Did he seem disappointed? Yet his words didn't imply anything of the kind. "Sure. As early as you want. Call me."

He didn't care about anything. Diane was the whole world to him, and he didn't know what the hell he was doing with her. What she was doing with him. Even when Doobs called him barely five minutes before he got in his apartment—leaving Diane when he would've rather been mutilated, seasoned and eaten by a cannibal—he couldn't say.

"The guy was married? For the last decade? And that was the one watching you two on the sidelines tonight like he wanted to slit your throat?"

"Yeah. She knows he's married, but he's not willin' to let it go. I can't blame him. He's been followin' her, us, constantly."

"About that…" Doobs started. "What the hell? You two were…"

"It's not real."

Doobs laughed loudly. "Sure in hell looked real to me."

"Guess that's the goal."

"To make this dude jealous? Why? Does she want him to leave his wife and marry her instead?"

"No! She says she'd rather die than that. She says it's over for her."

"Well, I believe her."

"What do you mean?"

"You got it bad, Mikey Lund, and she's got it just as bad."

"Diane doesn't feel that way about me. She sees me as a friend."

"Why wouldn't she see you as more?"

"She can't see me as anything but a tub of lard, boozin' his life away."

"You're not talking about yourself anymore. You're not that guy. She likes what she sees. That couldn't have been more obvious if I turned on the infrared, dude. Where was she if not with you by choice during all that? Because you have to know that wasn't pretend for her. She was *gone*. Stone gone. On you."

"The only reason any woman ever wanted me is 'cause you or Brett paid 'em to spend time with me."

Doobs laughed out loud again. "Um…what? Seriously, Mikey? What are you implying?"

"You didn't have to tell me. I knew it."

Doobs laughed, sounded shocked instead of amused. "You don't know anything. Dude, the ladies talk about you all on their own. Together. You're a sleeper. They say they don't know what hit them until they've been with you themselves. Trust me. I'm quoting what more than one of them has said to me about you personally."

"They were all drunk. Desperate. Horny."

"Since when does it bother you that horny women all want *your* number, bro?"

Mike didn't entertain the words as anything resembling reality. *Who would've guessed that fantasy would bother me? But the "since when" is since Diane. She's the only woman who's ever really mattered to me. I want more than friendship than her. More than some fantasy that gets me through an endless night. I want her to love me. I want her to want me to love her. Pathetic.*

"Look, believe it or not, Mikey, if a woman slept with you, she made her own choice—regardless of her emotional state or level of intoxication. Diane wasn't drunk or impaired tonight. And she sure as hell didn't look like she was pretending. You're not the man you used to be. Maybe she's not who she used to be either. Ask her out. Tell her how you feel. In fact..."

Mike started to groan, but Doobs talked right over him. "Next Saturday night, I don't have a charter planned. I'll take the two of you out on your own private, romantic cruise. The works. My treat. All you have to do is ask her to come and bring her on-board. The rest will happen on its own."

"Are we invitin' Diane's dud, Old Faithful?" Mike asked miserably.

"You idiot. You better get your eyesight checked and quickly, or you'll lose her. No woman wants to fall in love with a man who can't get over his unworthiness."

"Women don't fall in love with me. Period. They go *'Mikey? Mikey Lund?'* at the mere suggestion."

"Take my advice or regret it, bro: *Ask her out.* Don't ruin this before you give it a chance."

As Doobs hung up, Mike knew he wouldn't be the one to do that. Diane could never fall in love with him. She'd gone along with all that tonight because that creep had been there and she wanted to teach the stub a lesson for being possessive when he had no right to be.

Even as Mike thought all she'd done was playact, he remembered her reaction to his kiss in the cabin. *A kiss. Not sex. Not even foreplay. Yet she came...* Hell, that hadn't been a mere kiss.

That'd been his soul, hers, merging symbiotically.

He rolled his eyes at the romantic thought, crawled into bed, and put his phone right next to him, where he wanted Diane to be soon and for the rest of his life.

Wishing for the moon. Story of my life.

Chapter 12

"Roxanne?"

Her friend sounded exhausted, drugged and/or confused when she said, "What? Who is this?"

"It's Diane. Where are you? What are you doing?"

"Oh…I'm…I'm…"

Diane had called for purely selfish reasons. Mikey had left her alone when she didn't want to be, and she needed to talk to someone about all the craziness in her head. She realized suddenly that New York was nowhere near on the same time zone as Paris. "I'm sorry. Your show…"

"Don't worry about it. Is Mikey with you?"

Diane stopped breathing, her mind blank. "No," she said slowly, not sounding entirely sure to her own ears.

"But you want him to be. Tell me everything."

"Where are you, Roxanne? You're not at the show, are you?"

"No. Now shut up and tell me."

Diane had called with this very intention. Why hold back anything now? "Oh, Roxanne, Mikey kissed me. He *kissed* me."

"Oh, I knew I could count on that heartthrob. So Robert's history?"

"Forget Robert. *Mikey Lund* kissed me."

"That's great. He kissed you. Why didn't you let him do more than kiss you?"

"Because...because he kissed me and I..." She laid emphasis with her pregnant pause.

A second later, Rox murmured, "Ahh."

"Yeah. That's never happened to me before. I mean, with Robert... I didn't even every time with him. Rarely, in fact, and that's with the whole point. It was just a kiss. Mikey and I just kissed. That's all."

"Tell me everything," Rox demanded eagerly.

"He didn't touch me, didn't even move against me, if you know what I mean. It was just a kiss."

"I get it. Mikey's so good at all the foreplay stuff other guys pass over like they're not *everything* for a woman."

Just that suddenly, Diane was stark, raving jealous and she knew she had absolutely no right to be, especially with Roxanne. Rox had walked into their apartment and found her best friend kissing the only man she'd seriously ever fallen for.

As abruptly as her jealousy had come on, Diane's thought that Jamie kissing her had been nothing compared to Mikey's kiss overwhelmed her. But she had to know Roxanne wasn't planning to go after Mikey. Then it would be all over for her. "You don't know that from personal experience. Do you, Rox?" Diane asked meekly.

"No. I've heard other women talk about him. For what he

lacked in sexual appeal in the past, he more than made up for with sexual skill. He makes Don Juan look like a fumbling idiot." Rox rushed to add, "So I'm told."

"I'm sorry about Jamie!" Diane all but screamed, unable to hold the apology back. She'd apologized at least a million times for the same thing by now, but it'd never felt like enough to her.

"You've really gotta get over that, babe. Seriously. You did me a favor, truth be told. I knew he wasn't gonna stick around for the long haul. The fact that he would use you to convince me he couldn't be trusted only solidified my decision to forget him. I never blamed you for a second. Stop blaming yourself. Now, let's get back to that cutie-pie. I can't believe he finally took the bull by the horns and kissed you."

"Actually, I kissed him first each time, and he just kind of took over from there."

"Where were you two at the time?"

"On Jamie's boat. For the fireworks cruise. And Robert was there. I guess I didn't tell you he's been following Mikey and me everywhere."

"Whoa."

"What am I going to do, Roxanne?"

Just as she suspected, Rox possessed full clarity of direction. "What you should, what's only right."

"What's that?"

"Forget Robert Drake ever existed and fall in love with our Mikey."

Diane hadn't let the idea form fully in her own head. Yet her friend's words were as familiar as her own heart. "I've never... I couldn't have imagined..."

"Well, start! Don't mess this up just because you always feel guilty when you almost never need to, Lady Jane. Now I'll be back in a few days. Don't worry if you find out I didn't make it the Haute Couture show."

Though Diane had spent most of this phone call being selfish, she was suddenly concerned. "What's going on? Where are you?"

"Nowhere you need to be concerned."

"You don't sound good, Rox. Are you okay?" Roxanne had gotten in trouble before—with depression that led to drugs. "Tell me the truth."

"I'm fine. That's the truth. Trust me. I'll be home soon. There's nothing to worry about. If you really wanna make me happy, kiss Mikey silly the next time you see him. Don't stop. For any reason. Okay?"

Just like that, her friend hung up, leaving Diane with more to be concerned about than her own chaotic heart.

Mike was expecting anything but the words Diane greeted him with after calling him at six the next morning and asking him to come over. "I'm worried about Roxanne. Have you talked to her?" She pulled him inside and closed the door behind him.

In the kitchen, she handed him a cup of coffee. "Since that night you took the Ambien? No. Why?"

"I called her last night and she didn't sound good."

"Sound good, how?"

"She sounded sick. Drugged. Both."

"Uh-oh." Roxanne liked drugs. Most of the time, she did them with no obvious affects or consequences. But whenever she combined them with depression... "Isn't she supposed to be in Paris, for some big fashion show?"

"It is a huge fashion show, one of the largest in the world."

"Won't she get in trouble if she doesn't show?"

Diane tsked. "She's the bad girl of the fashion world. Everyone loves her though. She often says everyone hates her, too—because she's unreliable."

Diane looked so worried, Mike couldn't help worrying about her instead of Rox, who'd always taken care of herself, no problem. "You okay?" he asked, nudging her just a little bit. She instantly squirmed her way into his arms. Maybe he shouldn't have gone above his comfort zone because he couldn't help noticing she'd decided to forgo her fancy pastel business suits in favor of jeans that fit her rounded hips and butt as perfectly as the scoop-necked, casual shirt she wore did her voluptuous top half.

"I'm worried about her, but she said she'd be home in a few days."

"We'll call her when we get home from work," Mike offered reassuringly.

She nodded, smiling slightly and looking abruptly shy. "I had a good time last night, Mikey. The best time I've had in such a long time."

"Me, too," he offered.

Why can't I kiss her now? Why did I feel like I could last night but not now? 'Cause she kissed me first? Made it so obvious she wanted me to kiss her.

"I talked to Doobs after I got home last night. He says he doesn't have a charter for Saturday night. I thought, why don't we book him? He's got that one package option with dinner and a sail."

"Does he serve healthy meals?"

Mike laughed. "No. He knows one of the big-name chefs in the city. He calls in favors with the guy when he gets a dinner charter." *Romantic dinner. That's what Doobs specializes in. Diane must know that.* "Bad idea. Forget it," he said suddenly, feeling like two years stretched between them. She wasn't answering. That meant she didn't want to go on a cruise or anything like a date with him.

His phone rang, though it was barely six-thirty in the morning. He shouldn't have been surprised Brett would call him so early. His friend never slept well when he spent time with his family in Syracuse. He didn't like it there—it was a place of bad memories for him. He only made the effort because family was important to him now with Savvy and Harley.

Mikey murmured, "Brett" and Diane slipped away from him to refresh her coffee cup. Then she brought out fresh fruit and set it on the breakfast bar.

"We're comin' home," Brett announced, no surprise. "We'll be there Friday, and we really want a night alone. How do you feel about babysitting? Your apartment?"

Mike almost laughed at the kind of alone time Brett obviously had in mind for him and his wife. But Mike was thinking of Diane. He wanted to be with her tonight, tomorrow night, *every* night she wanted to be with him.

"Is he coming home early?" Diane guessed.

Mike took the phone from his ear and said, "Friday. And he wants a babysitter so he and Savvy can be alone."

"We could babysit Harley together. I'd love to."

Mike took a deep breath, trying not to do anything stupid in reaction, like dropping the phone, and brought the device back to his ear. "We'll do it," he said as casually as he could.

"*We* meanin' you and Diane? Works for me. Right after work. In fact, we'll meet you at the garage. You'll both be there, right?"

"Right."

"Good. Bring your car. Harley requires a full suite. You the man, Mikey. See ya later."

Mike hung up, and Diane eased her barstool three inches closer, her body turned toward his. She leaned her face closer. "Mikey, before Brett called, did you just ask me out and then *un*ask me?" she demanded.

His face burned. "I just figured…"

"Whatever you figured, I would love to babysit that adorable nine-month-old munchkin with you Friday night, then go on a romantic dinner cruise with you on Jamie's yacht on Saturday night."

"Really?" Even to his own ears, he sounded like he'd just stood up after having a speeding semi full-body-slam him to the ground.

Instead of answering, she leaned even closer and her strawberry-sweet lips covered his.

Chapter 13

Harley was an angel, and Diane loved the hours she and Mikey spent with the little girl. Feeding her, playing with her, taking a walk with her. Even giving her a bath and soothing her to sleep was amazing because Diane had dreamed of being a mother to many sweet babies and doing these parental tasks with her husband. As an added bonus, she saw Mikey in a different light, one she could never have imagined the man of old taking on. He was good with babies. He made the nine-month-old giggle, smile and sigh in happiness when he held her. Diane knew the feeling.

She'd gone through a blissful week, not letting herself think too much about what she was doing. She'd taken Roxanne's advice and stopped feeling guilty for everything—along with her advice to kiss Mikey the next time she saw him. She did that every time. She just let herself *feel*.

Letting herself go like this still stunned her because she'd never imagined herself falling in love with Mikey Lund, but often she thought, *Why not him?* He'd always been there for her. He genuinely cared about her. He'd listened to her talk endlessly about everything—including things he probably hadn't wanted to hear anything about. Regardless of how self-destructive he'd been back then, he was the same person now as he'd been then. He'd simply started moving in a healthier direction than he'd been going. Just like she had, thanks to Mikey's assistance.

The problem with not letting herself think too much was that they spent a lot of time kissing instead. She had a hard time being with him without wanting to end up in his arms, deep in his kiss. Though she always started things, he was the one who finished them. Yet he never asked her for anything. He still hadn't touched her the way she was dying for him to...though didn't really need him to in order to coax the same explosive reaction from her each time. He never pushed her for more than she willingly gave him. Just like Mikey to listen to her. She'd told him and him alone she never wanted to be in a sexual relationship that wasn't also "legal", and she knew he wouldn't step beyond that border unless she indicated loud and clear she wanted him to.

Holding back hadn't been easy. They spent most of their lunch breaks skipping the meal just so they could kiss—not in the office or the break room, but in the apartment that used to be Brett's and had been converted to a gym with a big couch. None of the other mechanics ever went up there for some reason. Unbelievably, neither she nor Mikey seemed to care about food anymore. They didn't even binge eat after they got home for the evening. Not when there were other wondrous things to do with their mouths...

"Has Roxanne called yet?" he asked after Harley fell asleep in her playpen in Mikey's bedroom and they closed the door so she wouldn't wake. He set the baby monitor on the end table next to the sofa.

"No. I'm really worried. Especially after she missed that fashion show and they're all in an uproar about her behavior. She does leave messages to tell me she's fine. She just never picks up when I call her."

Diane sat on the couch, her body already turned toward his in anticipation of being close to him when he sat down.

"I told Doobs. Well, he kinda asked 'cause apparently he also saw all the tabloids about her missing that fashion show. He seemed concerned, too."

Her eyes widened in surprise. "You don't mean…"

"Yeah. I mean, all this time he's acted like he's the one who wanted to break up with her because she was stranglin' him, wantin' more than he can give. But I guess after all the years he's known her he still cares about her. I never knew what it was that broke 'em up, but he claims he staged the event. He said he knew the only way to get her to see him for who he was to cheat on her and have her see him do it. Before that, he always seemed eager to be with her, almost like he was in love. I never saw him like that before or since."

Diane leaned against his chest, her fingers working against the buttons of his linen shirt. "I think it's my fault."

Mikey gaped at her. "Your fault? How could that possibly be your fault?"

"He came over to the apartment one night. When Roxanne wasn't there. And he just started talking, telling me it was over between them, and I was shocked. And then he was sitting really close to me, and just like that, he looked at the clock, then he kissed me. Roxanne walked in at that exact moment. She saw everything."

"That's what he meant. He staged it *with you*. Told Rox to meet him at your apartment at a certain time, showed up fifteen minutes early so she'd be sure to walk in on the two of you."

Even as a petty feminine side of her railed at being told yet again that Jamie Dubois hadn't wanted her at all—just used her to break it off with Roxanne—Diane was relieved. "I've always felt guilty for that. It happened so fast. I didn't know it was coming, and, by the time I realized it, it was too late. I guess that's what he wanted. But why me?"

"Because Rox might've forgiven him with anybody else. Not you. Everybody knows how protective she is of you."

"I guess so. How embarrassing. I don't understand any of it. They were so *whatever* with each other in college. They were close but never serious, you know, until they *were* serious, and then it was almost too intense. I couldn't be anywhere near the two of them without feeling like…"

Mikey laughed, allowing her not to finish the thought. But then he murmured, "I know the feeling" and his gaze went right to her mouth. Yet he didn't kiss her. Somehow she knew if she didn't initiate, he never would.

This is all so crazy. He needs me to tell him how I feel and yet I'm scared. This is happening so fast though it's not happening anywhere near as fast as I want. Even if I'm justified in getting on with my life after all that stuff with Robert, I don't feel right about jumping into another romance—especially not one like this, one that feels like everything, my whole life, right now, right here. Nothing else will do.

She drifted closer and the rest was simply magic. She lost herself in the kiss that stole through her entire body like Viagra.

She was a teenager who lived for "necking" again, yet she had the needs of a full-grown woman. *With a man so potently sensual, he only has to kiss me and I know the kind of fulfillment most women only dream of.*

Diane wasn't thinking of anything but giving every part of herself to him when she reached for his hands and put them where she needed them. The other women she'd seen him do this to faded from her memory. She was the woman in his arms now, the only one he wanted. The past didn't matter. Not when Mikey was whispering how beautiful she was, how perfect, how he'd fantasized about her. Non-stop. Never stopping…

Diane would have done anything. She would have died for this and more, all that Mikey would give her. And he was almost there. Her top was a mere memory, her bra breaking from the force of her own desire as he caressed her with just his slow, amazing, consummate hands.

Startled cries burst from the monitor nearby. Diane's mind recalled bits Brett and Savvy had warned them about Harley: *Night terrors. Frequently woke throughout the night, needing comfort…*

Mikey buried his face in her breasts, and she held him so hard he must have been in pain or suffocating. She didn't want to let go, didn't want to stop.

She almost sobbed when he eased her off him and said he'd be right back. On her knees in the middle of the sofa, she covered her face with her hands.

Rebound? That can't be what this is. Rebound means I'm still thinking about Robert and trying to forget him. I don't even care anymore—care that he looks like he's drunk every time me and Mikey see him staking us out in his car. One of these days, he'll probably be stupid enough to try to start a fight and Mikey will send him straight to the hospital.

"Take that back to your wife and explain it, why don't ya?" Unexpectedly remembering Mikey's words to Robert, she burst into fits of giggles.

"What?" Mikey asked when he returned from soothing Harley back to sleep. He had eyes only for her bared breasts.

Diane shook her head, drawing him down and resuming her place which settled him back into the one he'd left, and going further.

This wasn't rebound. It couldn't be. Because anything she'd ever felt for Robert Drake didn't begin to compare to what she was feeling now. She was in love, maybe for the first time in her life, really in love, and she wasn't going to feel guilty for it.

Mike wanted nothing to do with his friends' plans when they showed up before lunch at the garage Saturday—he was scheduled to work and Diane had insisted she wanted to come along, too—and told him in no uncertain terms *they* were taking him to lunch. He didn't want lunch. He wanted Diane. To hell with food. To hell with having his own insanely voracious sexual needs met. He could live just as happily satisfying all of Diane Hoffman's. As long as they were together, he didn't care. He just wanted to be near her.

"Diane..." he started.

"...is havin' lunch with Savvy, Darlene and Cherish."

"Cher..." He abruptly recalled the woman who wasn't much older than Darlene but wore her hair up in some fancy, old-lady bun and owned the flower shop Darlene worked. What he remembered most was that Darlene had intended to fix him up with her friend slash boss. Only Cherish had apparently seen him at some point before the date and changed her mind about going. "Not Rox?" he asked because he didn't want to think about the embarrassment of rejection.

"I don't know. She's not back from Paris yet, is she?" Brett asked.

"If she even was in Paris in the first place. I don't know either. Diane didn't say. But I guess she would've told me if she was."

Doobs had a troubled look on his face, but then he said, "The romantic dinner cruise is all arranged for tonight. All except you. You can't wear coveralls to this thing."

"I'm not wearin' a suit." Diane might go for dudes in three piece suits and oiled up shoes, but he didn't dress like that. Ever. He'd feel like an idiot in anything remotely like that. He remembered what she'd said about "moving up" from the sophisticated dudes. A joke, but he could only wish she'd been serious.

As stupid as he felt being taken *shopping* by his bros, he couldn't deny that, between Doobs and Jace, the two knew how to dress. They chose some nice dress pants that were sophisticated without feeling or looking awkward once on him. Mike especially liked the chambray shirt Doobs teased brought out his green eyes. The shoes matched the outfit but were far from the shiny, pointy things Drake wore like brilliant, shiny mirrors on his feet. Mike had wondered if the dude could see his own face in them or something.

Why would he want to? He couldn't admit he liked the clothes though—like it or not, he didn't see himself the way his friends told him he looked in them. The clothes were too sophisticated—*and I'm the opposite of what Diane wants in that regard.* "I'm gonna sweat so bad, I'll ruin both of these. I'll end up lookin' like Charlie Brown with hair."

"What are you nervous about?" Jace asked. "It's Diane. You've been friends all your life."

Well, not his whole life, but long enough that it felt like it. "That's probably what she's assumin' this is. Just friends."

"I get the feelin' you're lyin' even to yourself," Brett commented in a bored tone.

Mike had to look chagrinned because the dude had arrived Friday night to pick up his kid and he and Diane had looked like they'd gone more rounds than even Brett surely had with his wife in their hours alone.

Brett grinned. "Don't worry. She'll have her legs around your neck by the time the night is done...if she hasn't already."

"She hasn't," Mike said, annoyed that anyone would suggest something so crude about Diane.

Brett only laughed because he'd clearly said it to get this reaction from him.

"Flowers and chocolates," Doobs tried to steer the conversation to less volatile topics.

"No chocolate. Not healthy. Flowers."

"Wedding ring?" Jace asked.

Mike gaped at him, feeling almost guilty. None of them knew he'd already bought the ring. The weird part was, he'd bought the expensive engagement ring months ago with the money he'd saved from not drinking and eating so much. Back then, it'd been his goal to give it to someone—God only knew who. Since he'd made new goals for his future, including a healthier lifestyle and different interests, making a goal for his personal life had seemed just as important. He'd planned to give the ring to someone, to get that far into a relationship that he'd ask a woman to marry him. That was what he wanted more than anything. He had no clue who he'd intended the ring for, mostly because he'd never believed he'd get even as far as asking someone out. Unfortunately for him, the woman he wanted was Diane, and she might be the most unattainable one on the planet.

How often had he thought about proposing to Diane lately? He'd lost count. Almost as many times as they kissed and that was a lot. His mouth was sore, but he was far from complaining. It had to be too soon to be thinking about marriage, didn't it? They'd hadn't been on an official first date yet. Besides, she'd just chucked her married loser overboard. The last thing she wanted was someone already half down on his knees in front of her.
Right?

The fact was, he didn't know. He couldn't guess. He didn't have an inkling what he was doing. He was just going along, waiting for her to tell him what to do so he could do it without hesitation. Without her preapproval, he was terrified to do anything for fear this would all end if he chose the wrong course of action or the wrong words. He'd die if it did end, too. He'd already dug his own grave, anticipating the end. He'd be finished if she backed off now. *Sure as shootin'.*

By the time he got back to the garage—dropping all his purchases off at home first—he wondered if he'd survive his growing nervousness. Would she cancel their date as soon as she got back with Savvy, Darlene, and her boss? Would talking about it with her friends make her realize he was seeing this as a date and she didn't at all? Would she'd want to "protect" him again?

He felt confused once more about the whole thing until he remembered she'd even called it a date when she accepted it. The only time he didn't worry about her feelings for him was when they were kissing. Then he felt like everything was mutual between them—that they were both moving in the same direction: The one that got them legally hitched and holed up in any private room for three solid weeks, probably more.

Chapter 14

All the worry about her best friend for the past week wasn't relieved completely when Roxanne showed up in the garage office just before lunch. Instantly Diane knew something was wrong. Roxanne was gorgeous even when she was hideous, but she was skinny to the point of being bony, her face was dark and shadowed behind her makeup, and she was wearing a wig—something she'd insisted numerous times she never would outside of her work. She'd only worn one for modeling jobs because she hadn't been willing to let anyone dye her hair.

"Roxanne, why are you wearing that? That is a wig, isn't it?" Her friend's hair had never been that shade of blond before. Otherwise, the wig fit unnoticeably.

Her friend reached up. "Oh, just felt like a change."

"You didn't do a Britney Spears and shave your head, did you? Please tell me you didn't do that!"

Rox looked chagrinned. "It'll grow back. No worries, babe, and no big deal. Now, Darlene, Savvy and Cherish'll be here in five. Tell me everything."

"*What's* no big deal? What possessed you to shave your head? Is something wrong? Your agent's cleaning up a pretty big mess in Paris."

"Yeah, well, for all I pay her, it's the least she can do."

Diane frowned. "Are you sure nothing's wrong? You don't look well, Lady Jane."

"Now you're Lady Jane-ing me?" Rox laughed. "Stop. I'm fine. I wanna hear about you and Mikey."

Diane belatedly recalled what else her friend had said earlier. "Why are the girls coming here?"

"To take you to lunch, of course. And shopping for your big date with Mikey tomorrow night."

"How did you find out about that?"

"Everybody's talking about it. I'm sure *he*—"

He being Jamie Dubois. Diane recalled the things Mikey had told her, leading her to feel slightly relieved about the situation she'd spent years hating herself for.

"—told Brett, Brett told Savvy…"

Diane flushed. "Okay. I do need to go shopping."

She and Mikey had spent every free moment together. She hadn't had time to shop, but she knew she didn't want to wear a dress she'd at one time or another bought for Robert. She wanted something brand new. Unfortunately, she knew the girls wouldn't be content if she didn't spill her guts about everything during their time together.

And I'm not ready. Sure, I'd love to talk about all this to my girlfriends. But if I tell Roxanne I'm worried Mikey will always be like this—always accommodating, never admitting his true feelings for me—she'll run to him, and he'll say the words I need just because he knows that's what I want. That would defeat the whole purpose. Like it or not, my girlfriends won't let me clam up, so I have to tell them something.

No one commented on the first ever healthy, grilled chicken garden salad she ordered with low-fat dressing on the side. As soon as Darlene asked, "What about Mikey? Doobs told Jace you two were hot and heavy on the fireworks cruise. Brett and Savvy found the two of you with your skirt around your neck while babysitting Harley. And someone said Robert has been following the two of you like a stalker."

"Skirt around my neck…" Diane started in shock.

Darlene waved the words away with a hand. "You know Brett. If Mikey had lipstick on his face, he'd call it 'skirt around the neck'."

Diane sighed and started picking the fattening croutons off her salad to discard. "I don't know what's happening," she admitted, but she'd been looking forward to their lunch break together. She'd never been in a relationship like this before. "We talk about everything, anything." *And we kiss until I don't want it to end. I don't know how I've gotten it to halt since this thing started. All I know is, I would feel like I'd broken my vow to my morality if I did give in. I would know I really am one of those girls who fall in love and somehow convince themselves everything in love is right and good when that's as far from the truth as it gets. But with Mikey, maybe it would* be right.

As shocking as it was to her, she suspected it was Mikey himself who'd been holding them back. He knew she'd made a vow to herself not to have sex without being married first, and he wanted to protect her—from herself in this case. But she'd realized constantly how selfish she was being. One kiss with Mikey was enough to blow her mind literally. She'd wanted him to be satisfied, too, even knowing that could get out of control in a hurry. He wouldn't let her do anything that might compromise her vow.

"What is happening?" Darlene demanded. "I leave for a week and come back to hear you and Mikey are inseparable. But you were just devastated 'cause this Robert-love-of-your-life is married with kids. *What?*"

Diane took a deep breath, not lifting her fork as everyone else at the table had while she spoke from her heart. "Whether or not anyone but Mikey believes it, I never knew Robert was married. I thought he was emotionally scarred from his past and couldn't make the commitment I wanted him to make to me. I've been thinking a lot about that. I wrote down every time I saw him. I wrote it on the calendar and I looked back at those calendars. In the past ten years, I've seen Robert twenty-eight times. That's the grand total, and almost ten of those were in the beginning, when we first started dating. That means I saw him an average of twice a year. That's all. We talked on the phone more often than we saw each other—some of those times for work—but I think the fact that I almost never saw him made me believe everything he told me and I didn't consider any other alternative. I worked for the same company—the trips were legitimate and frequent. If he went home to his family while he was traveling, between presentations, he didn't log them in as work expenses. I told myself I was willing to wait for him to heal and settle down travel-wise so we could get married, and I did. I waited ten years. But, in addition to waiting, I've been grieving. I've been unconsciously coming to grips with the certainty that I would never get what I thought I wanted. I wouldn't get married and have children. Maybe it was the idea of marriage and romance and a family I loved so much. I don't know when I fell out of love with Robert. I only know that, as devastated as I was to find out he's been married this whole time, something inside me knew it was over long ago. It's as if I've been alone for ten years. Alone and waiting for the perfect man to come along, when he's been here the whole time and I just didn't see he's everything I've ever wanted in the man I fell in love with."

The funny thing about realizing she was in love with Mikey Lund was that it hadn't happened like a lightning-bolt shock out of a clear blue sky. It'd been deeply rooted warmth that spread through her entire body and being with a blissful certainty that this time she hadn't been foolish to fall in love.

"Mikey's such a sweetheart," Darlene said on a happy sigh. "So are you. The two of you together are the perfect couple. I don't know why I didn't see it before either."

"You tried to fix me up with him," Cherish reminded, and Diane leaned forward eagerly at this news. Cherish was extremely attractive. Okay, so she wore her hair in that strange bun that wasn't exactly appealing all the time. Without it, she probably would have been asked out more often. But Diane had always gotten the impression something bad had happened to her. Whatever it was, she avoided romantic interactions as a result.

"You never actually met him," Darlene said to her boss. "Never laid eyes on him. You should have given him a shot."

Cherish shrugged as if it was no big deal. "You know me. I have too much baggage. I didn't want to unload it on a poor, unsuspecting man, especially the nice guy you were describing."

Diane felt strangely jealous at the thought of anyone else seeing her Mikey as a prize—one they'd like to get their hands on. She'd realized Roxanne had never had any intention of going after Mikey herself. She'd been playing matchmaker all along, knowing Robert was exactly the wrong man for her and Mikey the exact opposite. Even all those things she'd said about considering a sexual encounter with him had been spoken to bring forth Diane's true feelings for Mikey.

Mikey is mine...or is he? Why won't he say anything? Why won't he tell me how he feels—if he's in love or he's just going along with this whole thing for who knows the reason? He told me himself he wouldn't know love if Cupid introduced himself and shot an arrow straight between his eyes. I don't want to hang my heart on another man who won't stand up for our love—just takes what he can get from me on his own terms. I want Mikey to barge in, guns blazing, the way he did the times he ran to my rescue. Only this time he'll end it by telling me he loves me and wants to marry me.

But maybe that's not what he wants. How will I ever know if he does or doesn't? He won't say. I initiate every time. I'm an old-fashioned girl. I want the fairytale. I want my knight in shining armor to sweep me off my feet—of his own volition. Because he wants me and nothing can stop him from claiming my love.

After lunch and a week's worth of gossip, she found the perfect dress at Macy's—a Calvin Klein sleeveless crew neckline with a pleated A-line skirt in a shade of red that highlighted the mahogany sheen of her hair. For the first time in years, she bought sexy high heels, knowing Mikey would still be taller than her when she wore them. The dress made her feel so pretty and slim. She'd lost weight and she'd been exercising. For once, she felt like she was exactly the right size.

"Mikey's gonna start foaming at the mouth when he sees you," Roxanne said when Diane came out of her bedroom hours later to show off for her date. Back in the dressing room at Macy's, Darlene and Cherish had swelled her head while awing and oohing at the sight of her. "He's spent more than three months getting ready for just this night."

"What do you mean?"

"That's when he started losing all the weight, wasn't it? Three months ago."

"That had nothing to do with me."

"No? Well, maybe not specifically, but he was getting ready to be the perfect man for some great woman. He didn't dare hope it might be you, but I suspect deep down if anyone had asked him and he'd been willing to confess, you would have been at the top of his list."

Was it true? She'd never been fair to Mikey, yet he'd always been there for her when she needed someone. *No, not just someone.* She'd needed *him*. She hadn't seen that before, not until he'd done what Roxanne said: Gotten himself ready to be every inch the man she needed. But now she wondered if she was worthy of him.

When the doorbell rang, Roxanne rushed to answer it. Diane held back, listening to her best friend and Mikey greet each other warmly. When the two came in, Roxanne was doing that weird thing that somehow always made sense between her and Mikey—she was riding him piggyback. As usual, Mikey looked totally embarrassed about it, too. Rox wasn't capable of embarrassment. She dropped off Mikey's back and plucked the colorful roses out of his hands, saying she'd put them in water.

Diane had never seen Mikey Lund dressed like this in her life. He wasn't exactly wearing a suit, but this was better. The slacks fit him as if they'd been made for his long, muscular legs, slim waist, and incredible behind. The soft looking shirt made his green eyes jump out at her. He was even wearing a pair of elegant, buffed loafers that somehow fit his casual personality.

Rox returned to the living room and set the flowers on the coffee table. Diane still hadn't gotten her fill of looking at him when she noticed he was all but choking. "What?" she asked in concern.

"You're *gorgeous...*"

I'll wait for him to take charge later. She threw her arms around him, laughing giddily at his compliment that was so much more than words. He was reeling. "You look so handsome, Mikey."

When they kissed, his hands were firm, molding her already pliable body to his and making her miss even more their lunch break nookie. She'd looked forward to that all morning—since he'd left her the evening before.

"I've heard about those kisses, Mikey, babe. Save something for the end of the evening," Roxanne broke in, teasing.

Mikey drew back first, and his face was as red as Diane's dress at being caught having discussed their white-hot kisses with her best friend.

The intercom buzzed. Roxanne went to answer it, calling a moment later, "There's a Mrs. Drake downstairs, asking to be let up."

Diane let out a gasp, sagging against Mikey holding her. Instantly, he said softly, "Tell her no."

Why would Robert's wife come here? Did she... Oh, no! Does she know? How? Diane's first instinct was to agree with Mikey.

Robert's wife was the last person she wanted to see. But she also knew she'd forever wonder and regret not agreeing to let her come up. She desperately wanted the woman to know she hadn't intentionally been involved with her husband for ten years.

Even as Diane told Rox, "Tell her to come up", she knew this was a mistake. No one would ever believe she'd had no idea Robert wasn't married, that she'd had no clue about it for ten years. Only Mikey believed that and possibly her closest friends. This woman would hate her—she'd scratch her eyes out now that she had the chance. *She deserves the chance. I'm not strong enough to do anything but let her.*

In the long pause while they waited, Roxanne opened the apartment door and came back to stand with her, where Mikey was already sheltering her. Tears of shame burned Diane's so carefully made-up eyes.

The woman she remembered at the door of the cozy house in suburbia New Rochelle stepped off the elevator and walked purposefully up the hall and through the open door of the apartment. Her hair was styled in the bouncy page boy and she wore a spring dress that might just as well have been armor. She wasn't beautiful, Diane realized, but she wasn't unattractive either. She was sweet and pretty looking—the kind of woman who got married and had a family and lived a pleasant life with a devoted husband. The fact that she'd gotten the opposite was a crime Diane couldn't condone.

Mrs. Drake stopped before the three of them in a tight line, her gaze on Roxanne initially when she murmured, "Not so concerned about sharing your religious pamphlets now, are you?"

She obviously remembered them showing up on her doorstep,

and Rox attempting to make her believe they were Jehovah's Witnesses.

Diane's mind was utterly blank. She only spoke because the words were there on the tip of her tongue and had been since she found out the truth. "I'm so sorry. You have no idea how sorry—"

The woman laughed out loud, ruthlessly and loud and slightly out of control. "Oh, now you're sorry. You've treated my husband as if he was your own for... How long *has* it been? Do you know how many times I asked myself that since you showed up on my doorstep and Robert gave himself away with his reaction? I thought about it endlessly, and I'm guessing this has been going on ten years. Ten years since I noticed a radical change in the feel of our marriage. He'd just told me they hired a new assistant at work. You, I assume. And that worried me. I didn't know why at the time. I wouldn't let myself consider it. And Robert didn't change radically toward me. He's always traveled a lot. That didn't change. He was still attentive and loving toward me when we were together and talked on the phone. But I knew. Somehow, deep down, I always knew there was someone else, someone who worked her evil magic spell over him..."

"Please, Mrs. Drake, I had no idea. You have no reason to believe that..."

"Oh, please! A woman like you must have no conscience at all, getting involved with a married man—"

At the same time Roxanne started to speak, Mikey stepped forward, forcing the woman to take a step backward in obvious shock. "Lady, you've got it all wrong. First, your ass of a husband is nowhere near the innocent bystander in all this you wanna make him out to be. If anyone's innocent, it's Diane. He seduced her, lied to her, went out of his way to create an elaborate deception about how scarred he was from his past and so he couldn't get married or start a family with her because of that and all the travel in his job. He was consummate, but the fact is Diane's too sweet and innocent to realize it was all lies. She was in love, too in love to see the truth. The second she found out he was married recently, that was it for her. She broke it off with him. But he wouldn't let it go. He's been followin' her everywhere since then, comin' after her, beggin' her to take him back. He even claimed he'd leave you if she agreed to stay with him…"

"No!" Diane broke in desperately, tears streaming down her face as she implored the woman not to believe that'd been the case. "He didn't want to do that. Believe me. He loves *you*. He didn't want to leave you."

Mikey snorted. "See, even now she doesn't wanna hurt you or your marriage. But, lady, your husband is a real creep. Even when he offered to divorce you and marry her, Diane wanted nothing to do with him. She never meant to hurt anyone, and she doesn't want any of this to break up your family. If she'd known before now he was married to you, none of this would've happened."

"It's true," Roxanne added softly. "Diane was hoping you'd never find out once she learned the truth. She didn't want you or your kids to get hurt. But I think it's good, you know. None of this is fair to you or your family."

The testimony of two witnesses seemed to have laid Mrs. Drake flat. Clearly reeling from the shock of discovering her husband wasn't who she'd believed him to be, she looked between the two them, then at Diane clutching her middle and sobbing at the thought of this woman and her children, their lives in ruin and shattered.

"I'm so sorry. I'll never forgive myself. There's nothing I wouldn't do to change what happened, to fix this for you and your children. I don't want you to lose anything. You don't deserve any of this. It's not your fault. I should have realized. I should have. I didn't. I'm so sorry."

The poor woman was shaking, her breathing irregular when she turned and all but ran from the apartment. Rox followed and closed the door behind her. Diane slumped into Mikey's arms, weeping helplessly at a confrontation she'd hoped would never come.

"What should I do?" Mikey whispered, sounding as helpless as Diane felt.

Roxanne patted his arm around Diane, then glanced with a grin at the "Robert shaped hole" in their apartment wall near the door. "Trust me, babe, you're already doing everything you need to."

"Are you sure you wanna go through this?" Mike asked for the countless time. They were walking along the dock toward the slip where Doobs's yacht was anchored, and they were seriously late. He hadn't expected her to recover from that encounter, let alone insist she wanted to go ahead with their date. But she'd fixed her makeup so there was no way to tell she'd cried for an hour straight and so hard, he'd worried she'd bust something.

"I wanted to hide my head in the sand about this, Mikey. I

hoped his wife would never find out the truth and never be hurt the way I was. But it was bound to happen, especially since he hasn't been home and obviously hasn't been going to work either."

The dude had been following them around constantly, lately looking like he was completely wasted.

"I'm sorry she had to find out, but... How long before he replaced me with some other poor, unsuspecting woman anyway? That he could do this all over again is even more unfair to her. She doesn't deserve what he's doing to her."

"You're a good person."

She leaned so Mikey put his arm around her to keep her standing upright, then she stopped walking and looked up at him. "I'll never forget what you did, Mikey. You stood up for me. You defended what was undefendable. That means everything to me."

"Roxanne did, too."

"I know. Neither of you would let Robert's wife leave thinking any of it was my fault. You're so good to me, Mikey. Having you stand up for me like that, I loved you so much."

If she'd hit him over the head with a pipe, he couldn't have been more shocked. But his mind immediately took her words and forced them into the proper slot—the place they had to fit. Friendship. She loved him as a friend. She'd appreciated him coming to her side as a friend. At one time that would have been enough—a dream come true in itself. Now...now he wanted more. He wanted everything. He didn't believe he could have it.

"Thank you," she added.

"Anytime," he choked.

It was starting to get dark. Even with all the lights along the harbor, he couldn't tell for sure but she seemed disappointed by his clumsy reaction to her words. He felt so inadequate the need to please her became desperate. He encouraged her to eat the whole, billion calorie meal Doobs served them—saying they'd been good for a long time; one night of indulgence wouldn't hurt them.

"I'm so full," she cried when slow, romantic music started and they got up to dance. "I didn't need that cheesecake. Or the steak…"

He hadn't either. The evening wasn't going how he'd hoped. Somehow he thought they'd spend ninety-nine percent of it in each other's arms. But, even now that they were alone on the stern, holding each other in the moonlight, he didn't have an ounce of confidence that it was really him she wanted to be with. She proved his worry was warranted when she said, "What do you suppose is going to happen now? Will his wife leave him? Take the kids? Why did he let it happen?"

"He didn't wanna lose you," Mike said rigidly.

"That can't be it. I was telling my girlfriends that I kept a calendar of each time Robert and I saw each other in the last ten years. Twenty-eight times—ten of them in the first few months we started dating. That's all. We didn't have a relationship. His phone calls were what he used to keep me with him. He'd say all the right things, the things that kept me strung along. Those phone calls were so perfect. Too perfect, now that I think about them. He was everything I wanted in those calls. He made me believe *that* was the man he was. Every dream I had, he spun it out into pure gold, so I was convinced he loved me more than anything and was only waiting for his travel to lessen, his scars to heal, before we got married. But when we were together, he made excuses. We'd go to 'our hotel', almost never out to dinner in the beginning, like we did that time Roxanne 'accidentally' met him early in our relationship.

He'd push for sex immediately, but once it was done the intimacy between us was over. He didn't want anything else. Usually. Once or twice, he asked me to...pleasure him...give him..."

Mike stared at her like she'd said the worst swear word in the world. Diane didn't talk like this. He'd never heard her imply anything crude like it before.

She shook her head, grimacing. "It was disgusting. *He* was disgusting."

He wondered if the act was what disgusted her, or the man. "And he never returned the favor," he guessed.

"I asked but he wouldn't."

He swore under his breath.

"What?"

Mike laughed, embarrassed but unable to stop himself from saying, "Just say the word and I'm there, lady."

Her face turned as red as his must have been, but then she continued talking—talking about the stub instead of their relationship. "Usually, we'd sleep together and wake up to sex one more time. He never wanted to talk about all the things we talked about on the phone—certainly not about planning our wedding. I realize now, he must have run home to his wife as soon as he was done with me. And then months and months would go by again. All during those months, he'd call me, probably when he was in some other city where he was trying to sell Global products, and he was probably bored in the hotel at the end of the day. So it was easy to call me and spend hours telling me everything I wanted to hear."

She bit her lip. "He didn't love me. I don't believe he did for a second. He just didn't want to lose. He'd spent ten years developing all my fervent, blind love for him. He didn't want to lose the image I fostered of him as the most incredible man in the world."

She sounded revolted, while Mike wished she'd shut up. He didn't want to hear another word about that worthless creep. Ever. He couldn't accept her words as anything but her crying over something that should have been dead long ago. But she'd gotten all dressed up like this, more beautiful than he'd ever seen her—and that was really saying something. He couldn't escape the conclusion that none of it was for him.

"Now his wife will suffer for his sins. His kids will. It's so unfair. I never wanted that. But in the long run, I can only hope something good comes out of it for her and her children."

Beyond his control, Mike felt himself shutting down like he had when she'd flirted with that office supply dude. He'd been fooling himself this whole time. He couldn't have this woman, no matter what it'd seemed like all these blissful days they'd spent together. In the rulebook of what kind of guys got the best girls, his name had never made a single appearance. It wouldn't this time either. While he was completely hers, he knew she'd never be his the way he wanted.

Chapter 15

Diane realized belatedly she'd made a mistake talking to Mikey about her feelings. He'd just been so quiet during dinner, she'd found herself going over and over that horrible episode in the apartment before they left. Even though she'd said things that should have relieved him, he was acting the way he had after she'd stupidly flirted with that guy Aaron, or whatever his name had been. Mikey wasn't simply quiet. He was locked down.

Why doesn't he want to hear I'm over Robert, that maybe I was never really in love with him in the first place? I was only in love with the idea *of him, of a perfect man, the one he tried so hard to make me believe he was? Shouldn't that make Mikey happy, especially after I told him I love* him?

But he hadn't reacted to those words any better than he had all her other confessions of closure. He certainly hadn't grabbed her in his arms, kissed her silly, and told her he loved her, too.

Why isn't he doing that? Maybe I've been all wrong. Maybe Mike doesn't love me. Maybe he's just been a friend all this time, giving me what he thinks I need as a woman so I won't be crushed by what Robert did to me and vow to never risk my heart again.

While it was true she was an old-fashioned girl and wanted to be swept off her feet by her hero, the fact was, she wasn't sure anymore—sure that Mikey was feeling the same way for her as she was for him. *How do I find out? I don't want him to feel obligated to me when he really doesn't want to be with me. But if I stay here, my heart will override my head, the way it always does. I'll ask him for more than he may want to give me.*

Though she hadn't formed a definite plan in her mind by the time she and Mikey were in his car parked in the quiet, deserted parking garage (at her request) just before midnight, she knew she had to take a pause in their relationship and give them both some space. Maybe the thought of being away from him for a single day was what made her so insane and unlike herself. She couldn't leave without something. Some kind of... *placeholder*...in their relationship.

The only thing she could think of was the way Mikey had said, "Just say the word and I'm there, lady." Somehow, she couldn't forget that for a second. She wanted him to know the most intimate act in the world with him didn't disgust her the way it had with Robert. Instead, the mere thought was wildly exciting to her.

Just as she expected, Mikey didn't reach for her. Based on the way he didn't get out of the car right away, he was waiting for her to make the first move. She wrapped her arms around his neck and kissed him with all of her heart. His hold felt real and tender yet fiery, just as much as his mouth moving forcefully against hers did. In seconds, he was leaning over her on her side of the car almost with his whole body lifted from the seat. Knowing Roxanne was at home, preventing them from their usual "nightcap" on her sofa, made her more anxious than usual. She slipped her hands over his gorgeous behind that'd been distracting her in those sleek slacks all night.

He all but gasped and she chuckled, surprised how throaty she sounded. All she wanted was to love him and touch him and bestow the pleasure he so unselfishly gave her. Nothing else mattered. Never before had she felt so determined. *Because I know I'm leaving. I'm going to give Mikey the space he needs to decide what his feelings for me are. I already know what mine are, what I want with him and him alone.*

Little more than a half hour later, Diane was in her bedroom, packing a suitcase. There was absolutely no way Mikey could be confused about her feelings. She loved him. She was *in love with him.* She'd said the words. She'd showed him her heart and desire for him. She'd proved beyond a shadow of a doubt that he was the man she wanted to be with, to be free to explore love in all its facets with.

"What in the world are you doing?" Roxanne demanded. "This is crazy. You do know that, don't you?"

"I know. But it's the only way."

"The only way *what*?"

"The only way to be sure."

"Of your feelings or his?"

"His. Just his. You're right. You were right all along. Mikey Lund is the perfect man for me. He's always been, no matter what else got in the way."

Rox shook her head at her. "What in the world did you two do tonight? I thought you had a romantic dinner on a yacht."

That and so much more. Diane looked away and quickly stuffed more things into her suitcase.

"Did you and Mike…" Rox asked, now looking shocked.

"No. But he knows I love him alone. Romantically. In every way a woman can love a man."

"So…what? Did that woman tonight upset you so much? Is that why you're fleeing in the middle of the night?"

"I'm not fleeing. I've been meaning to visit my parents for a while now, and this is the perfect time. I already called Brett—luckily he and Savvy were awake. I told him I'd finish organizing the body shop when I got back. My flight is leaving in a few hours. I'll have to call a cab."

"No you won't. I'll drive you."

"Thanks. You can come with me if you want."

"Maybe. Maybe later."

After you've run to Mikey and told him I flew off to Wisconsin? That would work just fine. Diane had factored the inevitably into her plans.

"My family always centers me. And this will give Mikey time to make up his mind."

"About what? What could Mikey Lund possibly need to think about where you're concerned?"

Roxanne couldn't understand. Diane wasn't even sure she did. "What I had with Robert for the last ten years wasn't real. You know?"

"Oh, I know, Lady Jane."

"It was like this *thing* trapped in a glass bottle. Never to change, if Robert had his way. Never to grow. Never to go away.

Never to become real."

"Okay..." Roxanne said like she understood but didn't.

"I don't want that ever again. I don't want anything like that. I don't want to go along with someone, never knowing whether or not they're feeling the same thing I am, wanting the same things I do. I have to know. Until I do, I can't do anything. I can't let myself go. So, until I know, I'll be at my parents' farm."

Mike hadn't recovered from the shellshock when his doorbell rang. He didn't even know how he'd gotten himself out of the parking garage.

Diane loved him. Diane Hoffmann loved *him*. She was in love with him and she *wanted* him. Everything he hadn't let himself hope for was true. He was the man she really wanted to be with, to give herself to, heart, body and soul. She wanted to give as much as she got.

He'd barely unlocked the door...had he locked it in the first place? he couldn't remember...when Rox pushed inside. "So I just dropped Diane off at the airport. She's going to Wisconsin."

Mike started to protest, looked at the clock, choked, spluttered...

Roxanne put her hands on his shoulders as if to steady him.

"What? Now? Going? Gone?"

Rox lifted a knowing eyebrow. "Bet you didn't expect that."

Ice rain fell down on him. Diane had gone from proving her

feelings for him to running home to her parents.

"All right, stop what you're doing right this minute, Mikey Lund," Rox said harshly. "I know you're trying to tell yourself she didn't mean what she said tonight when she told you she's in love with you. You're a new man. You deserve love just like everybody, maybe more so. You always have. You've always been a great guy. Any woman would be lucky to have you. You've got that girl hook, line and sinker. Now all you have to do is reel her in."

Mike shook his head. "I don't know…"

"You do know. You're gonna be patient. Until you can't be a second longer."

He blinked, not understanding. Nothing made sense right now. "Wha…?"

"I don't think she realizes it herself, but she needs a few minutes to clear her own head. And, once she does, you'll be there. You'll break on the scene like a juggernaut."

Juggernaut isn't exactly what I was goin' for. Not sure Diane would appreciate that either. "And what?" Mike demanded in shock.

"You tell me."

"I…go to Wisconsin?" he asked uncertainly, seeking confirmation.

Roxanne's expression encouraged him to keep going.

"I find her parents' farm? I tell her…I love her?"

"That's a start."

"Start?"

"Is that *all* you wanna tell her? Do you wanna *ask* her anything?"

Mike swallowed. "Marry me," he said in a whisper.

Rox burst into a grin. "There you go," she said, slapping him on the arm.

"Did she say she wanted me to follow her? I don't exactly got an invitation."

"Trust me, she expects you to follow. It's what she wants. And she'll roll out the red carpet for you the second you appear in her sights."

He shook his head. If she loved him, why would she run off to Wisconsin? Even as he marveled at her amazing gift—not realizing at the time of course that it was some kind of going-away present—he couldn't fathom her leaving meant anything good for him. "I don't know about this."

"And that's what's gonna be your downfall if you don't listen to me."

"What does she want me to do?"

"Open your eyes, babe. Ride to her rescue. That's all she wants. You've done it before, and this time..."

"What?"

Rox smiled, squeezing his shoulder. "This time, it'll be your own rescue, too."

Chapter 16

Diane had long forgotten how much she enjoyed being in the barn. Work or no work, she loved this place and the family surrounding her—her parents, and nieces and nephews, Penny's husband who'd been working the farm since he was as young as the other summer help her father hired every year. She even loved the smell!

The cows—all four hundred some of them—had been milked, and Diane and her mother and sister led them out of the barn, back out to the pasture as they finished. Then they cleaned the milkers, the floor, and everything was put up before they headed to the main house, where Penny and her oldest daughter were probably just putting lunch on the table.

The past two days had been wonderful for her. She hadn't had a single piece of fudge either, though she'd been offered it more times than she could count. Her mother apparently found her too skinny, but Diane felt better than she had in years. She'd been insisting that the freshly harvested vegetables from her mother's extensive garden not be covered, doused or even dotted with anything but a little salt and pepper or some fresh herbs.

More than anything, she'd wanted her phone to ring so she could hear Mikey's voice. The one time it had rang, Isaac Ravi had asked her if she was feeling any better. Without an ounce of compunction or tact, she'd told him she was in love—with the man who'd come to the office supply store with her—and she'd never be available to date anyone else. *Sorry for inadvertently leading you on, but please don't ever contact me again.*

More than once, she worried Mikey had taken her encouragement to ask out any girl he found attractive—because that female would accept in a heartbeat. Would he? Why wouldn't he? He hadn't said he loved her, but he'd been so flabbergasted before she left him that night, she was sure he couldn't have spoken coherently for hours afterward. Maybe that was part of the problem. Had she done the right thing? At the time, everything she'd said and done seemed like the best way to convince Mikey how much she loved him. Now, she was humiliated and doubted everything, especially her own appeal.

She hadn't told her family anything serious, of course. She'd talked a little about how she'd deceived herself with Robert, and all the while Mikey had been in the background. She'd talked endlessly about Mike. This time, they were insisting on meeting him. "I don't know when," Diane had said a million times. But she hoped…

As she and her mother approached the screen door into the kitchen, she heard voices—her sister's and her niece's. Her heart leapt, as if somehow guessing even without verifying with the sound of the male voice inside. Mikey was sitting in the kitchen and Penny and Millie were trying to shove fattening food down his throat, offering him this and that. His face was so red, he might have been sunburned the way Diane had been her first day here out in the field.

He'd never looked more handsome to her. She wanted to throw herself at him instantly. But she was embarrassed, cringing about the way she'd left him. How she smelled from the barn now. What he must think of her for her relationship with Robert, taking so long to get over all that, realizing she'd loved Mikey all along.

Ultimately, all that mattered was that he'd come. He'd done what she'd hoped and prayed he would once she'd dropped all those clues she'd hoped Rox would give him. *But she didn't push him into coming here, did she? I never considered that. I just needed someone to tell Mikey where I'd be, give him my parents' address...*

"I can't believe you're here," she said, then worried he would take her gushing words the wrong way. "Roxanne forced you into this, didn't she? She made you come..."

"Actually, she told me to wait."

Yet he was here. Diane grabbed his arm and dragged him deeper into the house. "I need to shower," she murmured once they were alone, though she knew her mother and sister could never be far enough away right now.

"Are you glad I came?" Mikey asked, so sweetly shy.

In response, she threw her arms around him. "I'm so happy to see you, Mikey. If you'd come an hour after my flight landed, I would have been thrilled."

"Really?"

"I wanted you to. You know I wanted you here." She swallowed. "I love you, Mikey! Don't you believe me? Or are you sorry...?"

Just like that, Mikey hauled her closer and kissed her ferociously so she couldn't have continued even if she'd wanted to. And she didn't. She was so happy, she wanted to laugh or cry. But neither seemed appropriate while he was kissing her into utopia.

His lips still against hers, he whispered, "I love you. I loved you long before. Forever."

"Why didn't you tell me? Even when I told you?"

"Do you have to ask? I'm me, you're you. You're an angel. I've loved you as long as I can remember. You're the only woman. The rest were never options. I was desperate. But you… Diane, I really wanted you. I never let myself believe you could want me."

She smiled feeling as if she'd stolen all the sunbeams directly from the sun. "Didn't I prove that?" she asked softly.

Their faces were so close, he couldn't have hid anything. "Diane, I want you. I want the same with you. I want everything."

"I'm yours."

His jaw tightened, and she worried because he said her name again, harshly. The pause killed her. Then he gave her her heart's desire when a part of her expected him to only be thinking about sex, which would be incredible between them but could never be enough for her. "Marry me."

Even before she could react, he backed up. "I'm sorry. It's too soon. I know it's too soon."

Diane grabbed hold of his arm. "Mikey, did you just *un*propose to me?"

He shook his head wildly. "I'm sorry. I don't know what I'm sayin'. I keep waitin' for you to…"

"…accept!" she said fiercely. "I accept, Mikey Lund, and you better tell me right now you *meant* to propose to me and don't you dare ask if I wanted you to mean it!"

Laughing sheepishly, he squeezed her tightly in his arms. "I meant it. I brought the ring if you need proof."

"You bought a ring?"

"Yeah. This is embarrassing."

"What is?"

"I told you I stopped usin' all my money for food and booze. You asked what I did with the money and I told you I saved it. That's not true. I did somethin' else with it when I had enough—and it cost a fortune. At the time, I didn't know why I did it. I was lonely. I've been lonely a long time. Lonely people do crazy things. But, as soon as you told me and showed me you loved me and then took off into the night, I knew I bought the ring for you."

"You bought an engagement ring with the money you saved? You bought it months ago? Before we even became friends again?"

"Yeah. It was like a goal. To give the ring to someone. You're the only one I ever could. I bought it for you. Regardless of *when* I bought it, I know *who* I bought it for. You're the dream come true I was wishin' for all along."

Diane sighed happily, blinking back tears. "You're my dream come true, too, Mikey Lund. I want *this* dream to be real and last forever."

Six months later

Their first Christmas as newlyweds, Mike took Diane right from work to the Christmas tree lot. They could hardly stop kissing long enough to choose a tree. The snow was coming down lightly, looking like diamonds falling around them. Diane's long hair beneath her hat glistened with the glittery flakes.

"Pretty soon you won't be able to hold me this close," she murmured, her eyes sparkling as she smiled into his. The baby growing inside her was a little bump now.

"I'll find a way." He kissed her again, not sure he'd ever get enough of her, of knowing she belonged to him and she *wanted* to. "And somehow we gotta find a way to fit a tree in my…our…small apartment. You sure you want one?"

"Of course. How can it be Christmas without a decorated tree?"

As soon as they came back to New York, they'd started planning their wedding. She'd met his family—something he'd never expected to go so well, and he usually joked that they only seemed to love him now because he was with her. Though they'd all been mad at him for never answering their calls, they'd forgiven him instantly when he called and said he wanted them to meet someone—his fiancée.

It was definitely true everyone in his family was completely smitten with her—down to his mother and sisters. But maybe Diane was right: He'd mistaken his family's inability to speak of their feelings, forcing food on him instead, and their seeming lack of attention, mild abuse, and failure to notice his addictions as a lack of love.

In any case, *her* family seemed to love him just as much and he'd warmed to each one of them after the numerous times they said Robert Drake was a complete waste of their precious Diane's time—and he was a knight worthy of her.

Though Roxanne had wanted the two of them to take her apartment, neither of them had wanted to. Besides that it was too big, they couldn't afford it. Diane had been working at the garage all this time, so it ran like a well-oiled machine upstairs and down, but she was looking forward to becoming a full-time mother once their baby arrived. In twenty years, they might be able to afford a better apartment and maybe even a house, but right now they were content in his tiny, one bedroom apartment.

"Let's invite Roxanne to decorate the tree with us," Diane said abruptly. "I'll call her right now."

They were all worried about Roxanne and no one knew if she was addicted to something, like she had been often in the past, or if something else was going on—something that'd made her shave her head and all but give up her successful career. She kept telling everyone she was fine and they were worrying for nothing. Yet she often disappeared for months at a time, so much so that, even if it worried them, they'd gotten used to not being able to get hold of her easily. Unfortunately, Roxanne had always been so independent, not one of them felt comfortable pushing beyond the borders she'd set.

"She's not answering," Diane said a moment later, her expression filled with concern.

Knowing the suggestion would relieve her, if only temporary, Mike said, "We'll go over there on the way home with our tree." But he knew Rox wouldn't answer the door, and Diane would end up even more worried.

They turned toward the rows of trees and crashed into another couple. It wasn't until they drew back, all apologizing at once, that Mike recognized the woman. Though her hairstyle had changed, it was definitely Robert Drake's wife.

"I'm sorry," Diane murmured, and Mike could tell from the soft, shocked tone of her voice she recognized the woman, too. But Mike had noticed something she obviously hadn't yet. The woman wasn't with Robert. The dude she was with was someone else entirely.

"No, I'm sorry." The woman reached out toward them, causing Diane to halt in her eagerness to get away. "Diane, isn't it? Diane Hoffmann?"

"Lund," Diane said in surprise. "This is my husband Mike. We're newlyweds."

The woman glanced at him, nodding. "Yes, I remember you. I suppose it makes perfect sense. I'm…I'm actually glad to have run into you. I've spent the last six months wanting to apologize to you."

"To me? Why would you need to apologize to me?"

"Because I realized you weren't lying. You truly didn't know Robert was married. I believe that, and not simply because your future husband here defended your honor so passionately. I could see how broken you were, how you reacted and your concern was for me and my children, not yourself. Not for Robert. I knew you were innocent mostly because I know Robert. I mean, I know the type of man he is. I just didn't want to accept the truth then. He deceived you, but you weren't covering your eyes, were you? You genuinely didn't know. He made sure of that. Just like he did with me."

Diane's eyes had gone wide. "What do you mean?"

"He was married before me. Robert and I dated for many

years. He traveled so much. Because of his job, we almost never saw each other. But we talked on the phone a lot. He hated all those hotels he had to stay while he was trying to make a sale. We talked endlessly. I believed every word. That whole time, I never had a clue he was married. It never occurred to me because it wasn't one of those typical affairs where he left clues all over the place. He was too smart. He only slipped one time, and that's when I found out he was married. When I found out..." Even in the growing darkness, the woman's face was flushed. "Well, you see, you have no reason to be ashamed, Diane, because you didn't do what I did. I let him divorce his wife and marry me instead. I told myself it was me he loved all along. That we were meant to be, and so that made our sin acceptable and justified. Our lives were so ideal. Even when I wondered if he was seeing someone else, I didn't want to believe he'd do something like that to *me*. And that's probably what happened with you, too. He slipped once, and that's when you saw the truth. You were an ignorant victim, just like I was, but you ended it when you should have." The woman smiled sadly. "When did you two get married?"

"August," Mike told her.

"It's our first Christmas together," Diane said.

"Congratulations. I actually just got married myself recently." She cast a warm look at the guy who'd been silent through all of this, but his protectiveness toward his wife had been blatant nevertheless. "Lionel was kind of in the background of my life for most of the years I was dating, then married, to Robert. Not that there was anything remotely romantic between us during that time..."

"No, of course not," Diane insisted.

"He was just waiting for me to see the truth about Robert."

Lionel hugged his wife. "I was hopelessly in love with her."

Mike grinned. "I know the feeling."

Just like that, both women were flying at each other, hugging and crying, saying "I'm so glad you got your happily-ever-after" and Mike and Lionel looked at each other with a kind of shared befuddlement at what was happening.

"So what is that jerk up to?" Mike asked Lionel.

"He was laid off only a few weeks after all this stuff happened. He's selling vacuums door-to-door," Lionel told him with relish. "In New Jersey."

"The kids tell me he's involved with someone," the woman drew back from Diane to say. "He's proposed to her."

"Poor thing," Diane said.

"I'm just glad we're not likely to run into him anytime soon." Mike had spent the past six months dreading the prospect.

As Lionel and his wife went off to find her kids, Mike said quietly, "I would've had to knock out some teeth if we bumped into the old stub instead of his ex-wife."

When the wind blew fiercely with the threat of heavier snow, Diane snuggled against him. "I don't hold a grudge. I can't."

"How can you not?" he asked in disbelief.

She turned and put her arms around him. "Because the best thing that ever happened to me came out of that awful situation. I regret ever meeting Robert Drake, getting involved with him, but, what happened afterward, when Roxanne asked you to run to my rescue if he ever came back around…well, that made everything completely worth it."

Mike couldn't help but believe, too. They were together.

Neither of them would ever be lonely again. Their love was worth everything that'd come before. "I'm the luckiest person in the world."

Diane smiled, shaking her head as she hugged him. "Impossible."

"How can you say that?"

"Because *I* hold that honor, good sir. I belong to Mikey Lund. No one else in the world can claim that privilege."

Chuckling, he kissed her, and felt worth his weight in gold.

Angelfire Series

Falling Star, Book 1
First Love, Book 2
Forever Man, Book 3
Only the Lonely, Book 4
Midnight Angel, Book 5
Shadows of the Night, Book 6
Promises in the Dark, Book 7

You can find ALL our books on our website at:
http://www.writers-exchange.com

You can find ALL Karen's books at:
http://www.writers-exchange.com/Karen-Wiesner/

Romance:
http://www.writers-exchange.com/category/genres/romance/

Series:
http://www.writers-exchange.com/category/genres/series/

About the Author

In addition to having been a popular writing reference instructor and writer, professional blurbologist and freelance editor, Karen Wiesner is the accomplished author of 156 titles published, which have been nominated/won for over a hundred and thirty awards. Karen's books cover such genres as women's fiction, romance, mystery/police procedural/cozy, suspense, thriller, paranormal, supernatural, futuristic, fantasy, science fiction, gothic, inspirational/Christian, horror, chick-lit, and action/adventure. She also writes children's books, poetry, and writing reference titles which have been repackaged in the 3D Fiction Fundamentals Collection. Karen will begin illustrating children's books starting in 2024.

Visit Karen's website and blog at https://karenwiesner.weebly.com/. Check out her Facebook author page here: http://www.facebook.com/KarenWiesnerAuthor.

If you enjoyed this author's book, then please place a review up at the site of purchase and any social media sites you frequent!

Only the Lonely by Karen Wiesner

Wounded Warriors Series by Karen Wiesner
Women's Fiction/Contemporary Romance Novels

Publisher Book Page:
http://www.writers-exchange.com/wounded-warriors-series/

Women who have faced pain, loss and heartache.
They know the score and never back down.
Women who aren't afraid to love with all their passion and all their strength,
who risk everything for their own little piece of heaven...
Men who live their lives on the blade's edge. Knights in black armor.
The only thing more dangerous than crossing these men is loving them...

RELUCTANT HEARTS, Book 1
What's a man to do when he's seen too much of life's dark side and suddenly finds himself believing in flesh-and-blood angels who can heal with a single touch? What's a girl to do when she believes in true love but can't trust the eyes of her own heart? Fall in love...reluctantly?

WAITING FOR AN ECLIPSE, Book 2
Steve Thomas has a self-destructive wife, three kids, more guilt than one man can handle...and a chance at true love for the first time in his life—if only he can allow himself to take it.

MIRROR MIRROR, Book 3
Twenty-five years ago, Gwen Nicholson-Nelson was in a car accident that left behind a strange gift. She can see the future, and death, before it comes to pass. She also has a disturbing connection with another psychic like her who not only sees into others but manipulates and destroys. When her nemesis targets the man she loves, Gwen must act—before her vision of Dylan's death comes to pass.

WAYWARD ANGELS, Book 4
What do you get with a former wild man who's committed his path to the Lord and a woman who has absolutely nothing to lose? It's either a match made in heaven...or a sure-fire heartache.

UNTIL IT'S GONE, Book 5
You don't know what you've got...until it's gone. Mitch has been playing a dangerous game. The lines between black and white, good and evil, saint and sinner are all blurred. Just when he thinks the stakes can't get any higher, in steps the only woman who could ever hurt him and the only one who can heal him. In the space of a skipped heartbeat, he can't imagine having more to

gain...and more to lose.

WHITE RAINBOW, Book 6

Jessie Nelson has been telling herself she doesn't deserve or believe in second chances, especially when it comes to love...until her white rainbow appears in a corporate pirate who conquers her, heart and soul.

www.ingramcontent.com/pod-product-compliance
Ingram Content Group UK Ltd.
Pitfield, Milton Keynes, MK11 3LW, UK
UKHW030632130325
456214UK00005B/159